"I love the idea but I've got to be practical. Where would we live? I can't afford this island."

"I thought you said I have a coin in my possession, somewhere, worth millions," Nick teased.

Taylor turned very serious. "Not until you believe me and start looking for it, we don't."

"Fair enough," he agreed. "I own a small cottage and just renovated the place to rent out. It's yours as part of your salary. It's already furnished. If you come to work for me for the summer, I'll try to find this coin you say I have."

"You're serious?"

"Very."

"Kate? Here?" she blurted out, smiling. "For the summer? She'd be in absolute heaven."

He nodded. "All right. We have a deal. Just remember what I told you about my old job. Diamante's hasn't gotten any easier. You'll earn every penny." Deep down, Nick knew this business deal was right for both of them.

And if he was lucky, maybe even the beginning of something more. "When can you start?"

Dear Reader,

Although fictional, Cantecaw is not only an island, it is a belief—a foundation—of heart, soul and family. Tough and independent, Taylor returns to the island to tell Nick a coin they found ten years ago is worth millions.

She walks into Diamante's Restaurant wanting things to be the same, as if she'd never left. Mama Bella welcomes her with open arms. But Nick? He doesn't believe her. And he's not ready for some fantasy to possibly ruin his plans for the future. But he does offer her a job because he needs her expertise to make those plans a reality.

Theirs was a spark that never had the chance to light. Can it now? Will Cantecaw provide the magic that brings them together?

Sun, sand and lasagna. What could be better? Except, perhaps, Cantecaw roots and Diamante hugs.

As a debut Harlequin author, I can't wait for you to welcome Nick and Taylor into your world. I hope you enjoy every moment.

Hugs,

Linda

REUNION WITH THE SINGLE MOM

LINDA J. PARISI

HEARTWARMING

Harlequin®
HEARTWARMING™

ISBN-13: 978-1-335-05156-1

Reunion with the Single Mom

 Harlequin Enterprises ULC
22 Adelaide St. West, 41st Floor
Toronto, Ontario M5H 4E3, Canada
www.Harlequin.com

Printed in Lithuania

MIX
Paper | Supporting responsible forestry
FSC® C021394

Linda J. Parisi enjoys creating unforgettable characters. Love conquers all, so an HEA is a must. She is the current president of Liberty States Fiction Writers and is thrilled to have realized her lifelong dream with her debut Harlequin Heartwarming novel, *Reunion with the Single Mom*. She loves to travel, tries to bake and lives in New Jersey with her son Chris, daughter-in-law Sara, and Audi and Archer, a pair of pooches who had her at *woof*!

Books by Linda J. Parisi

Harlequin Heartwarming

Reunion with the Single Mom

Visit the Author Profile page at Harlequin.com.

This book is dedicated to my Big Italian Family.

I love you all.

Never forget, big families are fun!

CHAPTER ONE

VOLUMES OF PAGES existed about love, yet no words could describe the feeling inside Taylor Hughes as she watched her daughter glide across the living room floor, dancing to music only the girl could hear. Her golden child pushed back a long strand of blond hair behind her ear, revealing the source of Taylor's serenity—earphones. Kate flashed her a huge smile and a sideways look with her bright blue eyes as she curved around a large moving box. Amazing how kids always knew when they were pressing the edge of whatever boundary had been set.

"Kate, honey. Please. You're supposed to be packing."

The pout. Kate had a master's degree in them. But this time, Taylor decided she wouldn't be swayed.

"A few more minutes, Mom? Please? I love this song."

Taylor opened her mouth to say no, but she found she couldn't even swallow past the lump in her throat. So much for tough love. Kate began dancing again, a sprite in a sea of clouds. Her daughter twirled with an innocence only a mother could appreciate.

Taylor sighed and rose from the floor. Stepping back from the open closet, she looked up. She'd forgotten something tucked away on the top shelf. A shoebox. She reached up, her fingertips brushing and edging the box forward. One last lift and the box tipped. She caught the cover in one arm and the box in the other, juggling the contents inside, already knowing what they were. She settled the box in her arms and brought it to the empty table in the middle of the room. The contents might be meager, but many memories filled the space inside.

"What's that?"

Leave it to a seven-year-old to ignore when she shouldn't and be insanely curious the rest of the time. "Just some old things."

Not some old things, not just memories, a summer of magic. Hanging with the crew from Diamante's, working her socks off right next to them, forging a bond she still remembered. There was a dollar store anklet from Jay, shells she'd found with Robin and Grace, a ticket stub to a movie she wondered why she'd bothered to keep, and the most special gift of all. The bottle with the bright blues and greens of sea glass inside that Nick Diamante had insisted she keep.

Kate peeked, leaned over the box and clicked her tongue, clearly unimpressed with the contents by the sound she made. But she did reach out and inspect the bottle—for all of three seconds, her average attention span these days. Taylor grinned at her loot and Kate returned to her dance. A shoebox with old junk wasn't much to interest a mini-ingenue. But for Taylor? The contents represented a world she missed terribly to this day: Cantecaw Island, just off the Jersey Shore. A spectacular beach, a decades-old family restaurant, and the best time of her life—Kate excluded.

Diamante's. Mama Bella, maker of the best lasagna, still, to this day, that Taylor had ever eaten. And bearer of the biggest, warmest hugs she'd ever known in her life. Taylor closed her eyes and heard the din of the crowd, the clink of their cutlery, and imagined the smell of the spaghetti sauce bubbling on the stove. She could feel the exhaustion of surviving another Saturday night, not wanting to move a muscle, but a huge smile covering her face because of a job well done. Best of all, though, were the crashing waves against the pier, and hanging with Jay and Robin and Grace and Tony. And most of all, with Nick, his black hair gleaming in the moonlight and his warm brown eyes understanding every feeling she felt.

Sometimes Rocco, Nick's brother, and his girlfriend, Beth, would stop by and they would all talk and talk and talk about the future, what each of them was planning to do with their lives, and the places they all wanted to see. Much of the time Taylor simply hung back and listened since she was the youngest, but she learned a lot from them and was grateful to be included as part of the crowd.

There were more crews from other restaurants on the Island and on one occasion they'd all built a huge bonfire in the sand. Nick had sat next to her the whole time. She'd loved the attention he showed, thankful for his protection when some of the crowd began drinking and smoking. And, of course, keeping her from getting caught when the cops came. Bonfires were illegal on the beach.

Taylor shook her head, focusing now on the present. Those days were almost a decade ago. She picked up the bottle and decided to pack it in newspaper. Although long dismissed, the bottle had never been forgotten. And neither had the kiss. She didn't even realize her fingers were touching her cheek. One kiss. One special kiss, one she wished had been under a moonlit sky but had ended up with the fog rolling in off the ocean.

Taylor set the bottle aside. She needed to get moving.

"Kate? Earth to Kate!"

Her daughter stopped dancing and pulled out an earphone.

"Go get cleaned up, please. I have to use the computer over at the library. My laptop is acting up again." She didn't have the heart to explain she was creating résumés and sending them to job websites. Yet. "You can take out a new book. Then I'm splurging. Latte or chai for me. What do you want?"

"An ice. No, cupcakes. No, an ice cream cone."

Taylor laughed. "Fine. You can decide when we get to the store. But we need to go now. I'd rather walk and I want to be home before dark."

"Okay."

With the high price of gas, Taylor didn't want to use her car except for interviews now. And picking up groceries. While her old security deposit covered the last month's rent on their current apartment, she'd had to take the security deposit and rent out of the bank for the new studio, which left her account on the thin side. Kate had taken to the downsizing like a trouper, thank goodness. And Taylor still had one more paycheck coming before she started unemployment. They'd get by.

She couldn't blame her boss Frank Foster, either. Breton, Pennsylvania, wasn't exactly Philadelphia. Or even the size of Hershey. Just a small municipality with a four-lane highway and Foster's Family Restaurant. The downturn in the town's economy wasn't Frank's fault, and despite her suggestions, he only knew one way to run the place. Funny, she'd been a godsend with her hospitality degree in hand and her experience from Diamante's and other restaurants under her belt.

He'd been a godsend to her, too, moving her up the ranks to hostess, then manager, yet understanding when Kate got sick or she needed off for school meetings and such. But there was no godsend for lack of patronage.

Frank had told her he would try to scrape up a week's severance pay for her, which would cover the bills for a bit. If he was able. But Taylor knew better than to count on the money. After all, she'd been running his business for a while and knew how much he owed to everyone else.

How interesting, she thought, *that there's what we want to do and then there's simply what is.*

Taylor ushered Kate out of their apartment, clasping her daughter's hand as they walked down the street to the library. Green had begun to spread across the vista as plants and grass came out of hibernation from a rather cold winter. The sun, warm during the height of the day, now cooled, and she zipped up her sweatshirt against the chill. Her daughter, thankfully, felt warm as toast judging by the hand she held. And Taylor couldn't help but smile as the girl let go, then hop-skipped along the sidewalk. Oh, to be young and lighthearted again.

The library resided in an old building, whitewashed, with unvarnished plank floors. It kind of looked like an old church from the outside. Inside, it smelled like books and something ancient, earthier, so much more real than some of those new contemporary places with their steel and chrome decor. However rustic, the place was inviting, and Lucy, the full-time librarian, had always been able to secure just about any book or resource as long as Taylor asked in advance.

While Kate searched for a new book, Taylor used the library computer to create another résumé and upload the file onto several job portals. Then she printed a few copies to have just in case. Frank had given her a really superb recommendation, so Taylor felt hopeful her job search would go well.

On the way home they detoured, stopping at Rollo's Confectionery, aka coffee shop and convenience store. She loved the painted pink-and-white brick and wrought iron windows. She loved the shelves filled with penny candy and huge, swirly lollipops. She loved all the sundry items, too, especially the fragrant, handmade soaps. The place made her think of the turn of the century and the inside was modeled after an old-fashioned soda fountain.

What a shame there'd be no more soap purchases for a while.

"Did you decide what you want?" she asked Kate, focusing on what she could buy rather than what she couldn't.

"Vanilla cone with rainbow sprinkles, please," Kate told the young woman behind the counter.

"And I'll have a vanilla chai, please. Oh, and

I'll take a newspaper." She needed it for packing those last few items, including the bottle full of sea glass.

Kate got her cone first. She sideslipped away, throwing Taylor a look.

"You'd better save me a lick, young lady."

Kate laughed. "Uh-uh," she answered, her tongue swiping a huge dollop of ice cream off the cone. Her daughter came away with ice cream everywhere, including the top of her lip.

"Get a couple of napkins, please," she told her.

Kate complied but Taylor had serious doubts about the napkins ever being used. The chai took longer to make, and as she waited, Taylor noticed a small television on the wall. The news was on and caught her eye. She listened to a story about a collector and a very rare set of coins. What held her attention was when the newscaster spoke about the collector, a dealer, looking for a coin missing from the set. A nickel. An 18-something nickel. How could she ever forget that date? Could it be the same coin she was remembering?

When the young woman came back with her chai, Taylor asked, "Did you just hear the news? What he just said?"

"Something about a coin." The server nodded.

"Did you happen to hear the date? The numbers?"

"Um, sorry. Not really. I think I heard him say twenty-one."

Taylor paid the bill. She must have heard wrong. There wasn't any kind of connection to… No way. Just a wild idea to get her heart to race for a moment. "Kate? Sweetie?" she asked, dismissing the memory of the coin completely. "Come on. Time to go home."

As they began heading back toward their apartment, Taylor asked Kate, "Hey. Where's my lick?"

Kate took off running and Taylor tried swatting at her daughter with the newspaper. Taylor chased, eventually winning a minuscule bite. They continued on home as the sun set, a glowing red ball in the sky sending out shards of pink across the horizon. She crossed her fingers mentally, wishing someone would like her résumé enough to offer her an interview. No doubt she and Kate would be okay, but she would have to be very careful to make ends meet.

A COUPLE OF weeks later, they were moved into the new, smaller studio apartment and Taylor had unpacked most of their things. But some boxes remained piled up in one corner because of the cramped space and Kate had already begun griping about the lack of privacy. And television rights.

With Kate in school, Taylor used the peace and quiet to sort through what she could, and in the process, came upon the shoebox with the sea glass bottle inside. Seeking a moment of solitude to revisit the joyful memory of Cantecaw Island, she unwrapped the bottle but noticed an article in the scrap of newspaper about a coin with the numbers 1821.

With moving, unpacking and job hunting, she hadn't paid attention to anything else, let alone gone back to see if her memory matched what must be a fairy tale on the news. But now she wasn't so sure. The article reiterated what she'd heard on the broadcast that day in the store.

Taylor searched for more details about the story on her phone. The set of coins was extremely rare and, even without the last one, incredibly valuable. But finding the last coin would make it practically priceless. Could it be…?

Taylor looked up the set on the internet. At first, she couldn't find anything. Figured. Things like this only happened to someone else. Not her.

Then she hit on a recent article in a rare coin magazine. Turned out the set was from the 1800s, the first coin from the turn of the century, the last ending with the Civil War. A nickel from 1821 was the missing coin in the set. Alone, the nickel was estimated to be valued at ten million dollars. The entire set? Between forty-five and fifty million. *No way. Impossible.*

She kept reading. A dealer was searching for the missing nickel, hence the newscast and article, and was willing to pay full price for it to complete the set.

Taylor looked again. There was a photo of another nickel, the same kind. She expanded it on her phone. The picture became grainy, but she knew that coin. And she would never forget those numbers. 1821. Their combined birthdays. The same coin she'd found on the pier and given to Nick Diamante as a memento in return for her bottle of sea glass. A coin he'd tried to give back. A coin he'd insisted they share.

Impossible!

Her heart started racing. She went to other sites on the internet. She checked and checked again. Sure enough, they all said basically the same thing.

No way!

All of a sudden, Taylor found she couldn't breathe. Her chest tightened, but her entire body seemed to be floating. Her hands trembled. The impossible seemed to be possible.

Taylor, with Nick Diamante's help, had just, well, for lack of a better description, hit the lottery.

CHAPTER TWO

TAYLOR SAT FOR some time, staring at her phone, wanting to believe her realization was true. Finally, she managed to still her hands and their apartment came into focus. Looking up at the clock in the kitchen, she gasped at the time. Kate would get out of school in less than an hour.

Taylor panicked. *Impossible. Impossible.* The word kept running through her brain. *This cannot be happening!*

All of a sudden, she exploded, releasing a huge whoop of joy. She started dancing and then jumped in the air. "Yes!"

Calm down. Calm down.

Taylor looked up at the clock again. She picked up her phone and searched her contacts. Finding the one she needed, she pressed the key and waited. "Lisa? It's Taylor."

The coin. The coin.

"Hi, Tay. How's it going?" her friend asked.

"I need a huge favor, please. Something's come

up. I have to go see my mother and I don't think I have time to get Kate."

What do I do? What do I do?

Lisa commiserated. "I understand completely. And you know Kate's always welcome. No worries."

"Thank you," she breathed.

"My pleasure. And don't rush. As a matter of fact, Rachel will kill me if I don't invite Kate to dinner. She likes to milk every second out of a playdate. You don't mind, do you?"

"Absolutely not."

"Good," her friend said with a laugh. "I'll even try to get them to do some homework."

"Thanks, Lisa. I owe you one."

Reality proved too much to take in and as she hung up the phone, her whole body started to tremble. Then it occurred to her she might now have a way to repay such generosity.

And then what?

Taylor had to protect her family. She imagined a wild horde of people hounding her for money and she started hyperventilating. *Breathe!*

Once she'd calmed her emotions, Taylor's brain kicked in. *Nick.* Nick Diamante had their coin. And until she knew that he still had it, Taylor was getting way ahead of herself. So, she had to talk to Nick. And if he did have the coin, then what? Would he still want to share? Of course he would.

He'd insisted. He'd insisted the coin belonged to both of them.

Taylor pulled on a sweatshirt over her blouse. Today wasn't a nice spring day. Gray clouds swirled outside her window, the wind kicking up. Her jeans would also keep her warm. She tucked her phone in her pocket, having saved the news report video, and got into her car.

Okay, problem number one? How to track Nick down. To find him, she should start on Cantecaw Island.

Problem number two? Taylor would have to ask her mother to watch Kate while she was gone. She'd explain about the coin and the story she'd seen but have to make sure her mother realized all of this could be one very enormous pipe dream. Deep down inside, though, Taylor knew Nick had the coin, so she had to try. She owed it to her mother and her daughter.

Kate. Kate would be curious about this sudden trip, but all her daughter had to know was that Taylor had an interview to go to, which would make sense, when she reminded her that she'd lost her job. Taylor hoped her mom was home.

She drove across town and pulled up to the one-bedroom cottage that her mother had purchased after her father passed. The small house had a certain charm, but it was in need of a facelift, she acknowledged. Blue paint, faded from the sun, no longer looked simply weathered, and the white trim around the windows needed a little tender loving care. And though her mother enjoyed gardening and tried to keep back the growth, a landscaper would really come in handy.

Taylor got out of the car and rang the bell, composing herself. When Cynthia, her mother, opened the door she asked, "Tay? Is everything all right? What are you doing here?"

"Hi, Mom," she answered, stepping forward. Inside, she noticed the faded yellow, flowered wallpaper, and remembered some plumbing issues that hadn't ever gotten fully resolved. "Everything is…well, as fine as it can be."

Yes, she decided. Her mother would love and deserved something newer, better.

"Kate's okay?"

"Yes. She's over at Rachel's for the afternoon. Mom, you're not going to believe this, but I have something to tell you. I—I don't even know how to begin."

If her mother was surprised, she didn't show it. "Then how about a cup of tea?"

"That sounds great."

Her mom smiled. "Always good to take advantage of those pockets of free time."

"Yes."

Her mother put a kettle on to boil and set out two mugs with tea bags. "So, what's going on that's so important?"

Taylor started with what was real. "Frank let me go."

And I don't care.

Her mom frowned, and Taylor tried to keep the bubble of sheer joy from bursting. Angst warred with possibility.

"You knew this was coming."

"Yes. And why I took the studio when it became available." Taylor stepped back, noticing the lines on her mother's face, her hair no longer completely blond.

I'm going to make things so nice for you, Mom. You won't have to worry ever again. I hope.

Mom sat down and reached out to pat her hand. "You and Kate can move in here with me. I know I don't have a lot of room but we'll manage."

Taylor squeezed her mother's hand, suddenly feeling tears gathering. *Yes, if this works out, I'm going to really make your life wonderful.* But she needed to find Nick Diamante first.

"Mom, listen, I have something else to tell you. You're probably not going to believe me. And frankly, I don't even know if it's true yet or not."

Her mother frowned. "Whatever you're trying to say, just say it. You're not making sense."

Taylor drew in a deep breath. Then she took out her phone and showed her mother the article, recapping her connection to the missing coin. "He may not have it, Mom. It's been ten years. For all I know, Nick may not even remember me." Her face must've fallen because her mother leaned over to offer a quick hug.

The kettle whistled and they both sat down at the kitchen table with the honey pot and mugs steaming.

"I need Kate to stay with you while I try to find out." Taylor swallowed hard, hating to lie to her daughter. "And I don't want Kate to know. I'm worried she might end up telling half the world. What happens if she does and the coin is gone, and can't be found? She'd be so disappointed. I'm going to say that I have a job interview in New Jersey. Atlantic City."

Her mother nodded. "For the best, I suppose. But it means I'm going to have to keep it a secret, too."

"Do you mind?"

Her mother smiled. "Never," she answered to both requests. "My lips are sealed, and I can't wait to have my granddaughter with me."

Taylor nodded, voicing her last fear. "Mom, listen. I don't want you getting your hopes up too high. If the coin is gone, then it wasn't meant to be. I'll get by and so will Kate. We always have. I'll get another job. Work three jobs if I have to."

"You've always done what was necessary. Made me so proud of you."

Taylor felt tears well up again and sipped her tea to hide them. "I may need a couple of days. I don't know if Nick is on Cantecaw, let alone how he'll react. But as I said, I have to try. For you. For Kate."

Her mother stilled and drew in a big breath. Taylor watched her as she let it go. "Oh, sweetheart. You're going to make me cry."

Taylor swallowed hard before saying, "I'm not trying to. It's just...we're all in this together, no matter what happens."

"I'm glad to hear that. I love...well, us."

They finished their tea and Taylor left. On the drive home, she thought about how fate could be both a blessing and a curse at times. What was supposed to have been a happy dance had repercussions that couldn't be ignored. Reality could be tough.

Taylor picked her daughter up at Rachel's. Kate waved goodbye for a third time before Taylor could put the car in Drive.

"Why are you picking me up in the car?"

Could her little girl be any more observant? "I had to go to Nana's."

"Is she okay?" Kate asked, alarm threading her voice.

"Yes. Yes, she's fine. I needed to ask her to watch you for a few days."

They pulled into their parking lot. Taylor ushered Kate inside their apartment before she continued. "Something has happened that we need to talk about." She took off her sweatshirt and went to hang up Kate's jacket. "I'm guessing you know by now I'm no longer working at Foster's."

Kate nodded as if she'd expected to hear the words. "I had a feeling, especially when we had to move in here."

So grown up. Taylor's heart swelled with pride.

"Then you understand I have to go on job interviews?" she said and Kate nodded. "Good. One of them happens to be in New Jersey. Atlantic City."

Kate startled. Seems her daughter wasn't quite as sure about their future as Taylor thought. "When?" she asked.

"Tomorrow."

"For how long?"

"Just a few days." That double-edged sword struck deep. She hated the crestfallen look on Kate's face. *Hopefully, I'll be able to make it up to you, too, kiddo.*

If Nick remembered her. If Nick remembered their coin.

"Okay, Mom." Kate leaned in and smacked a kiss to Taylor's cheek. Off she went to her desk to finish her homework while Taylor pulled out leftovers from the fridge to heat up for herself for dinner.

Should she simply try to call Nick? Perhaps. But Nick, the Diamantes… They deserved so much better. No, Taylor had to deliver this news in person. And she had to find out the truth in person.

Besides, if she were being honest, she wanted to see Cantecaw again. She wanted to walk on the beach and think of happy memories while she listened to the rhythmic waves roll in and out. And she had decisions to make. Lots of them. The coin, and whether Nick had it or not, could change their lives forever.

"It'll be so much easier, doing the interviews this way, than commuting back and forth. And if I get a job, then you'll see my old mug again way sooner."

Kate, usually the optimist, took the other road. "If we live in New Jersey, what about Nana? And Rachel? And Terri?"

Every name became a check in the con column rather than the pro. "Hey, let's not get ahead of ourselves, all right? And even if I do get an offer, I don't have to take it. Understand?"

Kate brightened. "I understand."

"Good. Then I need you to finish your homework and pack some clothes to take to Nana's." She waited for Kate's nod of agreement. "What did you have for supper over at Rachel's?"

"Chinese takeout. Rachel's lucky."

Takeout was expensive compared to cooking. "What dish was your favorite?"

"Spaghetti."

Taylor tilted her head, unsure. "Oh, like noodles? It's called lo mein."

"I *was* kinda confused. But it tasted good.

Maybe we could have it sometime." Kate swiveled in her chair and stared at the open book on her desk.

Taylor smiled. If she knew her daughter, Kate was already planning several different ways to get her grandmother to spoil her.

THE NEXT DAY, after leaving Kate's bag at her mother's, Taylor dropped her daughter off at school. She sank into their final hug and kiss, missing Kate before she even let go. But as she drove down the turnpike, she felt a sense of freedom take hold. She hadn't been anywhere without her daughter in a long time. Of course, guilt immediately overtook her, until she tempered the feeling by declaring to herself that parents had a right to their own space, at least once in a while. Didn't they?

She continued driving, though, and her guilt grew. Taylor had just lied to one of the two people she loved the most. Doing what was right had its own cost and for the first time since she heard the news report, Taylor doubted her decision to follow the coin. She shoved away the thought, admitting she still had an obligation to find out. For Nick, not just herself and her family.

As she headed east, the complications faded and she regretted not returning to Cantecaw sooner. Her memories of the Island and that magical summer were perfect. Had she been right in believing that new memories might spoil the perfection of the old ones?

Maybe. But for a long while now, Taylor's focus had been on other, more important things. There was her daughter, her divorce; she'd barely had time to blink. Greg was in the picture now only sporadically and when it suited him, never mind what Kate might want. Taylor had essentially become a single parent overnight. Thank goodness for her mother. Cynthia was a rock she'd leaned on heavily in the past.

When she reached the bridge leading onto Cantecaw, Taylor caught her breath. As the car crested the last hill that brought her onto the Island, she eased up on the gas and took a second to enjoy the bright sun shining in a crystal blue sky. She would never really be able to explain to anyone how the place made her feel. The world turned simple, problems melted away, the pieces of her life simply fell into place. Cantecaw made everything all right. No, still not quite correct. Cantecaw was home.

Shaking her head, Taylor pulled up to the light on Main Street. If she turned left, she'd end up in the more residential area of the Island. Instead, she turned right toward the more commercial side.

Smiling as she drove, Taylor noticed more houses than she remembered and fewer businesses lining Main Street. All things changed, didn't they? Especially after ten years. Hadn't she?

She was very happy to see McGill's Mini-Golf and the Bluefish Tavern still remained. However, Gull's Nest and the used-book store seemed to be missing. But, oh thank goodness, Shaker's had survived. She laughed softly. Not their old facade with the huge saltshaker, though. The storefront sported a more modern look. She could only hope they hadn't done the same to their pancakes.

As she approached Fourteenth Street, Taylor's heart began to slam against her ribs. She drew in a deep breath, letting the air out slowly, trying to temper her excitement. She made a right toward the bay side of the Island, and glanced at the clock on her dashboard. They should be open for lunch. With Memorial Day a few weeks away, she imagined Diamante's gearing up for the summer crowd.

The street widened and ended facing the bay, so Taylor swung around and pulled into a spot in front of the restaurant. All its features looked new and she wondered if it had been damaged in the hurricane a few years back. She'd watched the news, horrified by the devastation and destruction the storm wrought.

Turning off the engine, she took a moment to gather herself. She'd been away such a long time. Would they remember her? Would Nick? After a decade, she feared the emotions were all one-sided. She'd had such a crush on him during that wonderful summer.

Taylor opened the door of her car and got out. She drew in a lungful of brackish, briny bay air feeling that sense of peace and belonging descend again. She closed the door and let go of the breath and walked up the steps. She opened the front door of the restaurant, immediately assailed by the familiar smells of garlic, onions and tomato sauce. Diamante's was known far and wide for its authentic Italian food.

Coming from the bright sunlight into the dim restaurant, Taylor was unable to see. She blinked. And she blinked again. When her eyes adjusted, she realized she'd nearly run into him. She focused on his shiny black hair first, then recognized maturity and strength in his face. His warm brown eyes seemed to have a slight edge to them now. They widened and his gaze filled with shock, confusion, and oh thank goodness, a tinge of welcome. His lips parted but no words came out, so she smiled, hoping against hope he would smile back.

"Hello, Nick."

CHAPTER THREE

NICK DIAMANTE LIVED on an island bordering the Atlantic Ocean, not in a desert, so the vision before him couldn't be a mirage. He stopped, mid-breath. She'd been all arms and legs back then, like a thoroughbred waiting in the wings. Her long, multicolored blond hair fell in waves around her face, ending just below her shoulders. Those bright blue eyes, with the power to still haunt, put diamonds to shame. The line from her high cheekbones to her jaw still strong.

She'd grown into herself, become the picture he'd always imagined, and the result was incredible. "Taylor? Taylor Marchand?"

"Hello, Nick. It's Hughes now. How are you?"

She seemed like she had no idea how to greet him as her weight shifted from foot to foot. She lifted her hand to shake but Nick lifted a brow. In the Diamante household, there was only one way to greet a member of the family. He opened his arms and she stepped into them. She smelled like sweet perfume. He inhaled deeply, letting the pretty scent settle, then he wrapped her up in a big hug. Was that a sigh? No, just his imagination.

He let go and stepped back, he felt a huge smile on his face. "Fine. Fine." He kind of laughed to himself, the moment so unexpected.

"I stopped by to say hello."

Nick nodded. "Sure thing, I... Uh. Uncertain where to turn next, he walked back behind the bar. He needed a moment to gather his wits, so he started drying wineglasses and hanging them in the overhead racks. "Hello. Welcome."

She seemed nonplussed for a second, like she had no idea what to say next. He certainly didn't. Not after—what was it?—nearly ten years?

"I see you're getting ready for lunch."

"Not a huge crowd," he answered. "Wait until Memorial Day."

She took a hesitant step forward. "I need to speak to you."

Right away, he dropped the bar rag into the sink and leaned on the wood counter. He wondered what would have prompted her to come to Cantecaw now, in person. Without a phone call? An email? "I'm listening."

She shook her head. "No. In private."

"Private?" he repeated, surprised. Secrets never stayed secret in the Diamante household.

She lifted the corner of her mouth, understanding his point, no doubt. "Gotcha. But please. I'm asking. Perhaps you can grab a moment and we can meet at the pier?"

The place conjured memories of their one summer together and the way the sparkling blue-gray of the ocean matched her eyes. The look of fierce determination on her face when she took up a cause. And let's not forget when the tip of her tongue would stick out from between her teeth as she completed a task. Body and soul. Taylor put her entire self into everything she did.

Nick came back to the present, curious if she'd changed and knowing what a shame it would be if she had.

"Sure, but I still have lunch to serve. Then we have to change over, eat and get ready for dinner," he told her.

"Nick. Please. It's important."

What could be so earth-shattering that he should stop everything? "I understand that. But I'm shorthanded. We've been getting fewer kids looking for summer work these past two, three years. Everyone wants to be a tech wizard and make billions by the time they're twenty-one."

"I know what that's like. I've been dealing with eighteen-year-olds myself in the kitchen. So many don't know how to do anything unless a video can tell them."

Nick blurted, "That's amazing. You own your own restaurant?"

Twin spots of color dotted her cheeks before

she lowered her gaze. "No. I managed a family restaurant for the last seven years."

Was that a past tense he heard?

As he was about to ask, the swinging door to the kitchen popped open. Mama. "Nico? Aren't you done?"

Taylor whispered a one-word question. "Mama?"

His mother cocked her head and peered. She didn't see all that well without her glasses and the stubborn woman refused to wear them all the time.

"Taylor? Is it really you?"

"Mama Bella!"

His mother opened her arms and Taylor fell into a giant bear hug. Both of them started crying, while Nick's heart beat heavy in his chest. There couldn't be a more beautiful sight than such heartfelt emotion.

Taylor let go first and his mother patted Taylor's arms, sliding her hands up and down as if she couldn't believe Taylor was real. Then his mother frowned. "You have problem, *cara mia*? Is there trouble? You tell us. Mama Bella will fix you up."

His mother glanced over at him, her look daring him to refute her words, before focusing on Taylor again. "You will eat with us later, *cara mia*. Usual time."

Taylor seemed ready to argue. Of course, his mother could steamroll anyone, including the president and the pope. Nick knew the feeling all too well.

"Mama. Hold on. Taylor may have other plans."

"No, she doesn't." His mother turned to Taylor. "Do you?"

He watched Taylor flash his mother a warm smile with the ease of someone used to dealing with unexpected situations, without showing a hint of her inner feelings. She slipped her arm around his mother's and guided Bella back toward the kitchen. "Of course not. I wouldn't dare miss a meal with the Diamantes." With this statement, Taylor sent Nick a little dimpled grin. "Do you have any lasagna?"

Bella laughed. "I always have lasagna."

"Then I'll be here."

His mother disappeared into the kitchen and Taylor stepped up to him. "I've eaten in some very high-end restaurants."

"I ran some of them," he answered.

"I know." *She did?* For a split second, the ground fell out from beneath his feet and Nick walked on air. "Anyway, I have to say, no one's lasagna comes close to Bella's."

To hide his own emotions, he said, "You don't have to eat with us, you know."

She looked at him with a wry grin. "Trying to get rid of me?"

"No. No. Of course not," he backtracked. "But

we both know Mama can be—beyond persuasive?"

She nodded. "I'm a big girl now."

He couldn't help admiring the view. "Yes, you are."

She seemed unsure all of a sudden. "What's that supposed to mean?"

He smiled, hoping she'd realize his comment was a compliment. "Nothing. Nothing."

"Good." She straightened. "I can take care of myself."

"I'm sure." He returned to the bar and began putting glasses away. "Look, I'm sorry, Tay, I really need to finish up here."

"And I need to check into my hotel."

"Fair enough. What do you say we eat, keep Mama happy and I'll take a couple of minutes after we're done? Okay by you?"

"Sounds good. Three o'clock?"

"You know it." He smiled. "I'll see you in a little while."

Taylor left and Nick purposely avoided going back into the kitchen. He kept racking glasses until the shock of seeing Taylor again wore off. When he could no longer stay away, he walked into the bright, aromatic kitchen. Right into a "Mama Bella stare."

"You should have married that girl a long time ago, Nico."

He sighed. "Mama. Really? Did you happen

to notice the ring on her finger? She's wearing a wedding band."

His mother released a snort of disgust. "Sweet, hardworking girl. Not like that *svogliata* Lorraine. Ugh, such a lazybones."

Looking back at his brief engagement, Nick hated to admit his mother was right. He raked his hand through his hair and said, "I should've known better. You're right. Anyone who won't eat your lasagna can't be trusted."

Bella harrumphed and Nick laughed. "Mama, you need to let it be. Please. Things don't always work out the way you want."

She peered over her nose at him. "Says who?"

Nick knew better than to answer. He threw up his hands, admitted defeat and got back to work.

RIGHT ON THE dot of three, Taylor walked back into the restaurant. Nick hadn't really registered it before, but she wore a tailored suit with a collared shirt. He liked her large, octagonal sunglasses. They completed the look. But he liked her even better when she took them off and revealed her glittering blues.

She smiled. "What? Pimple on my chin?"

He chuckled. The last time she had asked the question, there had been. A nasty one. "Not this time, no."

The front door opened abruptly. Taylor swung

around and let out a squee of delight. "Rocco? Is it really you?"

"When Mama called," his brother said, "I had to see for myself." Rocco reached out and hugged Taylor. When he let go, he stared straight at Nick for a long moment, as if he couldn't believe she was here, before turning his attention back to Taylor. "Wow. You grew up."

Taylor made a face. "Happens, I guess, after nearly ten years." She smiled. "It's really good to see you."

"Good to see you, too. Mama doesn't always invite me for the pre-rush dinner," his brother said, grinning.

"You don't miss too many meals," Nick teased, patting Rocco's waist.

Rocco laughed. "Beth says hi, by the way,"

"Beth?" Taylor asked. "Oh, my goodness. You stayed together?"

Rocco's smile grew. "Married seven years. We've got a little boy, Roc Junior, and one in the oven. A girl."

"That's wonderful. Awesome," Taylor exclaimed. "I'm so happy for you both. And how's Beth?"

"Ready not to be pregnant anymore. We can't wait to meet the baby."

Something special danced around Taylor's lips as Nick watched her smile. "Your mother will never forgive you if you don't have at least five."

Rocco winced. "Don't tell Beth, or Mama will—"

"I'll what?" his mother asked, coming out of the kitchen. "Come. Eat. *Mangia*."

They always set several tables end to end in the middle of the room and Nick made sure to be near Taylor. Not as many tables as they used to have, he thought. Well past time to bring the restaurant back to overflowing as it used to be.

People began passing bowls around and Nick sliced off a large piece of lasagna for Taylor.

"You can't possibly expect me to eat all of this," she said.

Mama pulled her brows together. Uh-oh.

"Why not?" he asked. "You always used to." He also poured her a glass of the house red and she gestured for him to stop at half-full.

"Nick. Please. I really don't drink."

Rocco chuckled, beating Nick to the punchline. "You should know better, Taylor. In this family, wine isn't drinking."

Taylor took a bite of the lasagna and her face relaxed with pleasure. "Mmm. This is *so* good. I haven't tried to make my own in years." The excitement in her gaze dimmed for a second. "I guess I didn't have time."

Nick understood. Mama's lasagna took two days to make.

"I noticed the front of the restaurant looks new," Taylor said after a small sip of wine. "Was the storm bad?"

"Diamante's *è casa*. We don't abandon our home," Bella declared.

"We hunkered down here at the restaurant," Rocco explained.

"Got at least—what was it?—four feet of water in the storeroom?" Nick added. "And the power was off for nearly a week."

"The generator helped and we ran it as much as we could," Rocco continued. "People saw our lights on and came to us."

"We feed them," Mama added, nodding her head. "Neighbors are family."

"I'm sorry," Taylor said. "I watched on the news. Horrifying. Absolutely horrifying to see so many homes destroyed. I'm so glad the Island seems almost untouched now."

Nick sat back in his chair, becoming a little impatient. She had to know they all wanted an update about *her* life these last ten years, but she steered the conversation away from herself. It didn't seem like anyone had noticed. Impressive. Very impressive.

"So, Nick. How come you're not married?" she asked.

He wanted to explain but his mother answered for him. "No hope for my Nico. Not with that one he brought home who—"

"Mama." He tried to push off the topic, noticing his brother hiding a grin at his predicament. "I was engaged but it didn't work out."

They all continued eating until Taylor pushed back from the table. Half of her lunch was still on her plate. Mama looked ready to encourage her to eat more. And Taylor seemed to be bracing herself for Mama's well-meaning encouragement, but still, time for him to save the day.

"Mama, I have to go to the store for some heavy cream." He quickly followed that with, "Taylor, would you like to come with me?"

On cue, Taylor leapt to her feet. "I'd love to." She followed Nick away from the table, stopping next to his mother. "Thank you for the wonderful meal. It was as delicious as I remember it."

Of course, Bella wouldn't give up that easily. "I put the rest of your meal in a tin. You eat later."

Taylor beamed. "Thank you again."

Rocco stood, and he and Taylor hugged. She asked, "I'd love to say hello to Beth in person, if I could?"

"She'd like the company." Rocco and Taylor exchanged cell numbers. "Great to see you, Tay. Welcome home."

Something deep down inside clicked when Rocco used the shortened version of her name and said home in the same sentence. But Nick ignored the feeling and escorted Taylor out of the restaurant. He put on his sunglasses and watched her do the same. She breathed deeply and twirled her arms out wide. "What a beautiful day."

He looked only at her. "Yes, yes, it is."

They started walking toward the pier. "I couldn't help but notice," he began, "that you managed to get away without divulging one iota of personal information at the table. Well done."

"My life is hardly as exciting as a hurricane and its aftermath."

He smiled. "I can't believe Mama didn't force you to tell us all your news over the past ten years."

"Now that you mention it, neither can I. And now that I've survived one meal without an interrogation, I'm not sure I want to go back for another."

"Not even for more lasagna?" he teased.

"Tough choice."

They walked some more in silence and Nick couldn't believe how right things felt as she matched him stride for stride.

"You know," she told him as they approached the boardwalk, "I remember this journey being a great deal shorter."

"Me, too."

Once they reached the pier, which was just at the end of the boardwalk, Nick followed Taylor to the railing and looked out over the ocean. With the water clear today, Taylor couldn't know the striking image she made framed by sea and sky.

Of course, his next glance had to be of her gold wedding band. *Darn.*

Nick remembered how they used to talk, sometimes while they set tables, sometimes when they cleaned up the outdoor eating area on the deck. They discussed anything and everything, from baseball scores to their dreams for the future. They challenged each other, played tricks on one another. Boy, did he get an earful when sugar ended up in the saltshakers. Repayment for him almost pushing her over the bulkhead and into the lagoon. So long ago. "Good to be back?"

"Very," she breathed. "I'm completely land-locked. I live in Pennsylvania."

A detail niggled in the back of his mind and he dug it out. "Ah. Yes. That's right. Your mother's family is from there."

She cocked her head and stared at him. "You have the memory of an elephant."

"And the ears," he admitted with a rueful grin.

She leaned in, studying one side of his head, then the other, as if examining a painting or something. "No, I think they fit your face perfectly."

For a moment, Nick got lost in her gaze.

He stepped back with a shaky laugh and asked, "So, why did you come here, Tay? What brought you back to Cantecaw after all this time?"

She pulled out her phone. "You need to listen to me, okay? I know it'll sound weird, but the truth is here in an article I saw about a week ago. I even did a little research on him."

Him? Who? "You've lost me."

She presented the news article.

He frowned at the picture on the top. "That's a coin. A nickel, right?"

"Yes! Exactly!"

He was missing something here.

She started bouncing on her toes. "Do you remember that night? Right here? When I found a nickel stuck between two planks on the boardwalk? And I told you to keep it? I wanted you to have it since you'd given me the bottle of sea glass. And we kind of argued? You said the coin was mine but if I insisted, and I did, then it belonged to both of us?"

He looked at the picture again. *Had he?* Honestly, he had no idea. *It was a decade ago.* The next picture looked like a coin book, a set. One hole was empty. "I remember the night." Indeed, a warm feeling centered in his stomach. Funny how he'd never forgotten the one kiss he'd given her.

"Boy oh boy, am I glad you do."

Confused, he asked, "What do you mean?"

She started reading the article to him. With his mind half in the past, he didn't catch everything she was saying. Something about the nickel being expensive, part of a set worth even more, and a coin dealer looking for it.

"Now, I get that maybe you're not going to believe me. I didn't believe it at first, either. But *this* is the nickel I found. This is the nickel we argued about. This is the nickel you said you'd hold for both of us. Nick, do you know what this means? We're rich!"

Still half in a daze, he asked, "We?"

She stilled. She stiffened. And like a cartoon character, all of the air whooshed out of her. The color drained from her cheeks. The bright excitement dimmed in her eyes. "I see." Her words snapped with clipped precision. "I understand. You have no obligation to me. I gave the coin to you. Even though you told me it belonged to both of us, it's yours to do with as you please." She turned and began striding back down the boardwalk.

"Taylor, wait! No. Wait. Don't go."

"I was hoping you'd be fair," she said, pausing so he could catch up to her. He found no warmth in her gaze now. "You told me we would share it. But I did insist at first that the coin was yours."

Nick raked his hand through his hair. "Wait. You're wrong. I'm having a hard time processing. Please. Give me a moment. I'm not sure I understand any of this." Indeed, his head felt like it was under the ocean, all kinds of slow and muddled.

She nodded, her posture not quite as closed-off as before. "I came back to let you know. The coin is real. I could never make up a story like that. And I will never, ever forget that date on the coin. The dealer is looking for a nickel from 1821, Nick. 1821. My age. Your age." She took a breath and stepped toward him. "The news report might not be right about its exact value, but I know with every breath I take that this coin is the nickel I insisted you hold on to. Keep as a memento of our friendship from all those years ago."

How wild. Totally unpredictable. And a great story.

Not quite knowing what else to do, Nick started laughing.

CHAPTER FOUR

NICK KEPT LAUGHING and Taylor felt the hole in her stomach grow. She wasn't sure what to do. He'd asked her to wait for him to catch up with what she was saying, but he didn't seem to be accepting the truth. "You need to believe me, Nick."

"Great joke, Taylor. Really ingenious way to break the ice, I suppose. But *believe you*?" He kept laughing softly and shook his head.

Break the ice? Wait. What? "Read the article, Nick. Better yet, there's a video of a broadcast. The numbers, the year, is on the coin in the picture."

Taylor turned away. Her heart ached. Of all the reactions she'd anticipated, this wasn't one of them. No. Not Nick. Not the Nick she remembered. The man she remembered would have at least tried to understand. Find the coin. She remembered an honorable man. What had the years done to him? Everything simply became a blur. "Goodbye, Nick."

"What?"

"I can't force you to believe me," she called

over her shoulder, stomping away. "I can't force you to try and look for the coin. I'm simply telling you what I know. The rest is up to you."

"The rest?"

She stopped and faced him. "Do I have to spell it out for you?"

He frowned. "I don't know what you're talking about and I'm not sure I care."

"Easy for you to say."

He sobered quickly. He must have realized how upset she was. "Look, Tay," he said. "You don't need some kind of fantastic story to be accepted back into the fold."

"Hold on a minute. What?" She dropped her hand with the phone to her side and gawked at him. "You think I'm only doing this to get back into your good graces?"

At least he had the decency to seem contrite. "No. Of course not. But you've just dropped this announcement on me. I'm sorry. I'm not really sure what to think."

She glanced away. Okay, maybe he had a point. Taylor looked back at him and found him staring at his watch.

"I have to get to the restaurant. I'm already late. Mama will have my head." He sighed. "I'd like to walk you back, if you'll let me."

Taylor shook her head. "I'd like to watch the waves for a while. But thank you for the offer." Even she felt the ice coating her words.

"You're mad. I don't want you to be mad at me, Tay."

"I'm not mad. Well, maybe a little. But you did apologize, and to be fair, I didn't know how to react, either, at first."

He cocked his head and lifted a single brow, giving her the sideways look that always got to her. "Let's forget the whole thing for now, okay? We'll start again with the coin, later. Friends?"

It was the same grin he'd used too many times to get her on side. How did he do that? He could still charm the spots off a leopard.

"Always," Taylor said.

Nick gave her a quick, hard hug. When he let her go, he asked, "You'll be here in the morning?"

"Yes."

"Good. Shakers? Breakfast?"

She nodded. "I couldn't leave without at least one plate of pancakes."

"Excellent. Where are you staying?"

"The Sunrise."

"I'll pick you up tomorrow at nine."

He hurried off and Taylor found her interest more engaged in watching him walk away than the waves crashing into the shore. Finally, when she couldn't see him anymore, she focused on the ocean again.

How could she have been so foolish? She should have guessed that he might not believe her. How dumb!

Dumb? A bit harsh. Definitely unprepared. Thinking back, she barely remembered finding out about the coin. The past thirty-six hours seemed to be like zooming along a road, only recognizing a few mile markers along the way. The rest was blank.

Of all the expectations Taylor had carried as she drove across the bridge onto Cantecaw, encountering a skeptical Nick hadn't been one. And now? All she had was an article dredged up from the internet and a newscast he didn't want to see.

What's my next step? What do I do?

She thought about getting in her car and driving home, letting fate play out. It would serve Nick Diamante right. But then she thought of everyone else this discovery affected. She'd never forgive herself. Kate deserved better. So did her mother. So did Mama Bella and Rocco and Beth.

Judging by Nick's attitude, Taylor realized she had a great deal of work to do. She would have to get Nick to trust her again. Then she'd have to get him to search for the coin. The only way to win him over would be for them to get to know each other again. Could they rebuild the trust they once had?

She stared out at the ocean, awash not only in salt spray but memories. She'd admit, even to herself, her true nature was a cut above being very shy. Going for a degree in hospitality had been a means to overcome her shyness. She'd lived in a tiny cottage in Dennington with Dianna and Samantha, two friends from school, and taken classes during the day and waitressed at night. Her days were hectic, her evenings at the Dennington Grill long, and her free time filled with studying and sleep. In her most secret thoughts, Taylor dreamed she'd go back to Diamante's, degree in hand, and run the restaurant. With Nick. Her crush. How pie-in-the-sky it all sounded now.

With her schedule the way it had been, dating rarely happened. Every now and then she might manage a day at the beach with her roomies. Then she'd met Greg. He was in one of her classes. *Met*, she laughed to herself, didn't exactly come close to describe how she'd been bowled over. He was kind and so attentive. They'd gotten married and life couldn't have been more right. Several months later, though, he seemed distant, moody. She asked him what was wrong, but he never answered her. After that, he gradually lost interest in her, even Kate, and developed other interests she'd found out that had eventually driven a wedge between them.

Taylor tightened her fingers around the wooden railing until her knuckles showed white. How did a person know a mistake was a mistake until they made it?

The wind kicked up and she shivered. She stuffed her hands in the pockets of her jacket and started walking back to the restaurant and her car.

Mistake or no, Taylor had received the best thing that had ever happened to her, a nugget of pure, precious joy, from their union. Each and every moment with Kate was beyond a blessing.

Thinking of her daughter reminded her that she needed to call her mother and check in. "Hi, Mom."

"Hi, sweetheart. How'd the…interview go?"

Her guilt meter shot up again. She sincerely hated being deceptive. "Not too well, I'm afraid. He doesn't believe my story and he doesn't remember the coin."

"Don't be too disappointed if…well…" Her mother hesitated. Kate was probably within earshot.

"I know. But I can't help myself. I've got to get him to listen, Mom. For his sake and his family's, not just us. Might take more than a day or two, I'm afraid."

"I've got your back, darling. Don't worry. Kate only gets away with murder half of the time here."

More like three-quarters. But who was counting. "Thanks for understanding, Mom. And for covering for me. Can you put Kate on now, please?"

Taylor took two steps and a voice boomed in her ear, "Hi, Mom!"

She had to admit there was nothing shy or fragile about Kate. Her daughter's self-assurance came straight from her father. Only, in Greg's case, it was false bravado. "How's it going? I miss you."

"I miss you, too."

A wind gust rattled a nearby flagpole and trees, as Kate asked, "Mom? Where are you?"

"Just taking a little walk to get some fresh air."

"When will you be home?"

Taylor's heart hurt. She wished she was with her daughter. "I don't know. I just don't know."

"You sound sad. Don't be sad."

"All right. For you I won't." She heard Kate release a huge breath and Taylor realized the relief her daughter was feeling. "I'll call tomorrow and let Nana know what's going on."

"Okay. Maybe you'll be home tomorrow?"

"Maybe. I don't know. I love you, sweetheart."

"Love you, too. Here's Nana."

The sound of the phone being passed rattled in her ear. "You'll call and let me know what's going on?" her mother asked.

"Of course. I guess I'm frustrated. I didn't take the time to process all the possible outcomes. Now that I am, I don't want Nick to simply dismiss the chance of finding our coin. Am I making sense?"

"Of course you are," her mother answered. "I told you before. You'll do what you must. You always have. Hard choices are just that."

"Mom?" Taylor pulled the phone from her

ear to stare at the image on the screen. "Are you okay?"

Her mother gave a small smile. "I didn't mean anything by that, except to tell you how sorry I am that you lost your job. And now, when you expected…something new, it's so difficult. You've had to work so hard for everything you've wanted. I wish I could've given you more."

Tears filled her eyes. Now her heart hurt twice as bad. "Mom. Stop. Please. After Dad died, you had to struggle. Maybe it's part of being a Marchand. Didn't you tell me stories about how our family had to overcome so much just to get here?"

Her mother snuffled but Taylor was sure she wanted to smile. "I did. So much drama those stories held, but a lot of perseverance as well. I'll bet, if we did one of those ancestry searches, you could find out more."

She could. Any time she wanted. And she would not have to worry about the cost. What an amazing thought. *If* she could only get Nick Diamante to listen. "Yeah, I guess I could." Excitement filled her at the prospect. "Kate behaving?"

"Always."

That probably meant her daughter had only gotten one or two time-out threats, instead of the usual three or four. "Great. Thanks again, Mom, for helping me out."

"What was it you said about Marchand women? We take our responsibilities seriously."

LINDA J. PARISI   55

"Indeed, we do. Love you," Taylor said.

"Love you, too. Bye."

Taylor put her cell back in her pocket and found she'd arrived at Diamante's. She got in her car and drove over to the Sunrise, a small hotel just off the ocean, sandwiched in between several Victorian houses turned into bed-and-breakfasts.

Though some of the homes were a bit modern, others were true "painted ladies," trimmed in greens and pinks and purples. The inn was all white, with pink shutters and wrought iron railings leading up to a columned porch.

She parked on the block in the closest spot she could find and walked up to the hotel. A couple sat in white wicker chairs on the porch, playing a game of chess. Taylor nodded hello as she passed them and went inside the hotel. She breathed deeply as she recognized Cantecaw scents she would know anywhere.

A young man stood behind the reception desk wearing thin-rimmed glasses and a bow tie. "Mrs. Hughes?"

"Yes?"

"Nick said to give you this. And if I touched any, I'd be banned for life."

Taylor read the guy's name tag. *Henry.* "Oh, he did, did he?"

Henry lifted a huge bag with the Diamante's logo from behind the counter. "The rooms all have refrigerators and microwaves."

She knew. "Um, you do know he wouldn't ban you for life, right?"

Henry smiled. "Sure. I've been going to Diamante's since I was old enough to walk." He pointed to the bag. "You're lucky."

"And so are you. There's too much here for me to eat. Mama Bella probably included enough food to feed ten people. So, if you have a spare plate, I'll share."

"Are you kidding me?"

She shook her head no.

"I'll be right back."

Taylor peeked inside the extra-large bag. Half a bottle of house red, spaghetti, what looked to be either veal or chicken Parmesan, and the leftover lasagna. And a note.

When Henry returned with his plate and cutlery, she gave him the spaghetti and half the chicken parmesan. No one was getting the lasagna.

His face lit up like a little kid's. "Thank you, Mrs. Hughes. Thank you."

"My pleasure."

Once she got into her room, Taylor turned on the light so she could read the note.

Taylor,

I'm sorry I started laughing. Chalk it up to a reflex action. However, you have to admit your entire story is pretty out there. Espe-

cially when I remember the night, but I don't remember you giving me any coin. No matter the reason, let's forget the whole thing for now and start over again, like we said. Please.

Your friend always,
Nick

P.S. Mama put in extra food. Just in case.

Of course, she did. Taylor wasn't hungry just yet but half a glass of the wine called to her. She changed into jeans and saw a real wineglass inside the bag. Just like Nick to make the ordinary seem special. She went down to the porch to watch the sunset, glass in hand.

Odd, she felt antsy. She wasn't used to having time to herself. "I hope I'm not intruding," she told the couple playing chess. "I can leave if you'd like."

"No. Please don't. We're nearly finished. I'm Emily. This is my husband, Bob."

"Taylor."

She watched Bob sit back in his chair and shake his head. "Beats me every time," he groused.

Taylor sipped her wine. "Do you come to Cantecaw often?"

"Every year for the last twenty years," Emily

answered. "Although now, we come before or after the summer rush. Too many people otherwise."

Taylor understood. Before and after the tourist rush were the best times of year at the shore. "I love the Island."

"We do, too. Something special about this place," Bob commented.

"I know," Taylor agreed.

Emily looked like she wanted to ask something and finally did. "Was that package we saw from Diamante's?"

Taylor laughed. "Yes. I used to work there and stopped by for a visit. Mama wouldn't let me leave without food."

"Sounds like her." Emily laughed. "We're going over in a little while for dinner. We'd invite you," she said. "But you already have a lovely meal."

"Thank you so much for your kind offer. Maybe next time." She sipped her wine. "I have some thinking to do."

Her new friends rose. "No matter what," Bob told her. "Problems are easier to chew in small bites rather than large chunks."

"Leave it to Bob here to be right," Emily added. "But he forgot one thing. Problems always seem to work themselves out on Cantecaw."

"You're right. Both of you. Thanks." She smiled and shook their hands. "Enjoy your dinner."

"We will," Bob said with a grin. He patted his stomach. "We will."

Small bites. Chip away at the chunks. Or maybe she should be thinking in terms of mining gold. No matter what, she needed to get Nick to trust her. Then agree to look for that coin. Maybe the way to get Nick to see the truth was to bring up the subject of the coin but make light of the situation at the same time. Try to get him used to the idea first.

Taylor settled in one of the rockers, listening to the ocean and savoring her wine. She finished and went back to her room, eating what she could manage because Mama Bella would somehow know if she didn't. She fell into the deepest sleep she'd had in years.

TENSION AND EXCITEMENT simmered in her stomach as she waited for Nick to pick her up the next morning. The sun already warmed her face but the breeze came off the ocean with a chill. She thought back to that magical summer, when she'd been so awed by him at first, she'd barely said two words to Nick. As she got to know him, she'd found him to be genuine and honest, and his attention real, not fake. Soon she felt easy enough with him to tell him some of her deepest thoughts, which made them friends. Only, her heart wanted her to make it more. Then she'd think to herself, why would a mature twenty-one-year-old want to know more about an extremely shy eighteen-year-old?

Nick pulled up in a Land Rover and her mouth

fell open. She climbed inside, releasing a low whistle of appreciation. "Before you start to say anything—" he laughed "—Old Bessie here is a remnant from my corporate days."

"Old Bessie? I don't think so."

"You'd be surprised," he said. "Nearing a hundred thousand miles. I used to travel a lot."

"Wow. You'd never know judging by the outside."

He grew thoughtful. "When you appreciate a thing, especially over the long haul, you take care of it."

"Duly noted." Taylor lifted a brow. "Including pancakes? I'm glad the building is still standing."

He smiled. "I do miss the old saltshaker, though."

"Me, too."

The weathered redbrick facade of Shaker's seemed a letdown. They parked and Nick placed a hand on her back as he followed her inside. A frisson of...yes, anticipation, sizzled up her spine. Her first urge to hang back, became swamped by her second urge to straighten. Taylor chided herself. What was she doing, acting like she was an eighteen-year-old again?

A waitress brought a steaming carafe of coffee as soon as they sat down. Nick settled on a full breakfast while she ordered the short stack.

"I'm hoping my note will allow us to continue being friends," he said.

"The pancakes help."

He looked down, playing with the napkin on

the table, before catching her gaze. "I didn't mean to insult you."

"But you still don't believe me."

"Again, hard to do when I don't remember what you're talking about."

When she frowned, he tried to clarify. "Sorry, I remember the night. Talking on the pier. Seeing you home."

"Good. It's a beginning." Taylor nodded. "I thought about our predicament for quite a while last night. I decided a full-fledged kidnapping of you was in order."

He stared at her. "Seriously?"

"I was joking. What about a reenactment of that night? Maybe we can jog your memory some more. Then you can look for the coin."

"Do you really think recreating the past will make me remember?"

"Can't hurt."

"Maybe it can," he said, with a wary expression. "Even if I did believe you, what then? I have no idea where it is or what I might have done with it. Wouldn't it hurt even more to know it exists and not be able to find it?"

"Yes, it would," she replied, digging in her heels. "But I'm much more willing to chalk things up to fate than not to try at all. That night, well, you insisted the coin belonged to both of us. There are other people who will be very affected by our discovery. People we both love."

He still didn't seem convinced. "So, you just want me to up and go on a wild-goose chase, is that it? I have a restaurant to run. I can't get away right now, I can't even spare two hours of alone time. We're short-staffed and Memorial Day is in a few weeks."

"Not a wild-goose chase. Just a walk to see what we can remember. Please."

"Not sure what that will prove. I don't doubt the coin or coins exist." He shook his head. "Tay, I have no idea what's making you upset. I never said you weren't entitled to any of the money."

"You haven't said that I am," she shot back, knowing she shouldn't be angry but feeling mad, anyway.

"Because I don't remember the coin. I remember a beautiful night. I remember feeling on top of the world. I remember having a little bit too much wine."

"You were leaving for graduate school. The beginning of your grand plan. A master's degree in business."

"Starting a new chapter. I couldn't wait."

Taylor had no right but the emotions battering her then were hurting her now. How she'd wanted him to stay. The words clogged her throat. Not one came out. Not even after he'd kissed her goodbye on the cheek.

One thing hadn't changed—what a stubborn, stubborn man.

He made a face and sat back as if this was a topic he couldn't win. Then his brows drew together. "What about your husband?"

"My husband?"

The server came with their food. Taylor wanted to continue talking. But her stomach rumbled, so she started eating. She found the pancakes less decadent than she remembered. Or had the conversation ruined her appetite? Nick said little and soon finished his entire plate.

Nick paid the bill after they were done and said, "Let's head up to the ocean for a few, and we'll go over what I can remember."

"Thank you."

Once they were outside, he continued. "But first I'd like to know. Your husband? I couldn't help notice the ring."

Taylor looked down at her hand. She'd forgotten. She wore it out of habit. "Um—"

They reached the top of the dunes. The ocean spread out as far as she could see and the sun's rays glittered tiny diamonds across the surface.

"What's his opinion about this?"

"He doesn't know."

"What?" Nick's confusion was obvious. "You came here to tell me about a coin worth millions before you told your own husband?"

Now he thought badly of her. No matter what she did, when it came to Nick, it seemed she did it wrong. "He's not my husband anymore. We're divorced."

"Divorced?"

"You have got to stop repeating everything I say. I forget I even have the ring on most of the time."

"Right. Okay, let me see." He closed his eyes. "That night... You looked beautiful that night."

She felt a tinge of heat in her cheeks. "I remember. And?"

"I drank too much wine."

"You were certainly more relaxed than usual," she said, a touch of amusement riding her tone.

He opened his eyes and looked straight at her. "I walked you to your apartment. The moonlight glowed, your hair shone."

She hadn't forgotten a moment of that night. "There was no moonlight, Nick. The fog had rolled in and we could barely see in front of us."

"Are you sure? I thought..." He grimaced. "I guess I had more wine than I remembered."

Her hopes fell but she refused to give up. A certain someone was counting on her. "There's more, Nick. Besides the divorce."

He lifted both brows. "What? You're an ax murderer?"

She made a face. "Very funny. "Then she pulled up the photo app on her phone. "You're not the only one who has a bigger family. This is my daughter, Nick. I have a little girl. She's seven years old and her name is Kate."

CHAPTER FIVE

A DAUGHTER? NICK STEPPED closer to peer over Taylor's shoulder. Big mistake, since he inhaled a lungful of her perfume. Bigger mistake because he could feel the warmth of her shoulder nearly touching his chest.

There could be no doubt the child in the picture belonged to Taylor. The girl had the same hair, same high cheekbones and the same bright blue diamond eyes filled with impish delight. "She's beautiful," he breathed.

Nick wanted to move but couldn't get away from the heady combination of citrus and sea and warmth. He leaned forward again as if an invisible magnet drew him and he lingered for a shade too long. Taylor twisted to look up at him. It was almost like ten years in the past when they'd shared that kiss.

She had tiny laugh lines at the corners of her eyes now. Her features had matured, yet her skin looked as soft as ever. His heart began to thud low in his chest. He stepped back quickly. To hide the awkward movement, he asked, "Seven years old?"

"Yes." She smiled. "Just finishing up second grade."

"She looks exactly like you."

"I'll take your observation as the highest compliment."

"You should." Nick started walking again, watching Taylor slip her phone into her pocket. She seemed to beam with a glow from the inside. "She must be very special."

"She is."

Taylor followed and they both took a moment to watch the waves roll in and out. Nothing soothed better than the sea. Still, Nick felt he was missing quite a bit of her story. "Care to fill in the gaps? Obviously, there's a great deal you haven't told me."

She didn't answer at first and Nick wondered if his earlier behavior may have led to her holding back. "No matter what, Tay, we're still friends."

She tried to smile and ended up releasing a shuddering breath. "I guess I'm not used to having a friend. I have my Mom and the parents from Kate's class. But I don't think I've had a real friend in a long time. I'm not sure why."

Nick could feel his frustration waning and imagined himself to be a cocoon that could wrap around her until she was ready to fly away again.

Only, maybe he didn't want her to fly away. "I can be your friend, if you want?"

Taylor nodded, pushing the hair out of her eyes from the wind. "Thank you."

"C'mon. Let's go sit on a bench." Once they were seated, Nick put his arm around her. "I'm all ears." He rimmed the shell of one to make a joke.

Taylor laughed and her guffaws broke the ice. "I met Greg in college. He was in my accounting class. Business major." She looked over at him, lifting the corner of her mouth a little, sadness filling her gaze. "Isn't it amazing how at nineteen you know everything? But now that I'm twenty-nine, I feel like I know nothing?"

"Yes," he agreed easily, having gone through the same thing. "We all come down to earth eventually."

"I think I plummeted," she replied, making the sound of an explosion. The need to protect her filled Nick. But he couldn't, because the past was the past.

"Anyway, Greg and I started dating. And for the record, that man is still pretty convincing. But looking back, I fell in love with the idea of love."

Thinking of Lorraine, he answered, "I understand. I did the same."

"Yes, but you realized your mistake and got out."

One word, one answer. "Mama."

Taylor turned to him, looking full of regret. "I

wish she'd been there for me. Not that my Mom didn't try. She did. I kept plowing ahead certain I had everything under control. Until I realized I didn't and I'd made a rotten mistake. By that time, Kate was on the way and Greg stayed until she was born. We divorced a year later."

He frowned, inching his arm tighter around her, shoulders wanting to make that cocoon permanent. "You sound as though he's not really in the picture anymore."

"He is and he isn't," she huffed. "In his own way, he loves Kate. But sometimes I wonder if I don't have two children instead of one."

"So, things have been rough."

She straightened, the flare of a challenge filling her features. There she was, he thought. There was the Taylor he knew. And…okay, time to slow down and calm down. Truth be told, he didn't really know her well.

"No better or worse than any other life, I suppose. But with Kate, I wouldn't trade a moment."

The need to throw his support behind Taylor swamped him. A plan began to form in his mind. "I can believe that."

A look of pure love shone from her eyes. "I managed to finish three years of school by the time Kate was born. We shared responsibilities until we both graduated. Greg invested more back then, time and money."

She ended with an edge to her voice that surprised Nick. Yes, Taylor had indeed grown up. "So, you got your degree in restaurant management?"

"And hospitality."

"Tough business."

"Tell me about it." But then her expression softened. "I got a job at Foster's Family Restaurant. Greg helped out but for the most part, I took care of Kate during the day, my mom watched her at night." She stared out at the ocean for a long moment before saying, "I have a great deal to be grateful for."

Taylor, being Taylor, couldn't sit back and relax on the bench. No, she sat at the very edge, her back straight, shoulders proud. Independent and strong, yet warm and vulnerable. Never mind the ocean. Nick wanted nothing more than to look at her all day long.

"So, what about you, Nick? All we've done is talk about me."

Pleased at the genuine interest she showed, Nick said, "After I got my master's, I applied to all the big restaurant chains and hotels. My grades weren't top of the class but close enough, along with being raised in the business, it got me interviews. I ended up with two competing offers. Talk about an ego boost."

"Very impressive," she said, tilting back to look at him.

"Ha. Before you go asking me for an autograph,

each company knew exactly who they were getting and what they wanted to do with me. I knew I'd have to earn every penny."

"No free ride, huh?"

"Far from it." Nick rose and held out his hand and she took it. A burst of electricity ran up his arm as their hands clasped together. Her skin warmed his and her eyes widened before she suddenly let go. "C'mon. Let's keep walking."

Nick shoved his hands in his pockets to keep them from holding hers, the place they really wanted to be. "Anyone who tells you traveling for business is glamorous hasn't ever done it full-time for a living. The hours are long, stressful and, sometimes, very lonely."

"Oh, come on. Be serious. All those cities?"

"I am," he protested. "Sometimes I'd spend three weeks in Tokyo, a week in LA, then go back to Tokyo for ten days before I ever got the chance to come home."

"Lots of frequent flyer miles."

Nick smiled. "Too many. And you're right, I did get in sightseeing when I could, but I went to those cities to do a job. As you know very well, restaurant managers don't like being told they're doing something wrong by upstart young briefcases just out of college."

"You'd be correct."

She walked along the edge of the water and bent down to pick up a shell, the wind whipping at her hair and the sun creating a halolike effect around her. Lovely. Simply lovely. "For Kate," she said, grinning.

"When they realized I knew my stuff, they came around. Eventually."

"Not easy being a corporate whiz kid, eh?"

He chuckled. "You'd have fought me tooth and nail." They walked for a bit longer. "One day, the job became a grind and the work lost its luster. My heart wasn't in it after a while."

"Did you quit?"

"I guess you could say I tried. But they insisted on keeping me and cut back on some of the travel. Most of the time I stayed within the US." Now it was his turn to grin. "Until I walked into one of our flagships in Scottsdale."

"Sounds like an uh-oh."

"You could say that. I'd been dealing with Steve for years and I respected him. But he ended up in the hospital with an emergency surgery." At her look of concern, he quickly assured her. "He was fine. But without him, the operation began to deteriorate, so they sent me to restore order."

What an aggravating trip. His flight had been delayed, then canceled, and after being rebooked on a later flight meant he'd walked in just before closing, pretty exhausted. Right into…okay, Jules could be temperamental. "Jules, the head chef, was in the middle of a meltdown and Tony, the assistant manager, looked ready to commit murder."

"Total mutiny."

"I lost my cool and fired every single one of them. The entire staff. Of course, I rehired everyone the next morning. And I fixed the most immediate problems and managed to bypass total anarchy, but after the incident, I knew my days were numbered."

"A little too much to get away with?"

"Yeah," he answered, rubbing the back of his neck. "They finally let me go. I asked for Bessie as part of my severance pay."

"People and their cars. Love affair?"

"Total. I even lived in her a couple of times."

"*She* happens to be a truck." Taylor gave him a sideways look. "Lived?"

"I'll have you know, *she* happens to be the only one I've ever had a long-term relationship with who totally understands my needs."

Taylor doubled over, howling. How he loved the rich sound of her belly laugh. "You mean, sleeping in your truck didn't break your back."

"It did not!" he exclaimed. "Who else in the universe would allow you to drink a beer, watch a movie and get popcorn all over the place without a single complaint?"

"I don't know. But I also haven't figured out how to get my apartment through a carwash, either," she deadpanned.

Now he doubled over. "See? Instant bliss."

Ten years seemed to disappear as their byplay

brought him back to how much he loved being with her.

"You really are too much, you know."

"Guilty as charged." He sobered and added, "I walked back into Diamante's with my tail between my legs. Mama didn't say a word. She simply told me to put on an apron and get to work. One day I asked her if she was upset. You know what she told me? She said they lost two restaurants before Diamante's and they never considered either one a failure, just a stepping stone. Everyone in this world has to learn by falling and getting up again. She told me the only failure would have been deciding not to try."

Her pointed stare almost had him wincing. "You *do* know there's a reason why I love your mother so much, don't you?"

"Yeah, I do."

They turned and began heading back. They reached Bessie and Nick noted Taylor smiling with newfound respect for his vehicle. "Working all those years in a corporate environment showed me how to streamline production, manage inventory, and a host of other little things that make a restaurant profitable."

"I agree. The devil is in the details," she said.

"Mama said she only knew how to run the restaurant the way she and Papa learned it and it was time to add what I knew. Maybe that was the reason why I left and came back. She seemed pretty happy with it."

"Faith."

He sighed and leaned against the car, the metal already warm from the sun. "She's putting hers in me. I don't want to let her down." He looked up and couldn't believe the confidence shining in Taylor's gaze.

"You won't," she said.

He shrugged. "You know how hard the business is and it's impossible to predict. Revenue's up when you think it's going to go down and vice versa. So rather than count on markets and the economy, I've been canvassing customers since I got back. Unless you drive over an hour away, there are no upscale Italian restaurants in the area."

"There aren't many family restaurants, either," she observed.

"Not up to par with Diamante's, which has been our base since we opened on the Island. And keeps us going year-round."

"You want more."

Amazing how she knew what he was thinking. "Yes, I do. I want to expand the menu, upgrade the wine list—"

Taylor's jaw dropped and she reached out to stop him. "Whoa. Really? Your homemade red is better than a whole lot of expensive imports."

"I know." Inside, his excitement rose. "But

sometimes customers want the label, not just the wine."

"Why not create a specialty menu? Or make tapas and have tastings during the week? You could even create events and pair dishes with wines. Oh, Nick, yes. You could draw in new customers without pushing away your regulars. I think it would work."

"Me, too." He turned to her, barely able to contain his enthusiasm. "Which is why I need your help. I have to have someone capable of running the day-to-day so I can begin organizing the special events and find a chef to create the new dishes."

"A chef? In Mama's kitchen? Do you have a death wish?"

He stroked his jaw, considering what she had said. "When you put it like that, all the more reason I would need you. Mama likes you. And if you back me, I might be able to live through the aftermath."

"What about me? I like living, too, you know?"

He tried to hide a smile. "We'll have to protect each other, I guess."

She cocked her head. "Does this mean you're offering me a job?"

"Having you back at Diamante's would be perfect but you already have a job. At that place you told me about. Foster's."

She snorted. "Um, yeah, about Foster's. I have

a glowing recommendation, but the restaurant won't last another two months."

"You got laid off?" His heart started to pound as the idea filled his head.

"'Fraid so. Frank's the most delightful person and one of the hardest-working people I've ever met. But no matter how much I pleaded, he refused to change."

"That's wonderful," he murmured.

She reared back. "I'm not sure I would say the same. Frank offered me a job when no one else would."

He tried but couldn't help himself. He grinned. "Sorry. I feel bad. Honest." Thoughts flew back and forth inside his brain. "Do you believe in fate?"

"Yes."

"So do I. And I think fate brought you here. What do you say? Spend the summer. Let me see if we can pull off the changes for Diamante's."

She looked like she didn't know how to answer. "I love the idea but I've got to be practical. Where would Kate and I live? I can't afford this island."

"I thought you said I have a coin in my possession somewhere, worth millions," he teased.

She switched to being very serious. "Not until you believe me and start looking for it, we don't."

"Fair enough," he said. "I own a small cottage over on Tenth Street. Bayside. And I just renovated the place to rent out. Now you can have it as part of your salary. It's already furnished. You'd only need linens and things. If you come to work for us, I'll try to find this coin you say I have."

"Really?"

"Really."

"Kate? Here?" she blurted. "For the summer? She'd be in absolute heaven."

He nodded. "Perfect. We have a deal. Just remember what I told you about my old job. You'll earn every penny."

"I'm looking forward to the challenge already," she replied.

He knew. Deep down he knew this business deal was right for both of them. "Great."

He watched the tip of her tongue peek out from between her lips. "I promise to work as hard as you."

Game on. And if he was lucky, maybe it could be the beginning of something more. "When can you start?"

"I need to find out from Kate's school how soon she can leave and end the year. And I'll have to pack. Otherwise, I'm available right away."

"We'll work it out." Indeed, Nick felt he could do anything in this moment, so long as Taylor was with him. "Sounds like a plan."

CHAPTER SIX

TAYLOR DOUBTED ANYONE would understand, but as she crossed the bridge to go home, it felt like chains were trying to pull her back. She didn't quite understand it, either. Her ties to the Island had come about a long time ago. And yet, she felt bereft. As she sat at a traffic light, a face loomed in her mind. Nick's. With that spark of joy dancing in his warm brown eyes, with his long, slightly angular face filled with determination, and yes, even the ears he'd made fun of, whose imperfection only made the picture more perfect.

He'd changed, but the essence that drew her to him ten years ago drew her to him now. A moth didn't know any better, seeking the flame no matter what. Did she? Hadn't she been through one divorce already?

Taylor worried her bottom lip with her teeth. Could her need for a shoulder to lean on outweigh her need to know more about him? She went over and over it for most of the ride home and walked into her studio less certain than when she'd left.

And what about finding the coin? Now that she'd had time to digest this new situation, standing fast became more important than ever. She'd given the coin to Nick. He'd given it back. They'd argued, finally agreeing to share. But she'd been afraid she'd lose it, so she'd asked him to hold on to it for safekeeping. And he didn't remember the night?

She shook her head and began to unpack. The Nick she thought she knew wouldn't have laughed. And yet? For a split second, Taylor let go only to find the whole idea unreal. So, was his laughter unwarranted? Perhaps not. One thing she did know. The money would never be about filling a closet with shoes. The money had to be about being true to herself, helping others, and taking care of the ones she loved. He had to feel the same way.

After putting a load of clothes in the washing machine, Taylor called her mother. "Hi, Mom."

"Hi, Tay. Are you home?"

"Yes."

"How was Cantecaw?" Her mother's voice grew dreamy. "I've always loved the name."

Taylor knew. "The same but different. No more giant saltshaker. The hurricane."

Her mother sighed. "That's a shame. Though all things change."

"I guess they do."

"At least you don't sound too disappointed," her mother said. "Did you get the…uh…job?"

"Not exactly." Hmm, silence. Good or bad? "Well, sort of. Yes and no."

Her mother laughed. "Okay, I'm confused. Which part is yes and which part is no?"

"As I told you before, I went to Diamante's and spoke to Nick about the coin. He doesn't remember it."

"Okay. I assume that's the 'no' part."

Taylor continued. "'Fraid so. And here comes the 'yes' part. Nick offered me a job. A real one. In Diamante's."

"Host or manager?"

"Host. Probably only until October."

"Nice. This works. But where would you live? The Island's very expensive."

"Believe me, I know. He also offered a cottage for the summer. Can you imagine?" She rushed on. "Kate at the beach for an entire summer? You, too, as many times as you can make it."

"Oh my, that's wonderful! You're right. Kate will have a blast." Her mother paused. "But what about here? You still have to pay rent on the apartment."

"Without having to pay rent there, I can cover it here."

Taylor could hear her mom fretting over the phone, without saying a word. "I can handle my responsibilities, thanks to you, Mom. I've got this, okay? Marchand to the end."

Her mother laughed. "Okay." She then asked, "And what about the other? The coin."

"I'll have to keep asking Nick to look and remind him of how things went that night. I guess, from his point of view, what I dumped on him was pretty wild."

"But the truth, nonetheless," her mom said. "Sorry, let's focus on you and Kate."

"You mean," Taylor teased, tongue in cheek, "like having to invite Rachel and Terri and their parents for a visit?"

"You'd better. Or else Kate'll protest. Loudly."

"I know." Taylor pictured Cantecaw for a moment, a smile tugging at the corners of her mouth. She could almost see Kate running up and down the beach, kicking up the sand. "It's going to be wonderful. For all of us."

"Yes, it is." Ever practical, her mother asked, "When are you going to stop by to pick up her things?"

"I might be a little late. I need to make an appointment to talk to the school about how soon Kate can finish the year or figure out what to do if not, and there isn't a stitch of food in my refrigerator." She named a time that she'd be by.

Her mother replied, "I'll be waiting with the teapot. And if the school gives you a problem, Kate can stay with me and finish up her year."

"Thanks, Mom. You're the best," she added,

knowing she didn't say the words often enough. "I love you."

"My pleasure. I love you, too."

It turned out the vice principal, Mrs. Daniels, had an opening just after lunch. So, Taylor chose to have a cup of tea with her mother first, and a homemade scone, before walking into the school's main office. With a touch of trepidation, she said, "Hi. I'm Taylor Hughes. Kate's mother. I'm here to see Mrs. Daniels."

"I'll tell her you're here," said an older woman behind the counter.

Soon, Taylor was ushered into a small, rather cluttered room. A woman in maybe her forties, with short brown hair and glasses, rose from behind a desk. "Mrs. Hughes?"

"Hi. Thank you for meeting me on such short notice." They shook hands and Taylor sat down on a hard, very utilitarian chair.

"What can I do for you?" Mrs. Daniels asked.

Taylor explained the situation about Kate possibly finishing the school term early.

The vice principal nodded. "Moving?"

Taylor shook her head. "Not quite. I was laid off from my job and I managed to get a position for the summer. But it's in New Jersey." Mrs. Daniels didn't say anything, so Taylor continued. "My mother lives here but she works full-time, so leaving Kate with her will be difficult but not impossible. If I have to, that's what I'll do. Obviously, I'd rather not. So, if you can tell me how soon my daughter can be done, I'd greatly appreciate it."

Mrs. Daniels cleared her throat. "I checked Kate's file. Straight A's. Smart girl."

Taylor couldn't help beaming.

"The last day of school is Friday, June 18th. Those last five days are half days anyway. She'll have to attend this week, and the week including Memorial Day. Her final day will be Friday, June 4th. Meaning, I can give you the last two weeks."

Taylor couldn't believe her ears. "Thank you. This is more than generous."

Mrs. Daniels smiled. "Only because she's already finished her regular class work. I've been told she's been working on some third grade workbooks."

Taylor's heart was full of pride. She rose and shook hands with the vice principal. "Thank you, again."

Taylor walked out to her car, her steps lighter than they'd been in a long time. In spite of everything, Kate tried to excel. Did excel. Now more than ever, Taylor knew that spending time in Cantecaw would be wonderful for her daughter.

Children accepted life as it was given to them. Kate hadn't asked for her parents to divorce, and rather than feel sorry for herself, Kate simply tried her best to thrive. Maybe love had something to do with it? Taylor vowed once again to give Kate the best life she could.

And speaking of her daughter, Kate was one very surprised little girl when she found her waiting at school to pick her up as class let out. Taylor waved from the sidewalk. Kate saw her, squealed and ran to her. Taylor braced for impact.

"Mom! Mom! I missed you."

Taylor laughed, throwing her arms around her little girl. "I missed you, too."

Could there be anything more wonderful than her daughter's arms squeezing her, her daughter's face buried in the crook of her neck, and her little girl's giggling delight surrounding her? She let go and Kate did the same.

"You've been gone for, like, forever," Kate said.

"One day?" Taylor rebutted, enjoying the dramatics that seemed to come with her seven-year-old lately. Taylor shook her head and wondered what would happen at fourteen.

"Yes," Kate answered emphatically. "I missed you."

Taylor hugged her again, lifted her up, then deposited her on the sidewalk. Kate's backpack had shifted, so Taylor lifted a strap back onto her daughter's shoulder.

"Can I go to Rachel's?" Kate pleaded.

Taylor nearly laughed out loud. Now that Kate's world was right and the stars had realigned, Kate could go back to being Kate. "I'm sorry. Not today. I have to go food shopping so we have something to eat for dinner and then I need to talk to you."

Kate's brows lifted, then pulled together. "Is something wrong?"

"No. I have news and we have plans to make."

"You got a job."

"Yes."

Kate whooped and jumped up and down.

"Easy does it. We still need to discuss some things. And we still need to eat. Let's take care of shopping and we'll talk when we get home."

Kate was happy enough, but Taylor could see the wheels spin inside her daughter's head as their task wore on. The happiness didn't dim completely until Kate's shoulders slumped when they pulled into the driveway.

As soon as the studio's front door was closed, Kate asked, "What's going on, Mom?"

Taylor set the grocery bags down on the kitchen counter. She waved Kate over to have a seat at the table and joined her. "I went to a place I worked at a long time ago. Have you ever heard me mention Cantecaw Island?"

Kate shook her head. "No."

"Do you remember the bottle of sea glass from the box in the closet?" This time Kate nodded her head yes. "It came from Cantecaw Island."

"Oh." Kate wasn't exactly blown away but seemed intrigued. Taylor pressed on.

"Cantecaw is off the coast of New Jersey, part of the Jersey Shore. I got a job for the summer at a restaurant on the Island."

"That's great!" Kate shouted. Then her face fell and tears filled her eyes. "But then you'll have to live there and I won't see you for the whole summer."

Taylor took her daughter's hand. "No, sweetheart. This is the best part. We're going to be able to stay in a cottage. Right on the bay. We can go to the beach every day."

Kate's entire being lit up. She left the table and started dancing around the studio with joy. "I'm going to the beach. Uh-huh. Uh-huh."

Taylor waited for the celebration to calm. "But we'll have to sort out what you'll be doing when I'm working."

Kate nodded, coming down to earth. "Is Nana coming, too?"

Guilt ran through Taylor. "When she can. She still has to work. We'll figure things out."

Kate started singing again. "I'm going to the beach. I'm going to the beach."

Taylor left Kate to enjoy the moment and began unpacking the groceries.

"Can you make meat loaf, please? We haven't had meat loaf in forever."

"Meat loaf tomorrow. With homemade mashed." Kate loved mashed potatoes. "Chicken tonight. I'll broil some while you take your bath and finish your homework. And if you're real good, I might even be persuaded to make mac 'n' cheese."

Kate put her arms around Taylor's waist. "I love you, Mom."

She teared up. "I love you too, Katydid."

Kate dropped a kiss on her cheek, then went to grab her backpack, which she threw on the futon and flopped down on the couch. "When do we go?"

"You know, I had a feeling you would ask. How about homework first, washup second and dinner third. And I'll explain."

Kate shook her head. "Homework first. Dinner second. Washup third?"

"Deal."

Taylor finished getting their meal together while Kate did her homework. Not that her daughter had much, given it was almost the end of school. The television went on a bit too soon, but when Taylor checked, every assignment was finished.

As the chicken broiled, Taylor made her famous mac 'n' cheese. She'd learned many things in the restaurant business, taking home items no longer needed and making wholesome meals out of them. She encouraged employees to do the same.

She'd introduced Diamante's pre-rush meal to Foster's, and although she couldn't recreate Mama Bella's sauce or lasagna, she made soups and stews. Potpies worked out well, too. Nothing went to waste if she could help it.

Without realizing, Taylor's thoughts went straight to what she could do when, not if, Nick found the coin. She could get Frank out of debt. Update his restaurant, too. Sunday's fried chicken dinner with all the fixin's still drew a crowd.

Smiling, Taylor turned from the stove straight into a what's-going-on stare from her daughter. "I'm happy, Kate. That's all. Happy to be home. Happy to have a job, even if it is only temporary." *Happy to have found... No. Only positive thoughts. Nick is going to find the coin.* "I'm not allowed?"

"Sure, it's just…"

"Spit it out."

"You've been, like, really worried lately. Now you're not."

"A good thing, no?"

Kate smiled. "Very."

Taylor wondered if now was the time she should take the conversation further, as they sat down to eat. "Katydid, do you know what adversity means?" Her daughter shook her head no. "It means a time of difficulty. When there's a problem in front of you that's not easy to solve. Everyone faces adversity at some point. The reason I worried so much was I didn't want to make a wrong decision. It's important not to make bad decisions when things get hard. Even if it's only for the summer, this job is the right decision. Do you understand?"

"Sure. I face adversity all the time."

Taylor reared back. Kate? Her seven-year-old? "You do?"

Kate dug her fork into her mac 'n' cheese. "I try to be friends with both Becca and Joanie, but they're always fighting."

"I see," Taylor replied. "How do you handle the situation?"

"By getting more friends to hang out with us. That way they're just part of the group and don't go at each other."

Wow. How incredibly smart. "Does it work?"

Kate's fork was poised at her lips. "Most of the time."

"What happens when they don't?"

Kate chewed and grinned. "We run."

Taylor smiled and took a bite. "We can invite Rachel and Terri for the weekend once or twice. Nana can drive them unless Mrs. Baines or Mrs. McGuire also want to come. Just remember, weekends are my busy time."

"Really? Can we? I'd like that."

"And now, for the biggest surprise of all." She looked at Kate, expectation growing behind her eyes. "You get to leave school early, so I don't have to commute. You have to go back after Memorial Day, that week. But not the following two weeks. How does that sound? You get to miss the last two weeks of school."

"Awesome!" Kate exclaimed, pumping her fist. "Yes!"

"Hold on, hold on," Taylor admonished. "You have to remember that it's happening because I don't have a choice. Don't be boasting to your friends about it. Okay?"

Kate scrunched up her face, her excitement waning. "Yeah. I guess if I was one of them, I'd feel mad if somebody did that to me."

Kate seemed to be growing up faster than Taylor imagined. She wondered if two single parents had anything to do with it. "Can I ask you a question?"

Kate swallowed a bite of chicken. "Sure."

"Are you mad at Daddy or me for not being together?"

"Mad?" Kate frowned. "Sometimes I get sad. Especially when you fight about money. Most of the time when you're together you don't talk, which is okay."

Taylor's heart constricted and she sat a little straighter as she acknowledged the hurt. "We both love you very much."

"I know. You and Dad, you're like Becca and Joanie."

"How so?"

Kate scooped up another forkful of mac 'n' cheese before answering. "I think if you didn't fight about money, you could kinda be friends with Dad. Just like, I think if Becca and Joanie forgot about who could be the best, they could be friends, too."

Taylor picked up her plate and went to the sink to wash it so Kate wouldn't see her tears. This kid of hers made her so proud. There were times when children could be absolutely amazing.

Kate finished her meal and they had a water fight that ended quickly while they cleaned up. Taylor took her time drying the dishes. She hated what she was asking of her daughter and yet knew being divorced from Greg was way better than being with him.

Taylor ran a bath for Kate and listened with a smile while her daughter sang to a couple of songs on her phone. Once Kate was in bed, Taylor went outside to the front steps of the building to stare up at the stars and collect herself. She couldn't indulge herself for too long, though. She had too much to do.

Dialing Greg and listening to him pick up, she said, "Hello, Greg."

"Hi."

Taylor could hear some kind of sports game in the background.

"To what do I owe this pleasure?" he asked.

"I need you to work with me on something."

His tone suspicious, he barked out, "Work with you? What do you mean?"

"I got laid off from Foster's."

There was a dismissive grunt. "Look. I'm stretched to the limit. I don't have a spare dime."

He never did. Anything and everything for Greg. He had a sixty-inch television, while Taylor wasn't sure what she had qualified as a TV anymore. He had a lease on a new car, and hers got around on rubber bands and was held together with chewing gum. She felt a familiar surge of frustration. "I'm not asking for money."

"Then what do you want?"

His tone really hurt. "I have a summer job in New Jersey. I don't need your permission but I'm trying to be nice. I'm taking Kate with me. We have a place to stay as part of my salary, and she'll be able to spend the summer at the beach."

The silence on the other end of the line told Taylor he was sizing up what she'd said. Greg was all about himself, usually. Kate became the exception. Sometimes. "What about my visitation? I won't be able to see her."

"You have a car and you can drive. It's not *that* far." For the sake of peace, Taylor didn't remind him he wasn't exactly consistent with his visits. She would give him more access but he'd disappointed Kate too many times to make the offer.

"No alimony payments for the months you're away. You're getting free rent."

Free? Not exactly. And he hadn't made a payment yet this year. But she'd rather not argue—

getting distracted wouldn't help her here. "Fine. Whatever. But there's a condition." Again, silence. "You have to come at least once to visit. She'll expect you to."

He waited a long time to answer. "All right."

"Don't promise her and renege, Greg. I won't have you hurt her."

"I said all right, didn't I?"

"Yes." Taylor held little hope he'd come, but at least she'd tried. "We're going out this weekend to get settled and for Memorial Day weekend, then I have permission to take Kate out of school early. Did you know she's getting straight A's again this year?"

"No."

"Try to congratulate her, okay?"

"Fine."

Taylor had the feeling he was already back to watching his sports game. Once Greg got what he wanted, he was good at tuning her out. Problem was, he'd started tuning Kate out, too. "Thank you."

Taylor hung up. For Greg, the thrill was in the chase, in the winning. Taylor held no more significance now than a trophy sitting on a mantel. Now more than ever, Cantecaw seemed the right decision. The Diamantes—Nick, in particular—had no patience for playing games. Other people came first.

Taylor sent up a silent thank-you. For everything.

CHAPTER SEVEN

NICK LOVED CANTECAW. Sometimes people wanted to move away from where they were born, to be someplace new and exciting. Nick had seen the new and found it to be less exciting than the hype. Like the saying goes, there was no place like home. And after the hurricane, when an elderly couple had lost their vacation home and had had enough, Nick had jumped in to buy their property for full market price and then some. With the help of an old classmate who'd become a builder, he nailed structural beams, hung Sheetrock, caulked cracks and helped restore the house.

Nick's home was a block from the ocean. He thought of the view from the top deck, where he could see the water and the sky, and he could certainly hear the waves, enjoying how they often lulled him to sleep at night. He'd also made the house big enough so someday it could be filled with a family's laughter—and love.

Tonight, as he got out of Bessie and went inside, Taylor's face loomed. Surprising? Perhaps, but as he dropped his jacket on the back of a chair, Nick could see Taylor fitting into this space, teasing him, keeping him on his toes, even sipping a cup of coffee in front of the huge bay window.

Making him ask the next question: Why wasn't he more nervous about that? Any kind of permanence with respect to romance made him anxious. Because of Lorraine? Probably.

His doorbell rang and Nick glanced down at his watch. Kind of late for visitors. He looked through the glass next to the front door and caught part of his brother's face. Alarmed, he threw open the door. "Hey, big bro. Everything all right?"

Rocco put up his hands, palms out. "Sure. Fine. Sorry I scared you." They hugged and clapped backs before letting go. "Every now and then Beth knows I need a deck and the ocean."

Nick smiled, closing the door behind Rocco. "I've got both. And a cold brew coming right up."

They grabbed ice-cold bottles from the refrigerator and climbed the steps to the master to go out onto the topmost deck. What a rare treat, to sit with this view and his brother.

"When are you gonna tell Mama?" Roc asked.

Nick decided to play dumb. "Tell Mama what?"

Roc threw him a sideways look. "I'm not naive, Nick. You've been on edge for weeks now. Not hard to figure it must have to do with the restaurant. So, spill. What's the plan?"

Nick shrugged and swallowed a swig of beer.

"We've got to come into the twenty-first century. Mama can't run the kitchen forever. She needs to slow down."

Roc agreed. "One hundred percent. But she's gonna fight you tooth and nail."

"I know." Nick leaned forward in his chair. "Which is why I want to introduce my ideas slowly. I'm going to hire a chef, take part of the back room, and make it special. For the weekends."

His brother released a low whistle. "You really *do* know how to live dangerously, don't you?"

He grinned at his brother's teasing. "I did say *slowly*, didn't I? Just a special menu, better wines," he explained with a laugh. "Higher prices."

"Sounds wonderful for in-season. What about off-season?"

"Events. Tastings. Pairings."

"You could close down and revert the area back to the main restaurant," Rocco suggested.

"I've thought of it. But there's nothing upscale nearby for at least a half-hour drive, probably more, in any direction on or off the Island."

"You have a point," said Rocco, rubbing his chin.

"Not to mention the staff. They'll be counting on the work," Nick explained. "The weekends should be all right."

Rocco nodded. "Besides living dangerously, chefs are expensive."

"Tell me about it," he answered, his tone glum.

"Do you have enough capital?"

For a split second, Taylor's fantastic story about that coin flew through his mind. He shook his head. *If only.* "You know I sank every penny I have into this place. I was lucky to get the line of credit to fix up the cottage."

One of the things his parents had done was invest in the Island. Way back when, they'd bought a pair of cottages at a reasonable price and kept them as rental properties. Rocco had sold his and used the funds to pay off a large portion of his home. "I'm figuring I'll have enough collateral if I use the house."

"You certainly have a lot of nerve, I'll give you that." Roc's tone had a hint of awe.

Nick set his beer down and stretched his neck muscles. "I don't know how to tell Mom."

"Gotcha. Kinda like the time we broke that vase of hers."

Nick tried hard not to laugh.

"I don't have too much big bro advice on this one." Rocco shrugged. "Maybe just spit it out?"

"And then disappear?" Nick said, teasing.

Rocco laughed but then grew serious. "I think Mom's realizing she's not quite immortal."

Nick frowned. "What do you mean?"

"Beth took Mom to the doctor's last week."

Nick was stunned. Big-time. "Why didn't anyone tell me?"

"Calm down, it was just an appointment," Roc ordered. "Mom swore Beth to secrecy. But my sweet wife's conscience ratted her out."

Nick sat back and watched his fingers tremble. He grabbed his beer to hide his fear. "So, what did she say?"

"Mom's having trouble breathing," his brother replied. "Her heart is a bit shaky and she's got some circulatory issues."

Nick winced. "Probably from being on her feet all the time."

"The EKG result was acceptable but they put her on alert. She needs to slow down." Rocco sighed. "They say timing is everything. Maybe this idea of yours is a godsend, a way to get her to admit she needs to let go a little?"

Nick didn't answer because his mind had gone blank, his world spinning out of control.

"Hey, take it easy, bro," Rocco soothed. "I thought the same thing when I heard the news. Parents are invincible."

"Until they're not," he said under his breath. Nick rose, coming to a halt at the railing. "I hired Taylor Hughes. She's going to run the front while I focus on the back. She'll use the cottage for the summer and count it as part of her salary. She's got a degree in hospitality and restaurant management."

Rocco dropped a hand on Nick's shoulder. "She is? She does? Sounds too good to be true."

"In a way. Call it fate, I guess. She got laid off. She needs a job. Like you said, sometimes things happen for a reason."

Rocco downed a swig of his beer. Probably to hide a knowing grin, Nick guessed. He knew he was right when Rocco declared, "A match made in heaven!"

Now Nick knew for sure that Roc was pulling his leg. "I hope."

Roc swallowed another draft of beer. "So, being my lawyerly self, I wonder what brought her here, specifically. I mean, was she searching for a job on the Island?"

Nick wanted to tell Rocco about the incredible story Taylor had relayed to him about the coin but decided against doing so. Not that he didn't trust his brother. He did. With his life. But Taylor's story felt more like a ruse, an excuse, to close the gap on the last ten years than the reality of any coin. Which, for the record, he still didn't remember. He remembered her and the pier and hanging out with everyone, based on the previous discussions he'd had with her. But not much after and certainly not the coin.

Was he drawing a blank because Taylor hadn't ever come back to Cantecaw? A question to ask himself later.

"I don't know, and at this point, I don't care.

I need her expertise and she needs a job. It's not complicated."

Rocco didn't hide his smile this time. "Just looking out for your back, bro. As always."

"I know. I know. Always appreciated." Nick walked back to his chair and sat. "There's more. Turns out she's not married—at least, not anymore. She's divorced. Said she forgets she has the ring on."

"Ah. Gotcha. I was gonna ask."

"And…" Nick drew out his voice for effect. "She has a daughter, Kate. Seven years old."

Rocco sat down in his chair. "Wow." He grinned a huge, brotherly grin but it faded fast. "Single mom. Tough."

Nick nodded. "Which made the decision even easier for me. She's still family no matter how much time has passed."

Roc peered at him. "Just family?"

"We're two different people now."

Rocco snorted. "Older, yes. Wiser? TBD."

They finished their beers, talking quietly. Eventually the conversation came back to Bella. "Any other ideas about how to get Mom to slow down?" Nick asked.

"Tie her to a beach chair?" Rocco deadpanned.

"Very funny."

"I thought Luis was doing a lot of the prep work now."

"He is. But Mama still makes the sauce and

the lasagna. Maybe we can get her to at least not come in until just before lunch," Nick suggested.

"And have her pace up and down in the house worrying because she's not at the restaurant?"

"Hey, I'm lost here, bro." Nick sighed.

"Me, too. We'll have to keep thinking."

After Rocco left, Nick changed the direction of his thoughts. He'd asked his brother, were he and Taylor too different? Looking back, Nick realized no one felt right by his side, not the way Taylor had. And still did?

So much had changed. She'd grown up. She'd been through a great deal. She'd learned to live on her own, take care of herself and her daughter; she'd also succeeded. She'd grown into a strong, self-assured, self-sufficient woman, which only made her all the more appealing. One thing Nick knew for certain. He needed a partner, someone he could believe in, and who believed in him. He'd already survived the opposite.

Nick pictured Taylor sitting in the chair Rocco had just vacated. He could almost hear them talking about the day, the good and the bad. He could imagine them laughing about the mishaps and being proud of the things that went right. Always challenging each other to improve.

Not to mention the dimples her smile created and the shine of her hair in the moonlight.

Did he have it bad or did he want to have it bad? Nick wasn't sure. But he needed to find out.

Nick considered why he didn't want to find out anything about a certain coin. Taylor was determined. She said they'd agreed to share the coin, so, of course, they'd share in the proceeds. But if all that happened, what would she do? The answer rang in his head immediately: Taylor would leave Cantecaw. Why would she stay? Only, Nick wanted her to stay. He wanted to get to know her better. He wanted to work side by side with her and see if the old magic still existed.

All of a sudden, a clear memory popped into his head. A nickel. In the palm of his hand. And four very distinct numbers glaring at him. 1821. Her age and his.

CHAPTER EIGHT

Kate was unable to contain her excitement. It made Taylor smile as they drove up to the top of the hill just before coming onto the Island. Passing over the bridge, she waited for the familiar release of stress. But this time, her nerves held sway. Butterflies danced in the pit of her stomach. She so wanted Kate to like the Diamantes and for the Diamantes to like Kate. Of course, all Kate could think about was seeing the ocean and Taylor had promised ocean first.

She drove up Main Street to Fourteenth Street, but instead of making the right toward the bay, she turned left and continued to the shore. She parked and followed Kate as fast as she could, a huge smile growing as Kate paused to drink in the sight and then run down to the water.

The ocean looked calm today, glittering in the sunlight. Kate stopped at the edge, touched the waves, shivered and ran back to Taylor, whose heart swelled.

"It's cold," Kate remarked in between breaths.

Taylor laughed. "The water doesn't usually get warm until the end of July."

"I don't care," Kate announced. "I can't wait to go in."

Taylor cast her daughter a look. "You promised to help move in first, didn't you?"

Crestfallen, Kate answered, "Yes, Mom."

"C'mon, Madam Drama Queen," Taylor chided softly. "One afternoon won't stop you. You have all summer."

The look on Kate's face told a different story.

They got back in the car and Taylor drove over to the restaurant to pick up the key to the cottage. She warned Kate to be on her best behavior as they marched up the steps to Diamante's. Inside, Taylor watched Kate glance from side to side and all around.

"This is a nice place, Mom."

Taylor nodded and Mama Bella came bustling at them from the back. *"Bene,"* she said. "Taylor. *Si.*"

Taylor felt Kate edge closer to her. "Kate? This is Mama Bella. She and her family own this restaurant. Mama, this is my daughter, Kate."

"Nice to meet you," Kate whispered.

Mama wasn't one to stand on ceremony. All or nothing—that was Mama. She pulled Kate into a bear hug and bussed both cheeks. *"Molto bella. Ciao."* When Bella let go, Kate looked a bit overwhelmed but sported a grin on her face.

Mama turned to her. "Taylor, Nico say to meet

him at the cottage. He open for you." Mama reached into her apron and pulled out the key. "You come to dinner at three." It was more of an order than an invitation, but it was appreciated, nonetheless.

"No arguments from us." Taylor said to Kate, "Mama Bella makes the best lasagna in the universe."

"I love lasagna," Kate stated firmly.

"*Bene*," Mama said with a huge smile. "Good. Now shoo. Nico is waiting."

Driving along Tenth Street. Taylor knew the cottage right away. Painted white, it had teal shutters with a seahorse pattern cut out in them. A simple Cape Cod–style house. A low white fence surrounded the property, and stones covered the front yard. She pulled up, noticing Bessie and another SUV in the driveway.

Nick came outside, a warm smile on his face. Rocco followed, holding a little boy in his arms. Then Beth came down the steps looking very pregnant. Taylor cut the engine and jumped out, her heart high in her throat. "Oh, Beth. Look at you. You're gorgeous."

Beth made a face as she put a hand on her belly. "More like a beached whale."

Taylor hurried to her and they hugged. Time seemed to fly backward for a moment. She would never be able to describe how right this hug felt. The ever-present weight on her shoulders eased.

Taylor let go and she and Beth shared a look. One of friendship, understanding and motherhood. Then she introduced Kate. "Kate? These are old friends of mine. This is Nick, Rocco and Beth Diamante."

"Hello."

Kate wasn't normally shy but the Diamantes en masse could be a bit overpowering. Beth guessed the way of things and addressed Rocco and Nick. "Why don't you guys start unloading Taylor's car while I show them around the house?"

Beth took Roc Junior back from her husband. The child garnered Kate's interest right away. "How old is he?" she asked.

"Three." The little boy stared at Kate while he chewed on his fist. "He usually chatters like a magpie but I think he's rather taken with you," Beth answered.

"He's cute."

"Agreed." Beth ushered them inside. "Come on in."

The front door opened right into the living room. Typical shore furniture graced the room that led directly into a dining area and the kitchen. A queen-size bed took up a lot of the bigger bedroom and two twin beds rested against the walls in the smaller one. The tub-shower looked perfect for removing sand from a seven-year-old after a day at the beach. And there was an outdoor shower, as well. Even better.

"The couch has a pullout bed?" she asked.

Beth nodded, putting little Roc on the floor. Kate sat down next to him and started playing peekaboo. When little Roc started giggling, Kate did, too.

"It's so much more than I expected," Taylor continued.

Beth grinned. "I took over decorating duties. Almost ended up with cherrywood furniture and plank floors."

"Those men," Taylor groaned. "Gosh, it's really good to see you again."

"You, too," Beth replied. And they hugged again.

"Can you stay a bit? Do you have time for a cup of tea?" Taylor asked.

"As long as you-know-who behaves."

Taylor found a teakettle and by the time she finished pouring and put the honey pot on the table, baskets of linens lay on beds ready to be made, kitchen utensils and small appliances had been put away, and suitcases waited to be unpacked.

The group reconvened around the table. "You made tea?" Nick asked.

Taylor smiled. "By the looks of things, you both deserve something stronger."

Nick shook his head. "I truly enjoyed the ritual of tea in Japan but I think I prefer a cup of English breakfast with honey. And a biscuit."

"Japan? Really? It's so hard for me to picture all the places you've been. You'll have to tell me about it sometime."

Taylor got a mug for Nick as well but Rocco declined, grabbing a bottle of water instead. She set out a tin of cookies, which Roc Junior kept trying to steal from his father's lap. Taylor's heart warmed at the sight of cookie crumbs on the toddler's face.

Kate finished her juice box and asked to be excused from the table. Beth put out a portable playpen in the middle of the living room. Kate seemed fascinated by Roc Junior and continued to amuse him.

"I know we have a lot to catch up on." Taylor lowered her voice and gestured silently in Kate's direction. All of them nodded. "Up until a week or so ago, I was working in a family-style restaurant. I'd been with Frank since I got my degree but…well, an uncertain economy and a stubborn owner. You get the picture."

Rocco went next. "I'm a lawyer. I kept trying to make partner in a big firm in New York. Took a while for me to realize they weren't going to give it to me. So, I decided to hang out my own shingle right here."

Beth added, "I got my degree in environmental science and went to work for the state. Great job but no getting rich there either, I'm afraid."

"Beth and I saw each other again at an alumni

fundraiser. Very glad we did, too," Rocco continued.

Taylor watched the couple clasp hands and share an intimate look. They were meant for each other.

Nick had been pretty quiet, and as Taylor looked over, something clicked between them. She had to pull her gaze away or be swallowed by the warmth enveloping her. To quickly save herself, she picked up her story again, speaking softly. "I got married too young. No regrets." She cast a loving glance at her daughter.

Kate was playing hide-and-seek with one of Roc Junior's toys. The boy chortled with delight every time. Not too much later, though, he began to fuss. "We should head home," Beth announced. "We'll see you later at the restaurant. I think someone needs a nap."

Taylor smiled, remembering those days well. She'd curl up on the couch with Kate and they'd doze in the sun. "Beth? I have a huge favor to ask. My mother can't make it here until tomorrow, and I'm working tonight, so—"

"Not a problem. Ever. I'd be happy to have Kate over." They both rose and Beth hugged her hard. "Still family, right?"

"Absolutely."

"We're over on 25th. Number 118. We were able to snag a new construction town house back when, but with the family growing…" Beth paused and glanced down at her belly "We're looking to get a larger place. A detached house, we hope."

For a moment, Taylor thought of the money that the coin could generate. She came very close to blurting out the truth. *I can help.* "You'll find one. I'm sure of it."

"If we're all eating at the restaurant," Beth suggested, "why don't we take Kate from there?"

"And I'll pick her up at your place on my way home," Taylor replied.

"Sounds good to me."

Taylor was grateful for the generosity. "Thank you again."

Beth and Rocco left with Roc Junior. Once they were gone, Nick asked, "Can I help with anything else?"

"Yes, you can."

His face brightened. Wow, that grin. No matter how hard she tried, she couldn't get away from the charming curl right at the corner of his mouth. Now Taylor wondered if she really wanted to.

"I'm yours to command," he said.

"Be careful," she teased, finding it a bit hard to breathe. "I can be a tough cookie."

"Take my word for it," Kate chimed in.

"I can handle your mom," Nick said with an even bigger grin.

Kate laughed. "You haven't seen her in action."

Nick walked over to join Kate in the living

room. "Actually, I have. I knew your mom from before you were born."

"She told me you were all best friends."

Nick looked pleased at the comment. "We all worked together. So, I know exactly what she can dish out."

"I guess you do," Kate said, her tone thoughtful.

"How about you and me give your mom a hand outside while she finishes organizing in here?"

"Okay." Kate hopped up from the floor.

A minute later, Taylor peeked out the open window, watching Nick and Kate wipe down the small plastic table and chairs in the backyard. Kate didn't say a word at first. Then she asked Nick, "Were you born here?"

He answered right away. "Yes. And I've lived on the Island most of my life."

"Bet it was fun being able to go to the beach all the time."

"It was. But I had my share of work, too."

"You mean like cleaning tables?"

Nick laughed and Taylor's heart warmed. "Yes, indeed. Like cleaning tables."

Their voices grew faint and Taylor realized they'd gone to get the camp chairs out of the car. In the past, she'd taken Kate to a nearby lake to swim, but none of those times would ever compare to the Island.

Taylor heard Nick sharing some pointers about

the ocean and Kate giggled a few times as they arranged the furniture, then rearranged it a second time. She went to check on the duo. "Well done, you two."

Nick's proud smile made her heart flip. "Couldn't have done it without my partner. Right, Kate?"

"Yes, sir," Kate answered, snapping a mock salute.

Nick headed for the gate. "I have to go," he said. "Mama's waiting. But I'll see you both for dinner?"

"You bet." Kate sprinted into the cottage.

Despite Nick saying he had to go, he'd remained in the backyard. Taylor noticed how his gaze softened as he looked at her. Something lurked just under the surface that piqued her curiosity. Something she wanted to explore. Did she dare? "I'm glad you're here," she told him.

"So am I," he answered. He moved toward her and his palm cupped her cheek. His thumb brushing softly along her skin, making her heart flip again. Then he was gone. Taylor stood there for a long moment before going back inside.

"Your friends are nice."

Taylor turned and moved toward the couch. She smoothed a throw and passed it to her daughter, who was lounging there, reading a book.

Kate wasn't one to warm up to people right away. Then again, Taylor knew all about the Diamante charm. It seemed Kate wasn't immune, either. "Yes, they are. Thank you for best behavior."

Kate's next question told Taylor how comfortable her daughter felt already about being on the Island. "When can I go to the beach?"

"Tomorrow. You'll love it. I'll take you for a while until Nana gets here. Tonight, I have to work."

Kate dropped her book and turned on the television while Taylor continued to unpack. Then she dressed for work and Kate put on fresh jeans and a blouse.

As soon as they arrived at Diamante's, Mama Bella greeted them. "*Benvenuto*. Welcome to my restaurant."

"Hi, again," Kate answered. Kate seemed to take in the details more than she had earlier. "This place is kind of old."

"*Si*. You like my restaurant?"

Kate nodded.

"Come. I show you the kitchen and you can help bring out our dinner. Do you like spaghetti?"

"Yes," Kate replied with enthusiasm.

Taylor watched them exit through the swinging doors, then looked over to find Nick grinning. "Now I know where you get it from."

"Get what?" he asked, way too innocently.

"The Diamante charm." Taylor noticed Beth, who was also smiling.

"Don't go telling them stuff like that," Beth said. "They're bad enough as it is."

Nick pulled a face and locked eyes with Taylor, and everything else, including the restaurant seemed to melt away. All she could see, think and hear was Nick.

The doors to the kitchen banged open, breaking the spell. Bowls and platters bearing clams over linguini, heavy on the garlic, steak pizzaiola, and, of course, lasagna filled the table. Not to mention baskets of bread, a huge salad bowl, iced tea, and carafes of the house red.

Light filled the front of the restaurant as the front door opened. A man with auburn hair, about the same height as Nick, walked in. Everyone rose with calls of welcome. Taylor stood.

Nick began the introductions. "Taylor? This is Jason Bridges. My best friend. We grew up on the Island together."

Taylor smiled. "Nice to meet you." She wondered why she'd never met him before and shook his hand.

As if reading her mind, Nick explained, "Jason was going to law school. He was interning in DC the summer you worked for us."

Aha! Question answered.

"Not very glamorous. Patent law." Jason shrugged and said hello to the other staff. "Mama, I'm here for the usual order. The gang is starving. If I don't get back soon, they'll revolt."

"Gang?" Taylor asked.

"I'm head of the beach patrol for our township. I have a group of lifeguards I'm training. And boy, can they pack it away."

Taylor must've looked confused, because Jason added, "I split my time between my practice and the Island. I spend six months here and six months in Pine Lakes. Although, technically, I can work from anywhere as long as I have a computer."

Mama went with Nick, and he and Luis brought out several takeout bags containing food that smelled wonderful.

Jason took the bags. "Wish I could stay but, well, you get the picture. I'll see you all soon." He waved and left.

Taylor lifted a brow at Nick and asked, "I'm confused. Law and beach patrol?"

He shrugged. "I know. Kind of hard to explain but Jason couldn't give up Cantecaw completely. He owns his own practice and spends his summers here."

"He's lucky he's able to do that."

"Sure is."

Mama and Nick sat down again. So did she, noticing Kate tuck into her lasagna with gusto.

Mama lit up. Kate had always been adventurous trying new dishes and different foods.

"Good. You like?" Mama asked

"Mmm," Kate managed. But her mouth was full.

"Kate," Taylor admonished. "Manners."

"Delicious," the girl answered after she'd swallowed.

Mama laughed loudly and encouraged everyone to have seconds.

The noise level rose but Taylor didn't mind. This was what she remembered. The clink of cutlery and voices trying to drown out other voices. She looked up to find Nick's gaze directed at her, intense but welcoming. She shivered a little. To hide her feelings, she went back to eating, but didn't really taste a morsel.

Once they were finished, everyone joined in clearing the dishes and resetting the tables for the dinner crowd, even Kate, who never grumbled once. Taylor said goodbye to Kate. "You'll behave for me, please? Very, very best behavior?"

"Yes, Mom."

"I think some cookies are in order, don't you?" Beth asked Kate.

"You mean, baking? From scratch?" Kate asked, her face filling with excitement.

"Is there any other way?" Beth replied. She winked as they made for the door. "She'll be fine."

Taylor felt a twinge of guilt. "I hate imposing. Thank you."

Beth threw her a look. "Imposing? Never. You're—"

"Family. I know."

Nick walked up to her after Beth and Kate had

gone. "You ready?" With him being so close, Taylor found it hard to concentrate. She thought she nodded. She might not have.

A loud crash in the kitchen focused their attention, and Nick laughed, stepping aside. "I'd better see what the catastrophe is."

Taylor wondered if she wasn't eighteen again, the way her heart raced. With a determined shake of her head, she went up to the podium and viewed the seating chart. She swapped servers Matt and Tina. Matt was relatively new and all teenager, mostly long arms and legs that he tried to coordinate. Fewer tables to cover and him being closer to the kitchen would help.

The next thing Taylor knew, hungry customers started coming in and the night flew by. Business turned out to be crisp and steady. Some regulars, mostly vacationers beginning the Memorial Day holiday early.

She had a couple of dicey moments. The worst being when an arrogant silver fox type insisted he had a reservation when he didn't. Judging by the well-dressed lady on his arm, they had money and expected to get their way. Taylor caught a break when table three decided not to have dessert, meaning she could seat Mr. and Mrs. Entitled over there. Thankfully, most of the customers understood they were in for a wait if they didn't have a reservation.

Once the rush was over and the doors were finally closed for the night, Taylor blew out a sigh of relief and sat down, exhausted but satisfied. Nick came over with two small glasses of house red to join her and they clinked.

"To your first night back and a job well done. You were wonderful."

Taylor sipped and smiled. "Thank you for the compliment. You schmoozed your way around and charmed everyone."

"We make a great team," he said, and then drank his wine.

Taylor heard the swish of the kitchen doors. She couldn't imagine what Mama Bella was going to do with that statement.

CHAPTER NINE

NICK SAT AT a table after Taylor left, his fingertip circling the rim of his half-empty wineglass. He could feel his mother approaching and sense her concern, when he was the one who should be concerned. The bonds of the Diamante family were forged in steel and wrapped tightly by the heart.

A tendril of hair escaped from the loose bun at the back of her head. When had all the strands of gray appeared? Why hadn't he noticed? She sat down and squeezed his hand, which now rested on a pristine white tablecloth. Her strong grip made him feel better. Almost.

"Dimmi cosa ti preoccupa?"

Why was he so deep in thought? Did she really need to ask? He sat straighter in the chair and twisted toward her, patting the top of her hand. "Why didn't you tell me, Mom?"

She leaned back and let out a big puff of air. "Because no one keeps secrets in this family, and I know you find out sooner than later." She tweaked his cheek. "All right, all right. Because no one wants to admit they're growing old."

"You're not old, Mama."

Even as he said the words, he noticed her skin carried a pasty hue and the dark smudges beneath her eyes were even darker than usual. "But you do look tired."

She smiled, pulling her hand away. "I am. Getting ready for the Memorial Day rush, and the summer, is always tiring."

"I should have seen it."

"Maybe." She chuckled softly. "You not the only one, Nico. I try not to think, too, eh?"

Nick rose and got another wineglass from behind the bar, pouring a small draft for his mother. He sat down again, saluting her as they touched glasses. "It's been a long time since we shared a glass."

She smiled. "Too long."

His mama knew what was coming, had to know. "I want more of these moments, Mama. Please, you need to slow down. For us. If not for yourself." She frowned. "Rocco told me what the doctor said. If you keep pushing, you can end up with a heart attack. Or a stroke. Or both."

"Nico. *Bambino.* You blow things up. Way out of, how you say it? Proportion."

"Do I?" he shot back.

"Yes. No. I don't know. After a twelve-hour day, you tired, too."

"Which is the problem, Mama. You can't keep working like this anymore. The thought of losing you... I don't even know how to describe it. It's...it's like a cold knife to my heart. Please."

Her fingers trembled slightly as she picked up her wineglass and drank. "Who's going to run the kitchen if I don't?"

"I have an idea. Several, in fact. Some you might not like."

His mother growled out her next words. "I no like any of them already."

Nick stopped a laugh. "What if I run the kitchen with Luis? He's been working beside you for ten years. He's been begging for the opportunity, but I'm not the only one not seeing things, am I?"

His mother's jaw dropped. She looked away. "I didn't know."

Nick knew his mother was more observant than that. He played along anyway. "Now you do." He smiled to reassure her. "What if you took care of all of the purchasing and prep, the way you normally do, and you left dinner to us? I can handle the service. And Taylor's got the front covered."

She sighed and sipped. "Taylor is...*eccezionale*...the way she take care of people."

"Did you see how she handled the customer with the attitude?" he asked. His mother nodded. "Thought he could barge in and take over the whole restaurant. There's an art to managing a customer like him," Nick murmured, enjoying his wine. "So yes, she is."

"Perfect," his mother declared, a knowing gleam in her gaze. "And maybe she is, too, for whatever else is running around inside your brain."

"I never could get anything past you, could I?" His mother shook her head no and gave him one of her patented stares. He leaned forward and put one of her hands inside both of his. "I want more, Mama."

"More what?" she asked, a tight crease appeared across her brow.

He blew out a shuddered breath. "I want to bring Diamante's into the twenty-first century."

"I no understand." She really did look confused.

He knew. "I spent years learning how to make restaurants profitable, Mama. I want to make Diamante's more upscale. I want to take part of the back room, redo the menu and hire a chef."

There. He'd told her. Nick waited for the explosion. All she did was lift both eyebrows and ask, "A chef?"

"Mama, believe me. I'm not trying to remake Diamante's. Just Thursday, Friday and Saturday nights. Only part of the back room. Maybe fifty people maximum. Four tables of four and three seatings. And I want to bring in some more expensive wines."

She frowned. "And you think this would maybe make us more profitable?"

He could understand her concern. "No. But if the idea takes off, I'd open a second restaurant. Not to compete. To enhance." He drew in a deep breath and the words rushed out. "On the mainland. Not on the Island. I promise."

He could see the hurt in her gaze, recognize the pain even further as she paled. He steeled himself against it. She cleared her throat and focused on a spot somewhere over his shoulder. "The only failure is not to try. Your papa and I lost two restaurants before Diamante's."

"I know, Mama."

"Ah. But you don't know about your uncle Bruno, one of your papa's brothers. How he stole from us, took all our money. Your papa was so broken he didn't want to try again. But I made him. He had to know if we could succeed." She refocused on him. "So do you."

Nick knew by the bow in her shoulders, he had hurt her. "I don't want to upset you, Mama."

She frowned. "Upset me? Your papa and I dreamed one day of leaving both of you boys something built from hard work, but also built from our mistakes. Now, Rocco, his heart and head. They are in his law books. But you, *mi figlio*, you are the one to carry on for us. You want to make the, how you call it? *Un retaggio del passato?*"

"Legacy, Mama."

"*Si. Si.* Legacy. You want to make it better. And this makes me very happy. You have the fire. You've always had the fire."

She rose and kissed the top of his head. "I don't know if you right or wrong. But it is wrong not to try. So, I give you my blessing. We…we test the waters, yes?"

Relief overtook him. "Thank you, Mama."

"What you need now is to share your fire. You need someone to be your anchor. Sometimes life can get like the ocean, one day calm, the next choppy and filled with whitecaps."

Good grief. His mother wasn't even trying to hide her thoughts. "She works for me, Mama. For us. That's all."

"Whatever you say, Nico. Whatever you say." His mother finished the last of her wine and lifted both glasses to bring them back to the kitchen. "You will tell this chef not to mess with my kitchen, eh?"

"Yes, Mama."

"And we will give this chef a space." She grinned a very wicked grin. "A very small space."

He rolled his eyes and laughed. "Mama, stop."

"*And*, we make a deal. I will listen to that doctor if you will give Taylor more responsibility, eh? She good. Very good."

"Agreed." He half laughed, half sighed. "Anything else?"

"A grandchild would be nice."

"Come on, Mama. You're not even being subtle anymore." He roared with laughter. She gave him her best innocent gaze. "You *have* grandchildren."

She grinned. "Not enough. Never enough. Perhaps—?"

"Mama," he groaned. "Stop trying to be a matchmaker."

"Me?" she asked, putting her hand over her heart.

"You. Now, Luis said he'll drive you home tonight. You go and get some sleep, please. I'll close up."

She muttered her way back to the kitchen, so he wasn't quite sure what she said. Something to the effect of having eyes in her head. Well, he had them, too. But life had a way of being more messy and chaotic than muttered words becoming a reality.

When Nick was satisfied everything had been cleared and cleaned up, he knew he'd have a hard time falling asleep right away. Now that he'd gotten his dream out into the open, he had a billion ideas running around inside his head.

Taking the long way home, he wound up driving by the cottage. He wasn't surprised about that. But what *did* surprise him was the sight of Taylor sitting on the front steps. He shut off the engine and got out. "I just came by to make sure you and Kate were settled in. Everything okay?"

She seemed surprised but not surprised to see him. "Hi. Yes. Kate's sound asleep. I should be, too. Strange that I'm not."

"Me, too," he said, stopping in front of her and trying to keep his voice low. Sound carried on the Island big-time, especially near the bay. "I'm completely pumped." He pointed to the step. "Do you have room for one more?"

She slid over. "Sure."

Nick sat down. "Mama thinks we make a good team."

"Oh, she does, does she?" The side of Taylor's mouth lifted. "What does Nick say?"

Her slight frame screamed *fragile*. Nick knew better. "Nick says you know your stuff. I thought for sure that one guy was going to have a complete meltdown tonight."

She chuckled. "He definitely neared critical mass."

"How did you know?"

"Know what?"

"That the one table was going to skip dessert and leave?"

"Experience. Gut instinct. Something I learned over the years. The best signal is when people start to fidget at a table, then you know they're ready to go." She grinned. "The rest was easy. Kind of like playing chess. I keep the board in my head. Isn't this what you pay me for?"

He nodded, very aware of his knee touching

hers. He swallowed to calm his skipping pulse. "I've seen the best in the business work, but I've never seen someone so smooth. You performed effortlessly. Very impressive."

Her next words seemed almost a dare. "Is this all Nick has to say?"

On any other night, Nick wouldn't have hesitated. He'd have kissed her, but right now, there was a clear line that he shouldn't cross. Not when they both needed this job to work out for her. "Would you believe I don't know what else to say?"

"Nick Diamante speechless? Impossible."

"Ouch." He laughed. "All right, you were magnificent and I need you. You're the key to all my plans."

She beamed but then dimmed. "You spoke to Bella about your plans for the restaurant?"

He nodded. "Yes."

"You're still in once piece. Comparatively speaking, *that's* impressive."

Nick chuckled softly. "Only because you were the closer, the crucial part of the bargain. She wants you managing the front. She wants you to be in charge of the waitstaff, not just the podium."

"I see."

"I don't think you do," he replied, rubbing the back of his neck.

The soft glow of the streetlamp flickered and danced over her features, completely captivating him. Nick might never get enough of her outward beauty, soft and fair like a spring day. But her inner grit and determination? Those were the magnets pulling him closer and closer. "Taylor. I… Um…"

She smelled of citrus and something else uniquely her. A heady fragrance making him lose every rational thought in his head.

She drew back. "Nick? What is it? No way, we can't."

He leaned in but jerked to a halt. Forgotten what he'd just told himself about their circumstances.

"There's too much at stake," she went on without hesitation. "Your dreams. Mine. The coin. This isn't a good idea."

The coin. How he wished it didn't exist. Taylor was here. On Cantecaw. Working shoulder to shoulder with him. That's what was important. And, if he was being honest with himself, maybe there could be more.

"I've had worse ideas," he murmured. "But you're right." He rose and helped her stand. "Maybe we'll revisit it in the future?" He hoped his lighter tone would remove any possible awkwardness.

"I'm being serious."

"So am I."

"I have a daughter who needs me, Nick. I have to be there for her always. Now that she's old enough, she's been trying to understand the divorce, and I don't want to add to her confusion. She used to simply accept things the way they were. Now she's questioning everything." Taylor let go of a soft breath in a whoosh. "She's beginning to think her father's hit-and-miss behavior is somehow because of her."

"And instead, you're taking the blame."

Nick had to admit he had a hard time conceptualizing Taylor's and Kate's situation. He'd been fortunate to have such a wonderful childhood growing up on the Island, that he couldn't imagine life without a raucous, in-your-face family who fought as hard as they loved.

"Do you think I could get to know Kate? Maybe become a friend. You already know Mama's got her on her side."

She frowned. "Which worries me. too, Nick."

Stunned, he asked, "Why?"

"What happens at the end of the summer?" she asked in reply. "What happens when you finally realize that you should be looking for the coin? What happens when you find it?"

Nick didn't want her to leave. He wanted her to stay. Now more than ever. Because she wanted to, because she loved the Island, because she wanted this to be her home. "I don't know. Let's wait and see. There's no reason for you to go after the summer."

"Except Kate's entire life is back in Pennsylvania. All she's ever known."

The light bulb went on, cruel in its brightness. He paced, not quite knowing what to do with his hands. "Okay. But she still has the summer. Let's let her be a kid at the beach. There'll be no shortage of people to help care for her—me, most of all."

"Not Bella?"

"If you haven't figured out we *all* come after my mother—"

"I have. I have."

"And speaking of Bella..." he began. Alarm filled her face as he said the words. His expression must have given away his inner feelings, so he explained immediately. "No, no. It isn't something too serious, thankfully. The doctor says she's got high blood pressure. She needs to slow down."

Taylor visibly tensed. "She's okay, though. Right?"

"For now. But it makes me think of the future."

"Seems we both should." Taylor went up the steps to the screen door. "But one thing at a time. Let's make Bella our priority." Her gaze, always open, now had more than a hint of concern. "Good night, Nick."

"Good night, Tay. Thank you."

Once the door clicked shut, Nick thought about cause and effect. Too many what-ifs rolled around in his head. His mother. Kate. Taylor. What would happen if he pursued a relationship with her? He recalled her soft features, her fearless nature and how good he felt when he was with her, and he knew he wanted to try.

Nick had once left Cantecaw to learn how to fly, to spread his wings and establish himself on his own terms. But he'd returned to the nest and now the nest needed his help. Would his dream hurt Diamante's foundation? Or allow it to thrive?

Trying to find an answer worried him well into the night. Risk versus reward. Only time would tell.

CHAPTER TEN

TAYLOR WOKE UP to a very distinct bounce and roll. She cracked open one eyelid to find Kate jumping up and down on the bed. Taylor groaned as her stomach rumbled, and she tried to bury her head under the covers.

"When can we go to the beach?"

Taylor tried to gather her wits. She'd taken a long time to fall asleep, unable to calm her racing heart. Wow. The way Nick had looked at her in the moonlight.

"C'mon, Mom. Wake up. I want to go to the beach," Kate said, each word interspersed with a breath as she jumped.

Rising up on an elbow, Taylor admonished, "Kate. Stop. I can't think." The motion on the bed ceased. "I don't even know what the weather is going to be like today. And Nana's coming for an extra-long weekend."

Kate's face saddened at the mention of weather. She hopped down in front of her and said, "I'll check my phone." Then she slid off the bed and ran to get it.

"Is that coffee I smell?" Taylor called after her daughter. The girl could charm her into most things. Kate had learned how to make coffee early on, to the detriment of several coffeepots.

Walking carefully so as to not spill, Kate came back bearing one steaming mug of very fragrant brew. Hot, creamy and slightly sweet. Taylor sipped, feeling the liquid bring instant life into her tired bones. "You certainly know how to get on my good side, don't you?"

Kate nodded an emphatic yes. "My phone says the weather will be seventy-two and partly sunny."

"Which won't be until this afternoon," Taylor advised. She took another sip and set the cup down on the lone end table in the bedroom. Opening her arms, she invited Kate to snuggle. Her daughter took full advantage. "Tell you what. We'll do breakfast, then you go clean up and I'll take a shower. When we're both done, we'll finish unpacking. Shorts and a long-sleeved T-shirt. The wind off the water will probably be chilly."

Kate looked up at her, expectation in her eyes.

"We can walk on the beach and look for shells. Maybe Nana can take you for a dip later in the afternoon. Just a dip, though. I can guarantee you the water will be really cold."

Kate nodded and Taylor threw back the covers,

swinging her legs over the bed. Seems she was going to have to learn how to wake up early here, not that she didn't for school days back home, but there'd be no sleeping in when the ocean called.

A quick shower, fresh clothes, a touch of makeup and another mug of coffee had her feeling almost human. Once they were out of the house, Taylor cautioned Kate on walking to the ocean. On the bay side, there was less traffic, but crossing the main boulevard could be very dangerous.

"Rule number…exactly what number are we on?"

"Four hundred and thirty-six!"

"I doubt that, Madam Exaggerator. However, this one's very important. No crossing Main Street without an adult present. I mean it. There's a lot of traffic on this road and it's dangerous. Got me?"

"I understand." Kate nodded. "Is Nana bringing my bike?"

"I certainly hope so. I asked her to." Brisk traffic even this early in the morning concerned Taylor. "We follow crossing signs. And you never ride your bike up here without an adult. You hear me? You stay on our street by the bay."

"Yes, Mom."

Once they reached the beach, Taylor let Kate run ahead. The sun sparkled off the water, forcing her to shade her eyes even with sunglasses on. Kate had already divested herself of shoes and started playing keep-away with the edge of the water.

Taylor listened to the music of the ocean join in with her daughter's laughter, feeling her heart lighten. Cantecaw always made things better.

A few intrepid sun worshippers staked their claim in the sand and Taylor walked closer to the ocean. Kate came running to her. "Look, Mom."

Taylor felt Kate pulling on her arm, bringing her over to where a tiny crab dug into the sand. The waves kept trying to draw the crab back to the sea. "He's a fighter."

Finally, the crab was able to burrow out of sight. Safe for another day.

Kate walked the shoreline intent on her task of finding shells and sea glass. She brought something by for approval.

"Good one," Taylor said, inspecting the small but perfect shell. "We'll get a mason jar to put it and the others in. Maybe we can make you one like mine but with shells. I don't think you'll find too many pieces of sea glass."

Taylor put the shell in her pocket, one part of her brain keeping an eye on Kate, the other awash in memories.

From out of nowhere, a voice said, "Sometimes your eyes are exactly the same color as the sky."

Startled, Taylor spun and found Nick behind her. He wore shorts and a surfing shirt that was such a bright lime green color that Taylor had to blink twice. "And that color makes you visible for miles on the beach."

He rolled his eyes. "It's supposed to."

She laughed. "What are you doing here?"

"You can't tell?"

Sweaty and breathing heavily from his run, Nick shouldn't have been so appealing. Yet, her heart fluttered. "The question was rhetorical. You could've been running anywhere."

"But anywhere," he answered, his tone like rich syrup, "wouldn't have given me the opportunity to run into you."

Taylor tried to respond but not a word seemed to want to pass through her lips.

"And Kate," he added.

"Hi, Mr. Diamante." Kate stepped forward.

She watched Nick kind of smile and frown at the same time. "Mr. Diamante was my dad. Always will be. Please call me Nick."

Kate flashed her a quick look, seeking her approval, and she nodded. Kate said, "Okay,"

Kate started talking and whereas Taylor couldn't summon a word, her daughter was more than making up for it. Nick was attentive and leaned into whatever Kate was saying. You would think they were discussing strategies for world peace.

All of a sudden, Taylor watched them stop at the edge of the water. Each one, at different times, would bend and choose a shell and they'd stand close over the proffered palm. His black hair would meld with her blond for an instant until they did it all over again. The picture they made against the green of the ocean, the blue of the sky... Taylor's heart lifted.

"How's the hunt going?" she asked the duo as she approached.

Kate answered, "Got two perfect ones and a piece of sea glass. You didn't think I would, but I found one. Did I do well?"

"You did. Very well." Kate beamed at her. "Both of you."

Nick looked completely at home on the sand. He shared a look with Taylor, then turned to Kate. "Don't forget. Dinner is at three. Mama's expecting you."

"Yes. Thank you."

Nick waved goodbye and started jogging down to the water's edge, and Taylor forgot to breathe as she admired his athletic grace. Her lungs hitched and she drew in much-needed air. She looked over to find Kate staring. "What?"

Kate cocked her head. "You like him, don't you?"

"Yes. I also work for him." Taylor motioned for Kate to sit. Now seemed the perfect opportunity to ask. "Would it bother you if I did? Like Nick?"

Taylor settled in the sand next to Kate. She watched her daughter dig her finger into the sand and draw several swirly patterns before answering. "It would mean you and Dad aren't ever going to get back together again."

Taylor's heart clenched. "Regardless of Nick, that's right, baby. I'm so sorry. Daddy and I aren't ever getting back together again. We don't love each other."

Kate took her time replying. "There's a girl at school. Janey. She tells us all the time her parents don't love each other. But they're not divorced."

"Sweetheart, listen. You can't compare other people or their situations to ours. It's not fair. We're different and we're allowed to be different."

Taylor expected to have this conversation when Kate was older—much older. But she believed in honesty. "Kate, try to understand. I made a mistake. So did your father. I thought I was head-over-heels in love and he thought he was ready for marriage. We were both too young. Marriage is work and we didn't understand how much it would take. Not my fault. Not his fault. Your father has issues he needs to figure out how to deal with."

"What kind of issues?"

Aside from needing to grow up? she asked herself. "He likes expensive things he can't really afford."

Kate didn't answer right away. "I'll tell him not to buy me so many presents."

Taylor was grateful. Her daughter was so mature. Not like her ex. "Kate, you deserve presents. This isn't your fault, either."

Kate heaved the dramatic sigh of a seven-year-old. "But it's so great when we're all together."

Taylor quirked her mouth. "And not fighting?"

Kate nodded.

"You see, we try not to fight because you're with us. We try very hard. Now imagine what would happen if we stopped trying."

"Wouldn't be good, would it?" Kate said, her smile fading.

Taylor slipped an arm around Kate's shoulders. "Come on, sweetheart. You're a very smart young lady. You told me you try to keep the peace between your friends. Do you want to live the same way? Always in the middle? Always the negotiator? For the two minutes of harmony we might be able to achieve?"

Kate slumped. Her hand stilled in the sand.

Taylor tried again to explain. "I'm sorry you always end up in the middle. Your father and I shouldn't do that to you. But you need to understand that some people simply aren't meant to be together."

"Okay." Her daughter heaved a huge sigh, then turned to look at her.

"Kate. Your father loves you. I love you. But we don't love each other, and together we can't make the best life for you."

Kate nodded and rose, and it tore at Taylor to watch the sparkle drain out of her daughter. She'd recover. Kate always did. She had one of those bounce-back personalities. Taylor simply wished her daughter didn't have to use it.

In the meantime, maybe a Cantecaw summer with the boisterous Diamante family was just what Kate needed. Taylor certainly did.

Taylor watched Kate go back and play with the edge of the waves, felt the warmth of the sun on her face, and knew she'd heard the newscast about the coin for a reason—to be here on Cantecaw, to give Kate time to be a kid, to give herself time to be—herself? Perhaps.

And speaking of time. "Kate? Honey? We have to go. Nana will be here soon and we have to get organized before I leave for work."

"I'm coming."

They were just finishing cleaning and straightening the cottage when Taylor heard a car engine shut off and a door slam. With the front door propped open, she stood outside and watched her mother stretch and work out a few kinks. In light of what was happening to Bella, Taylor's nerves jangled. She swallowed hard and by the time her mother approached, she'd managed a huge smile and a strong hug. "Hi, Mom."

Kate came bounding out. "Hi, Nana!"

Taylor saw them embrace, full of warmth and love. "I should have come out here a long time ago," her mother said, letting go of Kate. "You were right. I'd forgotten. This island really is its own world. So lovely."

"I found a piece of sea glass," Kate began. "Two pieces, actually. And some shells. And the water is really cold. But I don't mind. You can take me to the ocean later. Mom said I could go swimming. Are you going to get wet?"

Her mother looked kind of helpless as Kate dragged her into the house. Taylor called out to her. "I've got your things. Go on."

Taylor hauled her mother's luggage into the house and began unpacking for her in Kate's room. When her mother joined her, she said, "I can take the pullout couch, Mom, and you can have my room if you want more privacy."

"And miss late-night giggles with my grand-daughter? Never."

"All right. But anytime you want to change, please let me know."

Her mother nodded. "You look much better. I never quite understood before, but Cantecaw agrees with you. Kate, too."

"It does," she said, already feeling the roots growing. "It really does."

As Taylor looked up, she studied her mother, smoothing the blanket on the bed and then refold-ing a blouse resting on top. "Mom?"

"Yes, darling?"

"I'm not so sure anymore."

"About what?"

"Everything. Kate's absolutely blossoming in this place."

"You know, when you came home from your summer away I felt like I was talking to a whole new person—a whole new you. You'd grown up before my very eyes and like the twist in a mystery, I didn't see the reveal until it was finished. But then, there you were." Her mother smiled and faced Taylor. "I'm certain I'm not explaining this right but that *you* is back again, the real you. And I'm glad. Greg took something out of you and you've been so unhappy lately."

Taylor lifted a brow. "I have?"

"Yes. A mother knows. A mother always knows."

Taylor understood. She'd know if Kate was hurting. "Yes."

Which made this summer all the more important. "Kate's been struggling, Mom. About me and Greg. She's been fantasizing about us getting back together again as a family. I keep trying to explain we're never going to be the kind of family she wants but maybe she needs to hear it from you also. Perhaps a little reinforcement at some point?"

"Of course." Her mother stepped around the bed and enveloped her in a huge hug.

She squeezed hard and let go. "Thanks, Mom." She stepped back. "I made a terrible mistake with Greg. You were right. I should never have gotten married so quickly."

Her mother shrugged. "We all have to learn by our mistakes."

"I know. I was in love with love."

"Which happens more than you might think. You're not the only person to fall into that trap."

"I'm sure." Taylor glanced out of the open doorway to find Kate engrossed in something on her phone. "But not all of the others have a daughter suffering because of their mistakes."

Her mother tilted her head and said, "You always take on the weight of the world, Tay. You don't have to. Kate will end up stronger for having experienced adversity."

"She may also end up not trusting men or relationships," Taylor replied, praying such a thing would never happen.

"Maybe. But don't discount the foundation you've given her. You've taught her right from wrong." Her mom winced. "Greg, with his infinite selfishness, has, too."

Taylor wished she could be sure. "I hope so. I really do." Time to lighten the mood, she thought. "We've been invited to eat at Diamante's at three. We'd better get moving."

"Great," her mother replied with an exceptionally bright smile. "I'm starving."

"The restaurant is on Fourteenth, we're on Tenth, so it is within walking distance. Not terrible. Just in case you ever decide you'd like to. Tonight, though, I think maybe we should take two cars because I have to stay and work."

They went to the living room, and Taylor heard

the back door slam shut. She turned and Kate walked in. "I put my bike in the little shed where the beach chairs are. Is that okay?"

"Sure, honey. Please go and clean up. And bring a sweatshirt with you. It may be chilly when you finish dinner."

As Taylor dressed, she thought about mistakes and how to rectify them. Could this one be fixed? All the money in the world wouldn't and couldn't build trust, especially not when it came to relationships. Maybe a bandage at best. Perhaps some Diamante love would help.

TAYLOR'S HEART HAMMERED as they got out of the car. She really wanted Bella and her mom to like each other. It seemed beyond silly, she realized, for ten years to have passed for this meeting to take place.

She needn't have worried. As soon as they walked into the restaurant, Bella enfolded her mother in a characteristic bear hug. By the time they reached the dining room, they were chatting like old friends.

Taylor spotted Beth, who gave her a hug, while Kate played peekaboo with Roc Junior. The place got loud with everyone talking, but the noise faded as soon as Nick stepped through the kitchen doors. Her heart, already on sprint mode, seemed to want to compete in the one-hundred-yard dash. He smiled and she smiled back.

Soon, Taylor came back to earth to find the decibel level had dropped. "Is it me or has everyone decided it's polite to stare."

"Both," Nick replied and laughed.

Heat filled her cheeks. She grabbed Nick's hand and pulled him over to her mother. "Mom? This is Nick."

Her mom smiled. "Nice to meet you. When Tay came home ten years ago, all she did was talk about you."

"I did?"

"I'm flattered," he said, giving her a smile that she knew was meant for her and her alone. She wondered what it would be like to cross the invisible threshold, take the next step, sink into the warmth of that gaze and let the spark ignite.

Taylor shook her head, letting the moment drift away. She was sure to be grilled later on but felt glad that whatever had been between them all those years ago was still alive. Rather than push it aside, Taylor let herself enjoy the feeling.

He knew. And he was doing the same.

But moments were simply moments, and quickly, reality had a way of intruding. Now, she suddenly wished she hadn't found the coin, because the numbers didn't seem lucky at all—just another missed chance at something wonderful that was never meant to be.

CHAPTER ELEVEN

NICK LOVED WATCHING TAYLOR. She talked with her hands, her smile lit up the room, and always, Nick found himself holding his breath without even realizing it. She burned with the brightness of a star when she performed her duties, completely in her element. He truly admired her strength and self-assurance. But Nick loved watching Taylor most when she dealt with customers and sticky situations, gliding through problems with the ease of a dancer, her take-no-nonsense persona wrapped in gilt velvet. She knew exactly when to hold her ground and when to bend. She seemed to almost have a sixth sense about how long patrons were willing to wait. A schmooze here, a free drink there, and at the end of the night, no one went home unhappy. Not even him, because her abilities made sure customers would return again and again. Amazing. Simply amazing.

"Sit and have a glass of wine with me?"

Taylor seemed to want to but was unsure. "Not

too long. Kate can be a handful. I don't want to overstep the privilege."

"Luis always offers to take Mom home for me. Tonight, I took him up on it. I wanted to talk with you." Alarm filled her gaze. "No. There's nothing wrong. Nothing new that's wrong, I should say."

"Your mom. She looked tired tonight. I see what you mean."

Nick went over and grabbed two glasses from behind the bar and brought over a carafe of the house red. As he sat down, he stared out the picture window facing the bay. How many times had he sat in this very restaurant, letting the lights of the mainland soothe him?

He poured two glasses of wine and set one in front of her. "I had a heart-to-heart with her, about how the doctor wants her to slow down. It was some tough negotiation, but I got her to agree. Sort of."

Taylor hit the nail on the head when she said, "She needs something else to do besides run this restaurant."

"I know. She enjoys Roc Junior. And Beth's tried to take her shopping but—"

"Disaster?"

He smiled. "Let's just say Beth looked a bit harried after she dropped Mom off."

"I get the picture," Taylor said with a light laugh.

Nick moved his hand from the wineglass to

take Taylor's hand, and her eyes widened. Taylor being Taylor, though, she refused to be diverted. "What about taking Bella out and letting *her* be waited on?"

"I tried," he said with a grimace. "She always complains afterward that no one cooks as well as she does."

Taylor huffed. "A steak is a steak, Nick. Atlantic City isn't far. Surely you have connections. Let her be treated like a queen for a night."

"I can't close the restaurant." He grinned at the face she was pulling. "Do you give that look to Kate?"

She nodded. "Works, too." She lifted a single brow, daring him to debate her.

"Mondays are our slowest day," he replied.

"And after Memorial Day, you won't get really busy until the end of June."

He drank his wine and then pondered the red liquid a moment. "I don't know."

"Make it a family affair," she urged, slipping her hand out from beneath his and squeezing hard. "Take Rocco and Beth. I'll watch Roc Junior."

"I'd prefer you come with us," he said, lifting his gaze to hers.

"Thank you for the offer. But I… We'll see." She stared at him, her ability to read his mind uncanny. "Nick, don't. I know you're feeling guilty. Your mother is who she is. Bella's happiest with the entire family around her, sitting at the table, making sure no one leaves early. She was so in her element at the pre-rush meal today."

He'd thought so, too. As he opened his mouth to answer, Taylor jumped in first to continue. "Everybody wants to be treated like they're special. Your mother is beyond special and deserves more love and attention every now and then."

He agreed. "You do, too."

Whatever thought his words had sparked, Taylor needed a sip of her wine before speaking. "I hate having to bring up the subject again, but the money from the coin could make all of her days special."

"The money," he repeated. Disappointment flooded his veins. "Tay, come on. Look, I understand and it's all right. I get it."

"Get what?" She frowned and tucked her hand back into her lap.

Nick hated losing contact, but it was time to face facts. "You could have called. You could have emailed. Instead, you used the story to break the ice so it'd be easier coming back to the Island, and seeing all of us."

"I did?" She reared back. "Do I look that insecure to you?" Her brows slammed together. "And what about you visiting me? Or does the road *not* go both ways?"

"I tried." He figured he'd gone this far, might as well go all in. "You were already engaged."

She sucked in a swift breath. "How'd you find out?"

"Your old roommate, Dianna."

She sat back, slumping in her chair. "I'm sorry."

Nick remembered the emptiness, the terrible letdown as he'd stared at his phone, his fingers wrapped so hard around the plastic he thought they would break. Letting go took a long time. Literally and figuratively. "I never found out, in the end."

"Found out what?"

"If you got married or not. Guess I didn't want to know."

She stared down at the table, her teeth worrying her bottom lip. "Seems to be the gift that keeps on giving. But I wouldn't change a thing."

"Kate."

"Yes. I just don't understand why you keep pushing back about the coin."

He nodded. "Because finding the coin's not my number one priority? There's the business, which I'm also planning on growing. And Mama—"

Her features tightened. "Now you're making me sound like a—a really horrible person."

Nick winced. She stood. He rose with her. "Tay, wait. Please," he called out as she turned to leave. "I'm sorry. I didn't mean to make you mad. I'll look. I promise."

She paused and turned back, but she focused

not on him, rather at something in the picture window. "You're afraid."

Wait a minute. Was he that transparent? "I'm what?"

"You're afraid of what the money will do, can do."

He half-laughed in disbelief. It seemed he wasn't so readable after all. "Maybe I am. Maybe I'm not."

She let go an exasperated breath, her gaze filling with what looked like confusion. "You have the most obstinate, thickheaded, block-of-wood for a brain I've ever come across."

Nick found her conclusions amusing and entirely captivating. "Pure concrete."

She opened her mouth to continue her tirade, he guessed, only for her to bark out what sounded like laughter, which morphed into a guffaw. "What am I going to do with you?"

He offered a teasing grin. "You're not the first person who's said that."

"How about tearing your house apart and forcing you to look for the coin?" she asked, her tongue pushing out the inside of her cheek.

"Not exactly what I had in mind—to be honest, but you're still welcome to come over."

She jerked her purse strap over her shoulder, shaking her head. "What would you do without the Diamante charm?"

He smiled and cocked his head. "Haven't had

to find out yet. So, how about we have breakfast tomorrow, then we'll take Kate to the beach?"

As if she was surrendering, she let her arms fall to her sides. "You're hard to get mad at."

He flashed her a brilliant smile, enjoying the win. This time. "Ten, okay?"

She looked like she wanted nothing more than to argue. "Perfect."

"There will be time for us to figure out everything, okay?" He walked her to her car. With her chin tilted up and her face in his sights, Nick struggled to not blurt out how much he admired her. "Deal?"

"Deal."

"Till the morrow, then." Clasping both hands over his heart Nick began to back away. She chuckled and got into her car and drove off.

Back inside the restaurant, Nick went to the table to clean up, unable to stop smiling. He swallowed the last sip of wine, straightened the table, then brought the glasses into the kitchen.

Getting his phone off his makeshift desk, he couldn't help himself. He began tapping his fingers on his browser, typing the words "rare coins" and the numbers 1821. "This is ridiculous. It can't be true," he muttered. Nearly an hour and a half later, he put the device down.

Something wasn't sitting well with Nick and he wondered what was wrong. Seeing Taylor, being with her, made the world right. When she stood next to him, he wanted to slay dragons, become the knight in shining armor she hopefully believed him to be. So why did he keep not wanting to find the coin?

He didn't want her to leave Cantecaw again.

All right. Duly noted. But there's more. Be honest, Nick.

He wanted the ten years to disappear. He wanted the free and easy flow between them, the unquestioning trust. But time *had* changed both of them. Was there too much history for them to find their friendship again? Possibly more?

Nick closed up, got in his car and drove home. He kept asking the question, and even while standing on his deck with the rhythmic lap and pull of the ocean waves, he couldn't find the peace he sought. Usually, the sound of the water cured the ills of the day. Tonight? Not so much.

TRUE TO HIS WORD, Nick knocked on the cottage door at ten sharp. Taylor greeted him, and the smell of pancakes had his stomach growling instantly.

"Sounds like someone is hungry," she said with a laugh.

"Someone is," he answered, accepting the offer of a cup of coffee with pleasure. "Good morning." He sipped. "Cinnamon?"

"A change of pace every now and then. And I splurged. Half-and-half, with a pinch of sugar."

"Delicious."

Cynthia entered the kitchen. Nick rose and kissed both her cheeks, Diamante-style. "Good morning."

"To you also." Taylor's mom picked up a wide-brimmed hat. "Enjoy your breakfast. I'm going shopping. I need a book."

"The bookstore on the Avenue is gone," Nick said. "They moved down to the Village on the Pier. And there's a bunch of stores with clothes and things, not just tourist stuff."

"Earrings?"

Taylor smiled. "You only have two ears, Mom."

Obviously, for Cynthia, certain jewelry purchases were a guilty pleasure.

"I'm allowed a vice or two."

Nick stifled a laugh for his own protection.

"A different pair a day," Cynthia continued, arching a brow. "Would mean I'd need three hundred and sixty-five pairs. I'm not even close."

Taylor wasn't one to give in so easily. "Closer than you think."

Cynthia shrugged. "We all have our quirks."

With not a second to waste, Taylor shot back, "Vices."

Nick watched them laugh and hug and realized their banter, though much quieter, matched the teasing his family enjoyed.

Kate walked into the kitchen. "Hi, Mr. Diamante." He frowned. "Sorry. Nick."

"Hey, kiddo."

Kate turned to Taylor with her face scrunched. "What's a vice?"

Cynthia sent Taylor a wicked grin before she practically ran out the front door. "Have fun!"

Kate called out, "Bye, Nana!"

Nick found Taylor in front of the stove contemplating the pancake batter she'd just poured into the frying pan.

Kate cocked her head at her mother, clearly waiting for an answer. Nick couldn't resist the opening. "Yes, Mom. What's a vice?"

Taylor turned. If only looks could kill. Then he watched as she focused on Kate, her gaze softening. "A vice is something that isn't good for you, but you can't stop doing."

Now Kate really seemed confused. "Buying earrings is a vice?"

"I was teasing Nana," Taylor said and sighed.

She went back to the stove and flipped several pancakes in the pan. Kate swung into one of the chairs at the dining room table where a place was already set. He waited until Taylor handed him the stack and brought them over before sitting down.

He tasted his first bite and smiled. "You really come close to Shaker's. Do I taste vanilla?"

"Just a dash."

Kate ate quickly, pushed her plate back and asked, "When are we going to the beach?"

"When Nick and I are finished with our breakfast."

Kate rolled her eyes and rose from the table. She put her plate in the sink before flouncing into the living room.

Taylor looked a bit defeated. He hated that look.

Nick caught her gaze. He asked her to trust him. She nodded, so he asked, "Kate, why did you hurt your mom?"

Kate seemed flummoxed. "Hurt her?"

Nick nodded. "Her feelings. You know she's only looking out for you. Now, you're a good kid. I haven't known you long, but anybody who can find the best shells is good in my books. So, whadd'ya say, you give your mom a break, maybe?"

Kate seemed to take it in. She sped over to Taylor and threw her arms around her. "I'm sorry."

Taylor smiled, her eyes filling, as she hugged her daughter. "Apology accepted, sweetie."

Together, the three of them took care of the dirty dishes. As a team, they cleaned and dried and put away the plates, bowls and utensils.

Kate wandered over to the couch and picked up her phone. Taylor plucked a few last things from the table. "Guess it's time to get ready for the beach."

"You go ahead," he said. "I'll take care of this." He took the items from her hands. She thanked him and retreated to her bedroom.

Nick found spots for the butter, jam and syrup in the fridge and cupboard and went to the living room to wait for Taylor.

Kate glanced over at him and frowned. "You're not my dad," she blurted.

"You're right," Nick said, treading carefully, knowing this was an important moment, not just for him and Kate, but him and Taylor. "Though I am your mom's friend. I'll bet you protect your friends when someone's being unkind."

Kate cocked her head. "Yeah. I do." After a moment, she added, "So, that was what you were doing for my mom a minute ago?"

"Yes."

"And I was being unkind, wasn't I?"

"Yes." He watched the little girl nod. "So, now you have to decide. Can we be friends?"

Kate's mood seemed to shift and she bounced up off the couch. "You like my mom, don't you?"

"Yes. I like your mom. Always have."

"Okay. Cool." Kate walked up to him and held out her fist. He made one of his own and they bumped. "Are you a baseball fan?" she asked.

"Of course."

Kate grinned. "I love the New York Yankees."

"You do?"

"Yeah. Most of my friends don't even like baseball. But I do."

"Hey, you know something? That's okay. And, for the record, the Yankees just happen to be my favorite team, too. Maybe we'll get to watch a game together. We can have hot dogs and popcorn, all the things to have fun at a game." Nick looked up to see Taylor's sweet expression and her eyes well up again.

She turned away and swiped at her cheeks. "Come on. Let's go, you two."

Once Kate was ready, the trio walked outside. Next to the outdoor shower, Nick had added a small shed. Kate's bike was there, as were beach chairs and sand toys, and a cart to bring them to the beach.

"For your tenants?" Taylor asked.

"For you."

"Thank you." She took a few steps and Nick realized he'd never forget the look on her face just then. Flowers? Champagne? No, not him. Beach chairs.

"To the beach," she announced.

He simply smiled.

Kate ran to the edge of the ocean as soon as they arrived. Nick told Taylor, "Go ahead. I'll set up."

She hesitated. "You've been so kind, gone above and beyond. I don't really have anything to give you in return."

He chuckled. "You came here to tell me about a rare coin, didn't you?"

"A coin you don't want to look for."

"Actually, I checked the internet last night.

Very interesting story. You were right. I should have listened to you."

She smiled and nodded, but then he watched Taylor turn toward the ocean and stop, shading her eyes from the sun. She swiveled to the left, then to the right, then sprinted toward the water. "Kate? Kate?"

Nick dropped the towel in his hands. He sprinted after Taylor, scanning as far as he could see. Kate wasn't by the water's edge or anywhere nearby. "I'll take north. You take south. I'll call Jason at the lifeguard station."

"Kate!"

CHAPTER TWELVE

TAYLOR DIDN'T FEEL the sand beneath her feet. She kept running and looking. Her heart pounded with every step, her lungs filling with air. But there wasn't enough as the pool of sickness swimming in her belly grew larger and larger. She tried to swallow. She couldn't.

Kate couldn't have gone far. She couldn't. And lifeguards were stationed every couple hundred yards because of the busy holiday weekend coming up.

Taylor knew all about children drowning. She'd been on a school trip at a lake campground when a boy drowned. She remembered the hush all along the beach as people watched, holding their breath. Worse still, she remembered the soft sobs of his mother, who'd only turned away for a second.

But Kate knew how to swim, was indeed part fish according to her instructor. And the lifeguards didn't become alarmed until she began calling for her daughter. But Kate could have wandered off and lost her bearings very easily, so Taylor stuck to the middle of the beach, scanning toward the water then up toward the dunes.

If she believed there were reasons for anything, she had to be thankful that Kate had insisted on wearing her new bright pink shorts set. If Kate was on the beach, she'd be hard to miss.

Taylor slowed to a walk, gulping air. Deep down below the sickness, she found the black hole of fear and worry—every parent's worst nightmare. She closed her eyes, shying away from the possibility of it becoming a reality. And when she opened them, she thought she caught a glimpse of pink.

Taylor ran.

She couldn't be sure, without checking the streets, but she thought they were about four blocks from where they began. She found Kate sitting on the sand with another little girl. They were playing. She slowed and sucked in her first draft of air in what seemed forever.

"Kate!"

Her daughter had the incredible audacity to stand and stare back and ask, "What's wrong?"

Taylor wanted to laugh, cry and scream all at the same time. "Kate! You can't go wandering off. You—"

Kate scrunched up her face. Taylor reached out and caught her daughter in a hug, squeezing tight. "You scared me half to death." Letting go, she put a hand on Kate's shoulder.

Kate looked around and tears welled. "I'm sorry, Mom. I didn't mean… I met… This is Jessica."

Taylor wiped at her eyes. "Hello, Jessica." The little girl didn't answer, but an older couple nearby, presumably Jessica's grandparents, sat on camp chairs and waved. "The beach can play tricks on you. Do you know you're about four blocks away from where we set up our chairs?"

Kate swung her head no and Taylor let go of her. "Hold that thought a moment." She pulled out her cell and dialed Nick. "I've got her."

"Oh, thank goodness," he answered, a huge breath blowing into the speaker. The sound warmed her heart. "I'll call Jason."

"Thanks. We need some Mommy-and-me time. Can you do me a huge favor and bring our chairs and stuff back to the cottage?" There would be no more ocean today for Kate.

"On one condition. Don't be too hard on her. It's really easy to lose track of how far you go on the beach."

"I know. And thanks." Taylor hung up and turned to Jessica. "I'm sorry. Kate's not going to be able to play today. Maybe tomorrow. Where are you staying?"

"Here. On Sixth Street."

"We're on Tenth."

"Okay." The little girl started tugging at one of her long brown pigtails. "See you."

"Bye," Kate answered.

Taylor directed Kate to the first beach access bench they came to. "Do you understand what you did?" she asked as she sat down beside her.

Her daughter had a very hard time meeting her gaze. "Yes, Mom."

Taylor shuddered as the shock of what might have happened set in. "And you know now how badly you scared me?"

"Yes, Mom."

"And you've figured out the Island isn't like home where you can go off and ride your bike and play with your friends up and down our street?" She paused a second. "Only after you ask permission?"

"Yes, Mom."

"Did you ask permission?"

Kate shook her head no.

"There are strangers on this island. People from all over come to this place to vacation. Mall rules apply from now on. You don't wander off, and you stay near me at all times. If you want to play with a friend, we set-up a day and time. Are we clear?"

"Yes, Mom."

"Good." Taylor winced, but a punishment was warranted. "No beach for the rest of today. No television until after dinner."

They walked back to the cottage. Kate was a great kid but sometimes she pressed boundaries. She stopped being contrite by Ninth Street and stomped into her bedroom with barely a nod to

Nick. Taylor motioned for him to join her in the backyard. "Sorry I left you with our stuff."

"Not a problem. That's what the cart is for." He seemed to hesitate, but then lifted a brow.

"She's used to our neighborhood. I should've explained the rules here."

He pointed to her hair. "I see several gray strands." He grinned. "There. And there."

Taylor swatted his hand away.

"Cut Kate some slack."

"Weren't you the one who just made the point about not pressing boundaries?" He nodded. "She scared you half to death, too."

"You noticed?"

He had tried to joke but Taylor still stood at the edge of the black hole. "I noticed. Thank you."

"It's okay to need help every now and then. You don't have to be strong all the time."

Taylor closed her eyes. A weight lifted from her shoulders, one she'd forgotten she carried. "I've been Mommy and Daddy for so long I don't even feel the burden."

He sat in a chair and she took the other one. "I can't imagine. And I won't be able to until I have my own. But we're both in the business of reading people and stepping into their shoes. I stepped into yours. At least, I tried, because I can't imagine the magnitude of your fear. I'm just pointing out the magic of the ocean. And a first real sense of endless sand."

She gave a small smile. "It's like walking into another world."

"Exactly. Pretty overpowering, especially for a seven-year-old."

He covered her hand on the armrest of her chair. He slid his thumb back and forth over her skin and Taylor stopped thinking completely. Intentional or not, the touch of his hand became her only focus.

Taylor cleared her throat, his reassurance finally pushing back the edge of her fear. "You'd make a great lawyer. But she still serves her time."

He laughed. Taylor loved his laugh, hearty and rich and full of life. His gaze warmed, turning the brown in his eyes to thick caramel with cocoa swirls. A woman could drown in a gaze like this. The world fell away. He leaned forward and her heart fluttered madly. To finally feel special again.

A car door slammed, startling them both. One side of his mouth quirked, filled with promise. No, almost a dare. Taylor smiled back, more than ready for the challenge.

"Hello!" The screen door creaked as it opened and her mother walked down the back steps. "Hmm. You're here and not on the beach and Kate's sulking in our room. What happened?"

Taylor explained and Nick added his opinion as Kate's defense attorney. However, her mom sided with her. "This time I agree with you, Tay. She needs to understand those boundaries."

Nick rose, reached out to Taylor and drew her up with him. "Since I'm completely outnumbered, I think I'll go bring Jason and his crew that tray of leftovers I promised for helping us look for Kate. I could use a little bro-bonding."

Taylor opened her mouth to insist on paying for the food, but Nick beat her to the punch.

"No, Taylor."

That they were on the same page like this sent tiny shivers down her spine. Taylor warned, "This time."

She watched Nick leave. "Men."

"You know the old saying," her mother said, claiming a chair. "Can't live with 'em. Can't live without 'em."

"Yes," Taylor said with a smile. "I've done both."

"I'm glad you're sticking to your guns. Kate is too precious to us not to understand that her actions have consequences." Her mother frowned. "I know I tend to indulge her."

Taylor didn't mind. "Oh, Mom." She reached out and hugged her mother. "Love is never wrong. And I still don't believe we can ever give children too much." She let go and walked up the steps. "C'mon. I need a cup of tea."

"You're on."

Taylor's phone buzzed. She pulled it out of her pocket and stared at the alert on the screen. "Well, I'll be. Someone's going to be happy."

Her mother asked, "What's going on?"

"I just got a message from Kate's principal. There's been a water main break. School is closed until Tuesday."

Her mother's expression lit up. "Guess I'm taking another vacation day."

Taylor frowned. "I hope that's not a problem, Mom."

"No, dear. Not at all," her mother reassured her with a smile. "I have a lot of vacation time, and they want me to take days."

Relief filled Taylor. "Thanks, Mom."

"Are you kidding? I'm really glad I'm here."

With the water put on to boil, Taylor set out two cups and the honey pot. She knew the instant Kate's bedroom door opened. She shared a quick glance with her mother, who nodded. "Hey, Kate." Kate's eyes were a little red, but defiance glinted in her gaze. Taylor wanted to ask her mother if she'd been this much of a handful. Her mom must have anticipated the question, because she flashed a wicked grin and mouthed the word "worse."

Once they all sat down, Kate said, "I'm really sorry, Mom."

"I know you are. Punishment still stands." Kate lifted her shoulders and let them fall. Yep, the girl was fond of drama. "But maybe we can make life a little more bearable." Kate sat up in her chair. "You're not going to believe this, but school is canceled tomorrow. There's been a water main break."

Kate grinned. "Really?"

"Yes. So I think I'm going to run to the store. The Diamantes have been beyond generous. Time to pay them back. What do you say we make a cheesecake for dessert for tomorrow's pre-rush dinner?"

Kate's grin blossomed into a huge smile and she started bouncing in her chair. "Yes! And I want to help."

Taylor's mother was a bit more pragmatic. "Where are you going to find a cake mold?"

She knew exactly. "McGinty's. It's really a five-and-dime and a pretty nice department store all rolled into one. They have every kitchen utensil ever invented. They have sheets and towels, clothes, even a really handy hardware section. And just about every household gadget and accessory you could think of."

Kate chimed in with, "You better get two. Just in case."

Hmm, it looked like her daughter had just licked her lips. "You bet."

With a clear purpose to occupy her mind, Taylor calmed to the point of almost feeling normal. Though a parent never forgot the absolute panic of a time when their child was missing. She'd had it happen accidentally when Kate was a toddler.

Kate had been strapped into her car seat, securely in the shopping cart. Taylor had turned her head to admire a blouse. Maybe she'd taken a few steps. The next thing she knew. Kate was gone along with her cart.

She'd looked all over, then rushed up to the customer service area. Off to the side was Kate and the cart. A Good Samaritan had thought Kate abandoned and brought her to the service area. To this day, Taylor still remembered how they wouldn't give Kate back to her. It took the hundreds of pictures in her phone to convince them. And the Good Samaritan did apologize, agreeing that Taylor hadn't been very far away, and maybe she'd overstepped a little.

Still, the terror and indignation and anger wasn't an emotional combination she'd forget anytime soon.

Taylor parked and walked into McGinty's, finding nothing had changed in the last ten years. The store still smelled like ocean, hardware and suntan lotion. She wandered the aisles proud to have made one of her earliest purchases on the Island with her first paycheck in this store. She found two aluminum snap-ring cake molds along with a set of mixing bowls exactly where she expected to find them. Perfect for what she needed.

As she walked up to the front of the store to pay for her items, a woman in a McGinty's smock stepped into her path. Taylor hit the brakes and said, "Oh, excuse me."

"Sorry, my bad," the woman said, pushing back

a strand of long straight brown hair. Their gazes met. "Taylor?"

Bewildered, Taylor wasn't sure but thought... "Cheryl?"

"Well, what a surprise!" The woman smiled and said, "Taylor Marchand."

"It's Hughes now."

The woman's smile got so big it took up most of her face. "You're married?"

Taylor shrugged. "Not anymore."

"I'm sorry."

Taylor waved away the comment. "Don't be. You know how it happens. Young and in love..."

Cheryl finished the sentence for her. "With love." She seemed to understand. "What are you doing here?"

"Working at Diamante's for the summer." Taylor paused at first, then recognized she had no reason to be embarrassed by her circumstances. "I lost my job. Nick offered. I jumped." She drew in a breath. "What about you? Married? Kids?"

"Divorced. No kids." Cheryl raised both brows. "What can I say? Still helping with the family business as you can see. You?"

"A daughter. Kate. She's seven."

Cheryl beamed. "That's wonderful."

"I can't believe it's been ten years. I don't feel any older." Taylor juggled the items in her arms.

Cheryl chuckled. "I do. Especially when I'm up

and down that ladder, stocking shelves. C'mon, let me ring you up."

"Thanks."

The final beep of the scanner on the register sounded and Taylor handed Cheryl her credit card.

"We should try to get together while you're here," Cheryl said, giving the card back.

"If Nick gives me a day off, I'll let you know. The restaurant business is twenty-four seven."

"So's this place. Why don't you give me your number?" Taylor did and put Cheryl's in her phone.

"I can't believe you're here," Cheryl said.

"Me, neither," Taylor answered. "So good to see you."

"Ditto."

Walking out of McGinty's, Taylor wondered at the vagaries of life. Ten years felt more like ten months and sometimes like ten days. Yet the years had passed. And Taylor had not only gotten her degree, she'd managed a restaurant for quite a few years. She'd created an incredible human being with enormous potential, the potential she'd felt when she was a kid.

Meeting Cheryl had brought back all the hopes and all the dreams she'd carried. Had her life turned out exactly the way she'd imagined? No. But as she headed back to the cottage, an older and maybe wiser Taylor knew one thing for certain. No one's life ever did.

CHAPTER THIRTEEN

NICK PULLED UP in front of the lifeguard station, leftovers on the passenger seat beside him. He turned off the engine and let go of the steering wheel, only to find tiny surges and frissons of fear still running through his fingers. He didn't understand why. Although, as scared as he had been, he couldn't imagine what Taylor was feeling, what she went through in that moment when she realized that Kate was missing. He loved his family unconditionally, but he'd never been responsible for anyone but himself.

Jason came out to greet Nick. They hugged and slapped backs. Jason saw the trays of food and frowned. "Bro. Seriously. Not necessary."

If Nick was certain of anything, this was it. "Bro. Seriously. Very necessary. Thank *you*."

Jason lifted the corner of his mouth with a slight shake of his head. "You know we won't say no."

"The thought did cross my mind."

"And Kate?"

"Oh, yeah. You met her at pre-rush." His friend grabbed a tray and so did Nick. They went inside the station. "She's fine. A little bewildered, I think. Her first taste of freedom on a beach. Went to her head, I guess. But she knows better now. At least, I hope she does."

Three young men and two young women who'd been lounging around staring at their phones perked up. Two of the guys rose and he watched Jason scowl. "Dinner," his friend explained. "For later." The pair backed off.

Jason put the food in the refrigerator, then they walked out onto the patio. The sun slipped behind a cloud and Nick shivered at the drop in temperature. Or was he still in reaction mode? They sat in wobbly plastic chairs and stared at the waves for several minutes in silence.

"I don't have to tell you," Jason began, "how lucky you are to have a happy ending. I've been part of several searches that didn't end as well."

Nick kept looking at the water, feeling untethered, like the ground had disappeared beneath his feet. "I'm having a real hard time understanding. I've always thought of the beach as my safe haven. We learned to swim when we were babies, that's a fact. And we never had somebody get lost or drown."

"But we did lose someone in the end," Jason said.

Nick reached out to clasp Jason's shoulder. "I

know. It's still hard to figure why things happen the way they do."

"Fate, I guess."

"It's why, to be honest, I'm struggling. Mama and Papa used to send Roc and me out here to play all the time so they could cook at the restaurant. You, all the cousins, were with us plenty."

"Yes."

"We were invincible." Nick noticed Jason glance away.

"Most of us."

"And we learned real fast when to be back. Pre-rush dinner only got served once."

Jason smiled, looking a little wistful. "I remember you bringing me a few times. Mama always said I was one of the family."

Nick threw his friend a look.

"Okay. More than a few."

Nick rubbed the back of his neck. "What I'm trying to say, I guess, is that sometimes ignorance really is bliss. Maybe it's never been important enough. Maybe I didn't have enough time to pay attention. But today was different. For a minute there, I was really, really scared."

"Caring isn't a crime, it's a necessity. Like Mama's lasagna," Jason joked but then became serious. "Consequences. If we thought about them all the time, we'd never leave our homes."

"No joke," Nick answered, finding his nerves

steadier now that he was talking. "Don't think I've ever taken things this seriously before."

"Also not a crime. You're entitled to do you."

Nick quirked his mouth, releasing a soft snort. "Entitled? I guess. Maybe. But way better off widening my perspective on things? Absolutely."

"That's something, bro. I've never seen you this thoughtful. Not even when you had all that trouble and lost your job. Taylor? The woman sitting next to you at pre-rush?"

Of course, he wouldn't be able to fool Jason. His friend might present a laid-back surfer persona, but underneath, Jason took his job and his life very seriously. "Yes. She worked at the restaurant ten years ago. The summer you went to DC to intern."

"Interesting. Made an impression, too." Nick didn't even begin to know how to explain. "Unattached for your sake, I hope."

"Yes. Divorced."

"Glad of the answer, bro, but not where I was going."

"What do you mean, then?"

Jason paused and looked at him. "Just a friendly word of advice. Remember everything you know about the ocean because it's unpredictable, just like life and love. But I'm betting you're ready to jump in with both feet."

Was he?

Jason rose, so Nick stood, too, and said, "Point made. Thanks, Jason."

"I've got your back, guy. And… I've lifeguards to train. Thanks again for the food. Good talk," Jason said, grinning.

Nick laughed. "Yeah. Good talk." He drove back to the restaurant and the feeling of confusion still lingered. Jason was right. The ocean could be dangerous even when it looked as calm and smooth as glass. Did he really want to jump in with both feet? He wasn't sure. With commitment came responsibility, and with responsibility came the sick feeling of fear when bad things happened. He wasn't sure how to survive it. Yet.

Mama greeted him as soon as he entered Diamante's. Her worried frown spoke volumes and Nick felt a little guilty, remembering his mother's heart. When he'd called Jason about Kate being missing, he should've known the Island grapevine would kick in.

"Kate. She is all right?"

Nick hugged his mother, needing more than he gave. "Yes, she's good. Not too happy, of course. Major time-out."

"*Si*. She knows not to go off alone now?"

"She knows." Nick nodded. "I feel bad for her, Mama. The beach. The ocean. Rocco and me. And Jason. It was our place, our safe haven. I can't imagine being punished for doing what comes naturally."

His mother's frown deepened. "I give you too much, I think."

"Freedom?"

"Si."

Nick asked his next question with a pensive tone. "Did we ever scare you like that?"

She smiled but the smile didn't quite reach her eyes. "From the day you and Rocco were born. I hide it well."

She put her hand on his arm and he realized she wanted to sit. So, he walked over to a table and pulled out a chair for her. "Even now?"

"Assolutamente!" She chuckled. "Especially now. All those trips. Planes. Foreign countries. I don't know how I ever survived." She patted his hand. "But you want the truth?"

He nodded.

"Driving. First Rocco, then you. I hated those driver's licenses. Every time you went out. My heart." She pointed to her throat. "I think I was relieved when each of you had your first accident. Little ones. I lived through them. I could sleep again."

He hadn't realized. Too involved with himself. A burst of guilt consumed him. "I'm so sorry, Mama. I never understood."

"You weren't meant to, *mi figlio*. Even the animals, Nico. They teach their young what they need to do to survive, then they must let go. Hard to do. But if I don't, if your papa, he don't? What do you do when we are gone, eh?"

"Mama…" he warned, not liking the direction of this conversation.

She waved away his concern. "*Si. Si.* I know. Not for a long time yet. But look at Taylor. What she must do alone. She must be a discipline… *superiore* and so much more all rolled into one. Not so easy."

"I guess not. She makes it seem so…so effortless. Obviously, so did you. And Papa."

"*Bene,*" she answered. "You must always think." She tapped her temple with her finger. "When you decide? You are like a train. You do not stop unless you have to and you follow the tracks no matter what. Straight ahead. No detours."

Nick laughed. "Mama, come on. I consider every angle, each and every one, before making a decision."

"Which is why you and Taylor are so good together. Like bread and sauce. Which needs to be stirred. And the bread needs to be sliced for the warmer." She rose and walked through the swinging doors into the kitchen.

Bread and sauce. How like Mama to put the entire scope of love and relationships into such simple terms. And yet, he thought, shouldn't it be?

No, nothing was simple. Life and love were complicated. Hurt or be hurt, wasn't that the way of the world? And consequences. They were the stepping stones.

Nick didn't have time to ponder, thanks to the evening rush, which turned out to be more like a steady flow than a typical summer Saturday night.

Toward the end of the evening, Nick noted Taylor seemed subdued. He hadn't factored the toll the day had taken. Oh, she'd turn on the wattage for the customers, but it seemed as though every time she turned on the light, turning it off made it even darker.

"You can go home," he told her. "It's not *that* busy."

She smiled slightly. "Thanks, but no thanks. I'd only think and thinking wouldn't be a great idea right now."

"I agree. Dwelling in the 'what-could-have-been' instead of the 'what is' isn't the best idea. I have a better one. If you insist on staying, how about a short walk after we close up?"

Nick focused on the image she made. Her eyes were wide and innocent, but her gaze was world-weary; her back was ramrod straight and strong, but her teeth were worrying her lower lip. He knew then that he couldn't take this lightly. Whatever was happening between them, Taylor wasn't meant for a holiday flirtation, she was meant for bread and sauce.

"No conversation unless you want some," he added. "Just a friend."

"All right," she decided. "I'd like to go. Very much. Also, just so you know, school got canceled tomorrow. Kate and my mom are staying an extra day."

"Kate's probably thrilled. I'm glad for her."

"Definitely took the edge off her punishment," Taylor said.

Later, after Nick locked the front door, he found Taylor waiting for him at the bottom of the steps. A light fog had rolled in, not dense, but enough to drop the temperature. "Are you warm enough?"

She nodded without smiling. "Yes. Thank you."

He hated seeing her so down.

They started walking toward Main Street. Some of the houses were empty. Others had cars in the driveway. They'd all be full soon enough.

"I know I promised no conversation, but I want, no, I need you to know how scared I was today." It was important to him, and he hoped maybe to her, too.

In the dim lamplight it was hard to see her face, but he thought her expression softened. "That's sweet of you, Nick."

"Despite being away from Diamante's for a long time, I always take my responsibilities seriously." He paused, noticing Taylor tilting her head. "And I did. For work."

"Not your fiancée?"

"I thought so. I was wrong. She wasn't family."

"So, you're saying I am?"

He smiled. "You've always been family."

She stopped walking. "That's sweet, too, but are you sure you're not mixing past and present? Still trying to be my protector?"

"No. I know exactly where I am."

Indeed, he did. In his mind, he could see the eighteen-year-old girl she'd once been, a bud ready to bloom. Honestly, he liked the rose better—he reveled in her strength and her fortitude. Even her thorns. "Although I will always want to protect you, you've grown up. You don't need me anymore. You're an amazing woman."

She let out a strangled laugh, her gaze filled with disbelief. "Nick. Seriously. You're the one who's amazing. You traveled the world, worked for a huge hotel conglomerate, and you made decisions that brought pleasure to millions of people. I'm jealous."

"Because you wanted to?"

"Yes." Her shoulders rose and fell but she looked far from defeated. A light filled her eyes, glinting determination. "But I got my shot. Not in the millions, of course, but enough to make the work worthwhile."

"Like we do at Diamante's every day."

"Yes. I don't think you see the impact you make," she said, her tone thoughtful. "When I was staying at the Sunrise I met a couple on vacation. They'd been coming to the Island for years. Over twenty, they told me. And eating at Diamante's the whole time. Your family has given pleasure to so many people." She began walking again. "I suppose, deep inside, I thought of myself as a failure."

He shook his head. "You're not."

"I know. I just took a smaller piece of the pie."

"I choked on the rest." Nick breathed in deeply. "Dreams aren't always the way we hope they'll be. I'm glad you didn't go the corporate route." He picked up the pace beside her. "I'm glad you didn't, because I would never want you to be burnt out. Unhappy. Lose that special spark of yours. They demanded everything I had and wanted more."

"Which is why you quit," she breathed.

Nick nodded. "It's so easy to talk to you. To be with you. The real you, not the face you show to customers or the world. But there's a piece of you, a door you won't open."

She slowed but didn't stop. "We're friends, Nick. We've always been friends. But I—I have to trust."

Nick faced her. "I thought you did. I thought, by telling you how upset I was today, I could make you understand. Why don't you?"

"Because you forgot something rather important."

"The coin," he muttered. "You're right. I did.

Because the thing doesn't matter. Whatever excuse you needed, doesn't matter. You're here now and all that's in the past."

Was the fog playing tricks on him or had he just upset her? Not his intention at all.

"Okay, you've made your confession, and now I'll make mine." She stepped back. "I wasn't sure if I had the right to Cantecaw or Diamante's, or my memories of both. I was wrong. I haven't exactly followed your avenue of success, but yours is only one of many. I have a daughter, a beautiful being. I did what I set out to do, manage a restaurant, and for a long time. Five-star? No. Michelin-rated? Hardly. Was I unemployed when I walked onto this island again? Absolutely. And proud of it. Because that restaurant should have folded years ago but I *managed*," she emphasized, "to keep it afloat."

"Hey, I wasn't trying to judge you, I was trying to explain that I care. About you, not the coin."

She huffed. "Your first mistake was to assume you can care about one without caring about the other."

He faltered. His mind opened. "Point taken."

"Your second mistake was to assume you know my feelings." Her mouth curved, but he saw no joy in her small smile. "Right now, I don't want anything more than an employer-employee relationship with a dash of friendship thrown in."

Okay. Talk about a twist of events.

"And for the record, you're very predictable."

He was?

"I'm not eighteen, gullible, and hanging on your every word anymore. I knew what you were thinking. Earlier today. Even now."

She did? "If your last statement was a challenge, I'm picking up the gauntlet," he said.

"No," she stated firmly. "No challenge. Just a warning. I think you've forgotten what it's like for someone outside your family to stand up to you."

He smiled. "You may be right. However, I've decided not to let the past stop me. Or the future."

A touch arrogant? Perhaps. But she seemed to follow his true meaning. She reversed direction and they walked back to the restaurant in silence.

When they reached her car, she said, "I'm very grateful for everything you did today. Running up and down the beach. Calling the lifeguards. Feeding them. So, I wanted to say thank you. Again."

"You're welcome." But as he said the words, Nick knew he didn't want her gratitude. He wanted more. "Is there a possibility for us to revisit…us?"

The glint in her gaze was telling. "Maybe. But not until you get your priorities straight."

He frowned. "Talk about single-minded. You're just as much on the same track as I am."

She smiled. "And here I thought you understood. Love drives everything I do."

CHAPTER FOURTEEN

NICK DIAMANTE. Taylor couldn't get the man out of her mind. She thought of him the whole time that she and her mom and Kate sat on the beach the next morning and especially in the early afternoon, after her mother took Kate back to Pennsylvania for school. It left Taylor with way too much free time on her hands.

She decided to head to the pier to think. The more she thought, the more convinced she became that she had to resolve the issue of the coin. It loomed like a giant shadow and she was beginning to get tired of the situation.

In all honesty? They'd both changed. They both had edges and experiences that led to their growing up in their own ways. And yet, Nick was still Nick, the one person she could pour her heart out to. If only he'd believe her, take her side, accept the reality of the coin and look for the silly thing.

Taylor missed her daughter and video-chatted with her every afternoon before she went to work. She talked to her mother, too, to make sure she was coping. Again, Taylor was reminded how great a mom her own mom was.

Each night, Diamante's had a steady flow of customers to keep her busy. And although she had errands and chores for the mornings, she really missed taking Kate to the beach.

She hadn't said anything about the coin for the past few days, but now she had no choice.

When she got to the restaurant for the pre-rush meal on Thursday, she put herself in his path. "Nick?"

"What's up?"

"I have to get Kate on Saturday morning. My mother has to work and can't come out until later, after her shift is over. I was hoping you'd take the ride with me?"

She watched the disappointment appear on his face.

"I'm sorry, Tay. I can't."

Stunned, she said, "I don't understand."

"I'm setting up interviews on Saturday. I'm getting together with an old friend tonight, in fact. Traci has a recommendation for a chef. If it sounds like a good fit for us, I'll meet with Jax on the weekend. We'll do a tasting. In New York. I'm going there after dinner tomorrow."

Traci. Old friend. Jax? A chef. "When were you going to tell me?"

A tasting. Without her.

Okay, her tone could have been a bit more neutral. He frowned, obviously not anticipating her reaction. "Tonight. After we closed. I just made the arrangements about an hour ago."

Why did his announcement cause her stomach to roil? Because—because she realized she wanted them to be partners, had begun thinking of them as partners. Did he not want to reciprocate? He had the audacity to look completely innocent.

"Traci's already here. I mean, she flew into New York on business, and I took her up on the offer to meet. Jax is the best chef and employee she's ever come across. Traci really doesn't want to lose her but Jax would like to come home. She's from New Jersey. And her father is sick."

"I see."

He stared at her, giving her a strange look. "I have other candidates in mind. There's another chef, Oliver, temperamental sometimes, but worth it. Definitely does his own thing, so I'm not sure how he'll fit in with this bunch. All I know is he cares about the food and needs absolute control."

She shuddered. "You do realize what you'd have to deal with if you hired a personality like that, don't you?"

Nick grinned. "Yes. But he'd make the place. So would Jax. Trust me."

She did. She only wished it went both ways.

"What's the matter? I thought you'd be excited. I'm finally getting the plan together," he said.

"I am," Taylor agreed. "I thought you'd want to include me in the interview process. My bad. I'm obviously overstepping my bounds."

A look of comprehension filled his face. "Oh. Wow. I'm sorry. I didn't mean to shut you out. When Mama said yes, I went ahead with making arrangements."

Taylor wasn't sure what Nick expected of her. "Your idea. Your restaurant."

Again, he looked confused and crestfallen all at the same time. "Now you're mad at me."

In reality? Yes. Would she tell him so? "No," she answered. "I'm still the hired help with a huge giant elephant in the room."

"Elephant?"

She put her hands on her hips. "I just want to get the coin out of the way so we can both get on with our lives."

"That's what I want," he said, clearly exasperated. "I'm trying to build a future here. With my own two hands. With you. Don't you understand?"

"I guess I don't. You keep avoiding the issue." Hurt seeped into her bones as she read the truth in his gaze. "Do you really believe I needed that much of an excuse to see you again?"

"Yes. No. I don't know."

He went behind the bar to start loading glasses into overhead racks. He'd done the same when they first saw each other. His way of coping?

"Tay, listen to me. Any normal person would've—"

Her jaw dropped. "So now I'm not a normal person?"

He shook his head. "That's not what I meant, and you know it. But you have to at least look at this from my perspective."

"Your perspective? All right. What should I have done? Hired a lawyer? Sued you? We said we would share the coin." Anger flared and she swallowed hard. "Not a flattering look, Nick. Not flattering at all."

"I know." He set the glasses down and leaned on the bar. "I don't know where the coin is. You have to believe me."

He did sound apologetic.

"You looked for it?"

"Probably not as hard as I could have. I have to admit it. But I've thought about everything you've told me, and I don't think I want the money. It's never been important to me."

"Really, Nick? Not even if it helped you open a new restaurant and fulfill this dream you keep talking about?"

"Would you believe me if I told you that I want to earn it on my own? You're the one who seems to believe I've had my success handed to me on a silver platter."

Now it was her turn to feel contrite. As mad as Taylor felt, he kind of made sense. Was he stubborn? Beyond reason. Was he telling the truth? She thought so.

"What about Mama Bella? She'd benefit so much. So would Rocco and Beth. The kids. Aren't you being a little bit selfish by not making the coin our priority?"

He huffed and went back to storing the glasses. "I don't know."

"I think you do," she insisted. "And if wanting a better life for my own family makes me a criminal, so be it."

"You're not a criminal." Nick had run out of glasses, so he raked his hand through his hair. "Can't you just accept that I care about you? I've always cared about you."

"You care?" Taylor bit out. "You care so much that you went ahead and started interviewing without me?"

"I said I was sorry." This time his apology sounded like lip service. Taylor didn't answer.

They barely spoke ten words to one another all night. Mama kept flashing looks at him, he kept turning away. So Mama focused on her. Taylor met the Bella stare with one of her own. Mama lifted a brow and shrugged, promising the third degree later on. But, coward that she was, Taylor left the restaurant as soon as she could once they'd closed for the night.

As she was exiting, Taylor caught sight of a very tall, elegant woman standing at a table, waiting for Nick to pull out her chair. Traci. Nick said something low and Traci bent her head. All Taylor heard was the sweet laughter in response. Her stomach hollowed.

She drove back to the cottage debating with herself. Nick didn't have to include her. Diamante's was his family's restaurant. Still, she hurt. She'd thought, especially since he'd been the one to ask for her help, that Nick would at least include her in his plans.

All right. Time to be honest. Nick didn't have to include her to that degree. But she wanted him to. She thought he did, too.

A jumble of feelings started to overlap and overwhelm her. Each way she turned she ran into the brick wall of the past. She'd created all the love in her relationship with Greg. Was she doing the same now? Taylor went to sleep with a heavy heart.

CHAPTER FIFTEEN

NICK SAID HE CARED. And yet? As she drove to the restaurant the next day, Taylor felt a surge of annoyance. For all her fighting spirit, she still could battle her way to understanding the man.

He had good principles, a good heart, great role models and still he couldn't see it when it came to a reality he didn't want to accept. Her feelings and the coin. Partners. Really?

And what about friendship. Friends had each other's backs.

All of which forced the question: Was she still in love with the idea of something rather than the actual something?

No, she decided. She'd taken off her rose-colored glasses a long time ago. Maybe a little because of the divorce, she admitted. She'd also grown up, accepted life and responsibilities, both of which had taken their toll.

Taylor walked up to the restaurant slowly. Maybe her memories and her reality were simply too entwined. Could she have mixed up her love for Cantecaw and Diamante's with what she felt for Nick?

The Friday rush pushed those thoughts out of her mind. Nick stared at her a few times. So did Mama Bella. Taylor did what Taylor did best. Deflect and defend. Until she realized she hadn't seen Nick in a while and now he approached her, wearing a dress shirt and suit jacket.

"Leaving in the middle of Friday night rush?" she asked, teasing.

Taylor watched as Nick call Donna over to cover for her. He reached out for her elbow, and as much as Taylor didn't want to admit it, his touch still sent tremors down to her toes.

He guided her out through the kitchen and onto the deck. "Actually, I wanted to talk to you."

She stiffened but tried to hide her reaction. "Is there something I need to know about?"

He opened his mouth a couple of times to start to speak but stopped. Eventually, he said, "I want to apologize. I'm used to making decisions on my own. I should have told you what I was planning and included you."

Watching the moonlight crown his head, seeing the stars shine in his gaze, feeling the graze of his fingertips on her skin, Taylor had to admit she wanted everything Nick had to offer. And none of it.

"Taylor, I—"

How easy it would be to simply fall into the

magic. How long had it been? To be close to a man? Too long. But without trust? How could she ever fall into that trap again?

Taylor stepped back, pulling away, but already regretting the space between them. "Okay, but I'm sorry, Nick. If you don't trust me, then…"

He frowned and took a step back himself. "I do trust you. And I'll prove it to you."

"Prove it to me?" She was confused. "How? There's only one way. Look for the coin. Really look for it this time."

"All right. I will."

She crossed her arms and squared her shoulders. It couldn't be this easy, not after all this time.

He crossed his arms over his chest as if to mirror her pose. "But first, I want to know something. Besides the coin, why didn't you come back sooner?"

Honesty. At last. Taylor drew in a deep breath, then let the air go as she said, "I'll be honest with you, since you're being honest with me."

"Sounds fair."

She stood up straight and looked him in the eye. "I was embarrassed. But not the way you think."

He cocked his head to one side as if ready to listen. "Go on."

"I wasn't embarrassed about Greg or Kate. How could I ever think of Kate as a mistake?"

"Sure. Then why?"

"Because I couldn't match your success. I'd always dreamed of being the corporate whiz kid, seeing all the cities, building all those restaurants. It took me a long time to be able to accept that my life was a success in its own way."

"You shouldn't have been embarrassed." It was impossible to miss the bitterness in his tone. "Like I told you, the reality wasn't worth the dream."

"I know. But it was my dream. I didn't live it. You did." A measure of calm took over and with the calm, she had the strength to say, "I wanted you to be proud of me, anyway, Nick. I wanted us to be equals."

His forehead creased right above his nose. Double line. "But I am. And you are."

"Okay." She quirked the side of her mouth. "So I had it backward. I don't have to live up to you. You need to live up to me."

"What?"

Taylor nearly laughed. He was completely bewildered. She wasn't surprised. "Family is what gets you through. Family is who you trust. I learned that the hard way. Well, like I said, you should trust me now. I'm not that eighteen-year-old girl hanging on your every word. I don't need you. You need me. Whether you can see that or not."

"I do. Every day."

"At the restaurant, sure," she told him, her tone a bit sad.

"No. You're wrong. What about our friendship? It means a lot to me. You have so much caring inside you. It's obvious in your warmth. In the way you love Kate and your mom and…"

She didn't know what more to say to that, wasn't sure he really got it, so she went back into the restaurant. She had a job to do and a future to figure out. With or without Nick Diamante.

CHAPTER SIXTEEN

NEED TAYLOR? How could he not? Of course he
did. On the drive up the Parkway, Nick found
himself surrounded by the past. Some memories
had weakened with time. Others were crystal
clear. Her quick, brilliant smile. Her laugh, not
forced but full and filled with joy. Her generosity and willingness to help even when he knew
she was exhausted.

See the woman and forget the memory of her
promise, her potential? Forget the day they all
went to the beach and how self-conscious she
was? And yet, he knew what she'd become, knew
she'd become whatever she wanted to be. Busi-
nesswoman, mother…partner?

She'd matured into everything he'd dreamed
of for her and then some. Taylor was right. The
eighteen-year-old she'd once been needed him.
The woman before him did not.

Her honesty forced him to take a long hard
look at himself.

Was he jealous of her? Yes! At least she'd been

surrounded by love and family. There were nights when missing Diamante's, missing his family, even missing the ocean gouged a giant hole in his heart that nothing could fill.

No matter what Taylor thought, he knew what the coin could do. He also knew what the coin *would* do. If he found it, Taylor would leave. But he needed her. For his vision of the future. Nick clenched the steering wheel tight. No, because she'd begun to fill that hole in his heart.

Unfortunately, procrastination seemed the best part of valor in this circumstance. As long as she wanted to be at Diamante's, she'd stay. Where that left him personally, he wasn't sure. But he did know that the longer they were together, the more they learned about each other, and the better his chances that she'd remain on the Island, and part of his life.

That was all he could ask for. A chance. So, this weekend trip to the city had to work out.

Nick pulled into a very familiar Manhattan garage. Tony, the attendant he remembered, was still there. He got out and they greeted each other warmly. "How you doing, old man?" Nick teased.

"Who you callin' an old man?" Tony shuffled his feet and threw a punch. "I can still go a few rounds with the best of them. Usual spot?"

"Please." He reached inside the passenger side of the car. The smell of Mama's lasagna filled the air. "Mama said to say hello." He held out the tray.

Tony's eyes widened and he smiled. "I got to meet your Mom one of these days. I just gotta. Tell her I said thank you."

"I will."

When Nick knew he had to go to New York to interview chefs, he'd called Brett Lawrence, his one-time intern who'd survived the job he used to have, and who was now on his way to becoming a vice president of the hotel corporation. Brett had told him he was away this weekend and Nick could use his place. Grateful, Nick took the second small tray of lasagna up to the apartment. Brett said he'd be home on Sunday and hopefully this would be a nice treat for him to enjoy.

Once inside the door, Nick found the ultramodern decor a bit sterile. He'd forgotten how cold the places he used to inhabit, suitcase in hand, could be. He put the lasagna in the fridge and dropped his stuff in the bedroom.

One thing he did appreciate was the view. Nick walked over to the window to look out at the lights of the city that never slept. Stunning, but he still preferred the stars and the ocean.

Was it a portrait somehow hanging in the window or wishful thinking on his part? A picture of Taylor behind the podium, her hair glistening softly in the lights, her smile entrancing customers like a siren of the sea.

The wail of an ambulance pulled him out of his reverie. She said he didn't trust her. She'd been wrong. He didn't trust himself. Nick drew in a breath and blew it out slowly. This was his shot. He dared not mess it up.

THE NEXT MORNING around eleven, Nick stepped into Dolce. Not sure what to expect from the swanky restaurant, Nick found he liked the mix of modern decor and the rich, dark wood of the walls. The bar was cozy yet welcoming.

Traci walked up to him, long limbs, sharp suit, looking as if she could have been on a runway. They greeted each other and he gave her a signature Diamante bear hug.

"Thank you for dinner last night, Nick. Besides wanting to meet your mom, you've talked about her lasagna so much I just had to make the drive down. Of course, you know I was going to try and steal her away from you." Traci laughed.

"She wouldn't let you. Never," he said, joining in on the joke.

"I can be very persuasive."

"Sure, but we're friends. Right?" A shadow crossed her gaze and it made him wonder. Did she want more? He lifted a brow, unsure. "Traci?"

She straightened his lapel, smoothing the cloth thoughtfully. "Nothing." Flashing him a brilliant smile, she took the arm he offered her, and they moved on into the restaurant. "We could have been a great together, you and I."

Taken aback, since he'd always thought of Traci

as a friend and nothing more, Nick didn't know what to say. "I'm sorry. I've been told I'm not very tuned in to people sometimes."

Traci grinned. "It's part of your charm. And believe me, whoever she is, I really want to hate her. But now you've gone and made me like her."

Nick didn't ask who. He knew.

"You really should tune in to folks, you know. There's a lot to see out here."

Nick had to admit she was right. Traci led him to a table with a place setting for one. A young woman came out of the kitchen in a pristine chef's coat, her multicolored blond-brown hair pulled back in a bun.

"Nick. This is Jax."

They shook hands. "Jax?"

"Jaqueline Anne Xavier." The young woman smiled. "Or, Jax, for short."

Traci pointed at Jax. "Warning, Nick. She's a superhero in the kitchen."

Nick liked Jax's firm grip. And he needed her superpowers. "Nice to meet you."

"My pleasure." She gestured for him to take his seat.

He unbuttoned his suit jacket and sat in front of the place setting, bracing himself for what he had to say next. "I'm not so sure." He paused for a beat, then continued. "I won't lie to you. There are a couple of issues that go along with this job. The first is my mother. She told me to go ahead with my idea, but Mama can be—well, I don't even know how to explain it. Formidable as a battering ram? An immovable rock? More temperamental than some of the chefs you've ever worked with?"

Jax laughed, but quickly tried to cover it. "Not a problem. I know my way around. I've got the experience. And besides, once a Jersey girl, always a Jersey girl."

"You sure?" He looked up at Jax. "She can be downright terrifying at times."

"I got you. You're her son. You're supposed to be scared of her."

Nick breathed a huge sigh of relief. "And the hours? I can't promise you more until I know how things are going to work out."

"My dad's sick. I'll need the extra time with him. It works out."

"All right, then," Traci said. "Let's do this."

Jax smiled. "For today's menu, I decided to begin with three crowd favorites. First out will be fried eggplant, mozzarella and roasted red peppers in a balsamic glaze. Next up, a shrimp cerviche with avocado, cucumber and cilantro. And last but not least, two-rib lamb chops crusted in a honey mustard sauce on a bed of arugula."

Nick savored every morsel. The eggplant was crispy and delicate, the shrimp crunchy and salty-sweet with the avocado, and the lamb chops perfectly seared, with the coating melting in his mouth.

Jax came out of the kitchen. He wanted to hire her on the spot. But he owed her the rest of the tasting.

"Coming up is a pasta course. I won't try to compete with your mother. Sounds kind of impossible. So I selected a primavera. And for the main course, three more dishes. A Wellington with mushroom duxelles, pan-seared duck breast in a blueberry wine sauce over mashed cauliflower and potatoes, and a seafood paella I learned how to make in Portugal."

Nick was a happy man. The duxelles was perfect, the duck wasn't overpowered by the sauce and, again, melted in his mouth, and the paella tasted authentic. He couldn't find a flaw except maybe the scallops in the paella were a little softer than he'd like.

"You've already got me thinking of wines for pairings." Nick rose and approached the chef. "You're hired. I'd love to have you in our kitchen, Jax."

Jax beamed and they shook hands. "You bet. Thank you."

"I'm going to introduce you and your menu to a small part of Diamante's. The idea is to get the crowd hungry for more. I've been looking at property. To open another restaurant. On the mainland so I don't compete with Diamante's. It's also why

I'm in the city today. You may end up with more than you bargained for."

"Sounds good to me."

Traci joined them. "I knew you'd love her." She turned to Jax. "I'm sorry to lose you. You'll be hard to replace."

Jax grimaced. "I don't want to leave, either. But the commute, even from here, has been too much. I need to be closer to my dad."

Traci smiled. "I understand. Hurts something bad, but I understand."

"I was planning on July Fourth weekend, okay, Jax? That'll give you enough time to move and for Traci to find a replacement," Nick said.

"Gee, thanks," Traci deadpanned.

Nick offered an alternative, it was the least he could do. "I was going to interview Oliver St. Cloud tomorrow. Want to take my place? You will be down one chef."

Nick watched Traci's gaze flare. "He's a spoiled child with an ego the size of Manhattan."

"He's brilliant. He's unique."

"He's a brat." Traci rolled her eyes and Jax guffawed. "Okay. I'll take your interview. Where?"

"Azure Blue. No tasting. Just a business meeting."

Traci shook her head. "You see? That chef's got such a huge reputation, he feels he doesn't even need to prove himself. Ugh."

"We'll be in touch?" Jax asked.

Nick nodded. "Great. I'll see you soon. Thank you."

"No, the pleasure is going to be all mine, I'm sure."

Nick said goodbye to Traci and thanked her again. He walked out of the restaurant full and feeling on top of the world. Mama was on board, Jax was on board. Now he needed Taylor to join in. That made his next stop at the lawyers' office of Connor & Winston even more important. Bless Jason's heart. And Rocco's. They were behind him one hundred percent and had really come through for him, doing the research and finding the perfect piece of land for sale on the highway. He simply had this feeling in his gut, the rock-solid feeling that he was making the right decision. For Diamante's. For his family. And hopefully, for himself and Taylor.

Meeting over, he set course for the parking garage. The only matter weighing on him now was a major apology to the person he cared about most. Taylor.

Nick found Tony sitting in his usual chair, listening to a baseball game. "Hey, Tony!"

Tony grinned and stood. "What's up Nick? You ready to go?"

"That I am, my friend. That I am."

"It was great to see you."

"You, too." They hugged Diamante style.

Tony grabbed the car keys and brought Bessie

down a few minutes later. He paused and smiled. "She beautiful?"

"Who? Bessie?"

Tony guffawed, then narrowed his gaze. "You know what I mean."

Nick sighed and thought of Taylor. "Yes."

"You gonna invite me to the wedding?"

Nick startled. "What?"

"You heard me. You got it written all over you like a billboard in Times Square."

"I do not," Nick denied.

Tony scoffed and handed him the keys. "Sure. And your mom don't make the best lasagna in the world."

Nick shook his head. He remained in complete denial through the Tunnel, down the Parkway, and onto the route that led to the Island. Then a touch of reality sank in.

Whatever he felt or didn't feel, he couldn't go forward until he rectified the past. Climbing up over the bridge and turning onto Main Street only confirmed his decision. That when he walked into Diamante's, he would head for the kitchen. Then he'd make a call to Cynthia.

He needed both mothers' help.

CHAPTER SEVENTEEN

TAYLOR DREADED THE drive to Pennsylvania. Saturday afternoon traffic, even though she was going west and coming back east, was sure to be a nightmare. But Bella needed errands run for the restaurant and Nick was still in New York. She was looking forward to picking up Kate, though.

When her mother called, all Taylor could think of was how soon could she get to them. "Hi, Mom."

"Hi, sweetheart. Look, there's been a change in plans. Kate and I talked and she's going to spend the day with Rachel until I get out of work, and then I'm going to bring Kate to you, instead of you coming all this way out to get her."

"But—but I don't understand."

"It's not a problem, is it?"

"No, Mom. Of course not. I—I don't know what to say. Thank you. And yes, you're making my life a lot easier. It's bound to be a little hectic tonight at the restaurant, but I hope I can be home in time to catch you two before you go to bed."

Dead silence. Then her mother said, "I'm sure it will be."

Was that—did Taylor hear a chuckle in her mother's voice? Was she insinuating something between Nick and her? Shaking her head, Taylor chalked the confusion up to a lack of sleep. "Um, great. Tell Kate to call when you guys get to the bridge, so I know you're here."

"Will do. Love you."

"Love you, too."

Taylor ended the call and realized she needed to get the cottage ready for her mother and Kate. She dusted, did the laundry and remade the beds. Just about finished, she heard her phone buzz in her pocket.

Nick. Nick? "Hello?"

"Hi. I realize you're probably busy, but I wanted to let you know I've hired a chef."

His announcement still stung a little. Shouldn't, but it did.

"I'm on my way back. I can't wait to tell you all about it." He sounded happy. "Even with traffic, I should be home in a few hours."

Having no clue why Nick felt the need to tell her these details, Taylor hesitated. "All right?"

"I'd like to take you for an evening out. I've made arrangements. Tonight, if that's okay with you?"

Stunned, Taylor tried to form an answer. "Arrangements?" Her first thought went to Traci. She bit her tongue, banishing those little green monsters. Her second was the realization that he was including her in future plans for the business. Her third? Diamante's. "Who's going to run the restaurant?"

"Mama. Luis. Rocco. Donna will take the front. They'll be fine."

What? She paused, thinking she was in an episode of some kind of science fiction television show. "It's a Saturday. It's the weekend. It was the other reason your announcement about going away didn't make sense." He never left the restaurant at one of its busiest times.

Nick just laughed. "They'll be fine. It's all about trust, right?"

Nick sounded almost cavalier. Nope. Things had definitely just gone wonky. "Are you sure?" she asked.

"Very. It'll be an evening out at the shore. I'm wearing something nice."

An evening? Wow. Up until now, Nick's apologies had been Shakers at best. "What if I say no?"

"Your prerogative."

And then she realized… "You called my mother." She could picture him grinning.

"Of course. And mine. And my brother."

"Not fair."

"Wasn't trying to be. But I knew I wouldn't get you to come any other way. And I have a surprise for you."

Completely steamrolled, Taylor almost didn't ask. "Surprise?"

"Can't tell. Yet."

Her curiosity piqued, Taylor agreed. "You had me at Saturday night off."

His tone turned soft. "I can't wait to see you."

Taylor shivered. *Uh-oh.* "Same here. See you soon."

Kate called less than a half hour later, and shortly after, her daughter was running into her arms. Oh, how she loved Kate hugs. And Mom hugs. And Nick hugs?

To be continued....

She let go of her mother and eyed her up and down, but she just shrugged and said, "He sounded very sincere. I couldn't say no."

"You could have let me know, so he couldn't blindside me. You even got out of work early."

Her mother shrugged a second time. "He asked me not to. Then he explained he needed to apologize and why. I gave my word."

Taylor pressed her lips together. "I'll just bet he did."

"Give him a break, Tay. No one's perfect."

She lowered her voice so Kate wouldn't hear. "Mom, he says he needs me, but only talks about our friendship. We haven't made much progress with the coin, and yet he tells me I'm the reason he hasn't kept looking. Then he wants me to be his partner, except he goes off and does every-thing on his own, anyway. It's so confusing."

Her mother looked at her knowingly. "But he's clearly learning. We all have to."

The problem was, and always would be, trust. In order for Taylor to have terra firma under her feet, she had to believe she trusted the person she was with. Right at this moment, Taylor only trusted Nick so far.

Being honest, Taylor asked herself if she would trust Nick more if he found the coin. The answer didn't surprise her. No. The heart of the matter wasn't the existence of the coin, it was his will-ingness to look for it. He kept putting it off and she couldn't understand why.

Nick had told her he didn't want her to leave, that he appreciated her help at Diamante's. He'd also mentioned the future. Was he trying to tell her there might be more?

A picture of him gazing at her filled her vision. Not fair, not when he looked at her like she was the most important person in the world. To him, though? Or Diamante's? He probably thought that if she found the coin she'd be gone in a heartbeat. Her head and her battered heart started warring with each other. She finally put an end to the bat-tle by deciding to protect herself, until she could be sure one way or the other. Nick would have to win her trust before he could win her heart.

CHAPTER EIGHTEEN

TAYLOR HEARD THE sound of a car in front of the house and her heart beat a low thud inside her chest. She could see Bessie through the slats of the window shades and smiled. A part of her wanted to remember the hurt, but she found the pain fading into a background of mixed emotions. She would never know what he truly thought if she didn't give him the chance to explain.

The front door opened, and Nick stood before her, his hair gleaming, eyes twinkling. He reacted to her dress and sandals exactly as planned. Who said she couldn't wear her own kind of armor?

"You look beautiful," he breathed.

"You did say beach chic, didn't you?"

He nodded. *That's one point for me.*

"Although, you didn't tell me specifically where we were going," she said.

He lifted the corner of his mouth with that boyish grin she so loved. "If I told you, it wouldn't be a surprise."

She decided to play it coy. "Maybe I don't like surprises."

"We'll see."

He ushered her out to his truck and lent her a hand to get in and drove down Main Street in the direction of the bridge. Taylor appreciated his leaving the top up. It would grow cool once the sun set.

"Bessie seems to know where she's going," she groused.

Nick laughed, putting a gentle hand on the dashboard. "Come, now. Do I hear a hint of jealousy in your voice?"

"Never," she insisted.

They crested the bridge. No matter when, no matter whom she might be with, the pull of the Island tugged at her. She noticed that he was looking at her and she said, "You feel it, too."

"Of course." His fingers tightened on the steering wheel. "I learned the hard way. All those years traveling." He paused. "I took Cantecaw for granted when I was growing up. Even now. Life is messy and painful. It's not perfect. But on Cantecaw? I don't know how to explain it. It's special."

"I do get it. Anything is possible. Cantecaw is strength. Roots. A foundation for everything life throws at you." The memories had her smiling.

"You *do* understand."

She swallowed hard. "Which is why, what you did hurt so much."

He didn't answer. She felt she'd made her point. Then he pulled off onto a main county route and a few minutes later, they were in a beautiful clearing in the woods. He cut the engine.

"Come on," he said, and soon they were in the middle of the clearing, holding hands.

"Welcome to 1821."

Taylor turned her head in several directions. Nothing but trees. Pretty, but... "I'm not following."

"Sorry," he said. It looked like he could barely contain his excitement. He let go of her hand and turned in a circle, his arms out wide. "This was the other reason I had to go to New York. I'm negotiating to buy the land."

"Oh, wow."

"You're the first to know. Except Rocco, of course. After all, he is my lawyer."

Taylor was shocked. She didn't realize this was all happening now.

"My way of apologizing," he said.

"Except you didn't ask me. Again. You didn't even discuss the idea."

He nodded. "With Jax, I didn't think, didn't trust you. And I'm sorry. I should have. But I'm trusting you now. I want—no, I need—your input." He settled, his tone serious. "So, what do you think?"

"We're a bit off the beaten path," she replied. It was the first thought she'd had.

"I know. Looks pretty desolate, huh?"

She nodded.

"But…the zoning board just approved a section for shops and businesses about a quarter of a mile up that way." He pointed north. "And some lovely houses are going to be built that way." He pointed south and west. "The restaurant will be the only one around for several miles in any direction."

"Lovely houses?"

"Off the Island, but close enough to travel here for a Friday or Saturday night. Far enough away and for a different clientele, so as not to take business from Diamante's."

Taylor frowned. "You've already purchased the land?"

Staring deep into her eyes, he said, "No, I made enquiries. I had to find out if the plot was still available. That's all."

"And if I said I didn't think it was a good idea?"

He picked up her hands and rubbed the backs with his thumbs, sending sparks shivering through her. Very distracting.

"Then I would ask you about your objections because I value your opinion. You're the one with this kind of experience. I'm counting on what I can see, but you know more about the kind of traffic we could expect to get in this type of neighborhood. I understand upscale and established. You've got insight into location and clientele."

"No matter what, I think we'd do fine during the summer. Even late spring and fall. It's the off-season that's worrying me."

He smiled. "You said *we*."

Taken aback, Taylor breathed. "I guess I did." She huffed. "Don't think you're completely out of the doghouse yet, though."

"I understand. All I need to know is if you're with me, if you want to be my partner? Can we make a go of it?"

The emptiness in the pit of her belly disappeared and she smiled. "I'm betting on it. It's going to be midweek that'll make or break us."

He beamed. "Us," he repeated as if he couldn't quite believe she'd said the word.

A spark lit inside, ready to burn. "All right. Supposing I agree. Wouldn't the coin—"

"Yes, it would. But would you mind if we don't talk about it tonight? Tomorrow. I promise." He gave her hands a squeeze. "Let me finish my apology tonight, let me make it up to you. No more talk of land or restaurants or customers. Let's just have some fun."

How could she argue? It was what she wanted, after all. "So, what's the plan?"

"To be honest, I have more of an idea than a plan. You with me?"

She nodded. "I am."

Nick drove them back to the Island. If leaving always hurt, returning over the bridge, coming home, was a celebration. Instead of turning right to go south on Main Street, he turned left to go north and drove all the way up to the tip of the Island to the lighthouse.

The structure itself was closed but the grounds were beautiful with spring flowers. The ocean broke against a rock wall that featured a path between the water on one side, and sea grass and trees on the other.

"I'd forgotten how amazing the inlet looks."

He stared at her, not the ocean, and said, "I hadn't. We came here for lunch that day. Do you remember?"

"I remember the thunderstorm. I couldn't believe how cold the rain was."

"You were shivering. I gave you my jacket. I've never been more jealous of a piece of cloth in my life."

She whipped her head around to gaze at him for a moment before he took her hand.

"C'mon," he said. They held hands all the way back to the car. "First course, coming up. Hope you're hungry."

She was but her thoughts centered on the feel of his fingers, the rough calluses, and softer skin. They climbed into Bessie and drove to the park next to the bay. They walked together, holding hands again and swinging their arms, until they reached the water.

Orange and yellow streaks filled the sky as if a painter were creating a masterpiece. Gray replaced the blue above the sun, yet like a jewel, it shone brilliantly for all to see. Dropping lower and lower in the sky, the sun became a fiery ball of red, then a line along the horizon, until it was gone.

"There are sights in this world that can't be duplicated," she remarked.

"Unmatched."

Unmatched. Nick was right. About the sunset, at least.

"C'mon," he said, finally. "You must be starving."

They returned to Bessie, where Nick brought out a picnic basket from behind his seat.

"I thought you said you only had *sort* of a plan."

He grinned. "A beginning."

There was a white and green gazebo near the water. They headed for it. A small picnic table and benches were inside.

"That day was something else, way back when," he said, covering the table with a black tablecloth, and arranging matching napkins, china plates and two crystal glasses. He poured them each a glass of red wine.

Taylor chuckled. "We were soaked by the time we got to this point. You tried to keep me warm. You must've apologized a hundred times."

He flashed her a rueful grin. "The foolishness

of youth. We should have parked by the lighthouse, not over here. I felt terrible."

"I know." Taylor remembered being cold and wet but never angry. "How could you have known there'd be a passing thundershower? Besides, half an hour later the sun was shining and we dried out pretty quick." She watched as Nick set out an entire antipasto with cheese, salami, olives, marinated artichokes and a loaf of fresh bread.

They clinked glasses and ate.

"What happened to us, Tay?"

She had only one answer. "Life, I guess. Ten years."

He shook his head. "No. I mean *us* us. It was so easy to talk to you. No hidden meanings, no agendas. I used to look at you and you would look at me, and the next thing we knew, we'd be laughing our heads off. For no reason."

"We were kids."

"We were friends," he countered, turning serious. "And friends don't hurt one another the way I hurt you. Even by mistake. I should've realized. I'm really sorry."

Hearing Nick's heartfelt apology cracked open something inside her. A door. To a wall she'd built around her heart. "Apology accepted."

"Thank you."

They finished eating and sat sipping the wine. "Are you still hungry?" he asked. "I know a place we could go for tapas if you'd like?"

Taylor hesitated.

"Or the diner down the street? Burgers and fries?"

She shook her head. "I'm fine. Let's just watch the sun go down together." *Together.* What a wonderful word. And so right for this moment.

"Tell me about Kate. What's she been like growing up? As a baby? All I know is that your ex wasn't around much. And she's turned out to be a great kid. Your doing, by the way."

A sear of pride ran through her. Although she knew Kate herself had a lot to do with it.

"Kate? You know I'm going to say she was the best baby ever. But, of course, she had her moments, like every kid does."

Nick smiled. "Go on."

"She didn't really have the terrible twos," Taylor continued, her heart warming as she remembered. "She had the meltdown threes. Not often, thank goodness. But, boy, could she throw a temper tantrum when she wanted." She shifted her gaze from the dark horizon and the emerging lights in the distance to see his features soften. "Nick?"

He startled. "Sorry, I was just imagining."

"She's so smart," she added, wondering exactly what he was imagining. "Sometimes I'm speechless."

He reached out and clasped her hand. "Gets that from her mother, too."

Taylor wasn't quite as certain, but she let it pass. "You know what I want to do?"

"No, what? The night is yours."

"Let's go down to the amusement park."

He laughed. "Skee-Ball?"

"Skee-Ball."

She rose and began to pack up the food and dishes, but he motioned for her to sit. "No. My turn. Let me wait on you for a change."

Once he was finished, they hopped into Bessie again. She almost couldn't believe the scene when they reached their destination. The amusement pier. Nick parked Bessie in the huge municipal lot. Taylor couldn't stop taking it all in. So much had changed. There was a water park next to the rides and Taylor knew Kate would just love it. There were many more rides than she remembered. And games. She barely noticed how much the sky had darkened, for all around her, lights shone, and the ocean mist enveloped her as would a cocoon. She felt protected by the man holding her hand and the Island beneath her feet.

Nick slowed to a stop and said, "I've been waiting for that look ever since I saw you again."

"What look?" she asked, arching a brow but knowing exactly what he was talking about.

"You're happy."

His palm cupped her cheek and his thumb rubbed her skin. She couldn't help herself. She leaned into his touch. "I am."

He nodded and they started walking again, heading for the arcade first. Bells, whistles greeted them, the bounce and clang of pinballs, and the ever-present shouts of joy and defeat.

He had to stay close so she could hear him and his warmth felt right. "You're sure this is what you want to do?" he asked.

She gave him an emphatic nod. "I recall getting slaughtered at Skee-Ball every time we played. However, I have a child and we've played this a fair amount. I've been practicing."

He chuckled. "Well, I haven't played in years."

She won two out of three games, sinking the last ball for a high of fifty points. Nick twirled her around in celebration and the arcade faded. She sank into his gaze.

"Nice shot," he murmured.

With a huge smile, he claimed her hand and their tickets and they went to cash them in. She was about to choose her prize, when she stepped back and gestured for him to pick. He pointed to something far down in the case.

The young girl behind the counter produced a ring that sparkled in the light. "You're lucky, mister. You have enough points."

He took the ring. It was meant for a child, but it fit perfectly on her pinkie. "Partners," he breathed.

A thousand butterflies took flight inside her

stomach as he lifted her hand to his lips. Her gaze landed on his. *What magic was this?*

Together, they left the arcade and continued down the amusement pier. Kids and adults alike were enjoying the rides, food and all kinds of games.

Nick stopped at a dart and balloon game. He put a bill down on the counter and picked up three darts. Before Taylor could realize what had happened, all three darts had landed perfectly, breaking all three balloons.

The kid running the stand gaped. "You get the last row, mister. Choose whatever prize ya want."

"Show-off," she teased.

Nick grinned. "I'm lucky I hit anything."

"Yeah, right," Taylor said, pushing an elbow into his ribs.

He grunted, but also grinned. "I learned in London pubs. It's your turn to choose. Pick out a prize."

Taylor selected a gray dragon with red eyes and a red tongue who tried to look fierce but seemed more like he needed to be cuddled. Kate would adore him.

"For Kate," she told Nick. "She's into dragons. Although I think this guy's trying to be dignified in spite of being in a carnival game."

Nick laughed. "A dignified dragon?"

Absolutely," she replied, trying hard not to laugh with him.

He picked up her hand again and squeezed. "If you say so."

A sense of peace filled her. "I do."

They moved on toward the Village and shops. Clothes, jewelry, souvenirs and beach bric-a-brac filled each place they went into. They strolled along the wooden boardwalk. The ocean dancing, as it came in and out.

"One more stop. Coffee?" he suggested.

"Kind of late. Tea?" They found a small bakery. "Elephant ears!"

He purchased one pastry and two cups of tea. They sat on a bench to enjoy their dessert. He split the elephant ears into two and Taylor took her half eagerly, biting into the flaky pastry with tons of cinnamon and sugar. "Oh my goodness, so delicious. Just as I remembered."

He chewed a huge piece and swallowed. "They tasted even better when I was a kid."

Taylor nodded. "Everything tasted better when we were kids."

They made short work of the treat and sipped their tea in silence. Nick brushed his hands off and said, "C'mon. One *last* stop."

She wondered for a moment but only a moment. *The pier.*

There were teenagers hanging out on the beach and a few couples watching the ocean. Nick parked and they went to the railing to take in the sky. Clouds raced by, opening at times for the moon to peak through.

"Do you know how beautiful you are right now," he murmured, looking at her rather than the stars.

She didn't answer. Instead, she leaned in when he bent his head closer to hers. How wonderful and content she felt.

He pressed his lips to hers and she deepened the kiss, knowing no matter what else happened, she'd never forget this moment. She welcomed the embrace, and the sound of the ocean and everyone else around them faded. Nothing else existed but the two of them.

He stilled and in a not too steady voice said, "I'm not sorry about that."

She wasn't either, and yet... "We shouldn't complicate matters."

"You're right. Whatever is growing between us isn't simply something that'll go away."

"Agreed. We have some matters to resolve first."

Time passed before either one of them spoke again, but eventually, they went back to his truck. That was when the force of her words and his actually hit her.

During the ride home, Taylor held on to the dragon for dear life. Oh, my. What was she going to do now?

CHAPTER NINETEEN

NICK STOOD IN his living room, thinking about his evening with Taylor. They'd had fun, sure. But he'd wanted to recreate that special connection they'd once had. The memory of her deep cobalt blue eyes, the color he'd only seen in the Caribbean, swam in front of him, almost as if waiting for him to dive in.

And when he'd kissed her? He knew he held the greatest treasure in the world. Some old coin? What coin? She was his everything.

Nick shook his head, trying to regain his senses, and pivoted on his heel. Over at the bar he chose sparkling water. Drowning his feelings in whiskey wouldn't work.

When Taylor had first arrived back on Cantecaw, they'd been standing on opposite banks of a raging river. Tonight? Tonight, they'd started to build a bridge to meet in the middle. So, jumping into the rushing current might only hurt one or both of them, not to mention possibly destroy any chance at finishing that bridge.

He was grateful. Tonight had been about memories and getting to know one another. Tonight wasn't only plots of land and new restaurants, it was about recapturing the spirit they'd once shared.

Nick went up to his deck to look out at the ocean. He'd forgotten the energy and excitement of the Island, forgotten his roots in his craving for the glitz and the glitter. He realized how the craving had diminished once he'd found out the things on offer weren't what made him happy. The cities, the work, sure, it was all interesting, but it wasn't real. At least, not to him. Reality, what made him truly happy, was hopefully sleeping soundly in a bed a few streets away.

Taylor had talked about trust. Her need for it. Was that what would hold their bridge together one day?

Nick drank the last of his water, thinking of the past, knowing he owed Taylor so much, and he didn't want to repeat history by losing her or just walking away. Was he taking advantage of Taylor's kindness and knowledge now?

He certainly didn't want to.

She'd come to his restaurant with a purpose, not with her hand out. She'd needed a place to stay but never asked for him to give her the cottage. All she'd asked was that he look for the coin.

If he did, and he found it, would he lose her then? His gut clenched. He had it bad.

They'd kissed, but really, did she feel the same way that he did? Perhaps it was time to find out.

THE NEXT MORNING, Nick picked up his phone and dialed Taylor. "Good morning," he said when she answered.

"Good morning," Taylor replied.

She certainly didn't sound as bad as he felt. He hadn't gotten much sleep. He stared at his coffee maker, willing the brew to somehow reach his cup. "Did you have a good night?"

She laughed. "The same as yours, I'm sure."

"How about you come to my house for breakfast?"

"I'm not exactly hungry. And Kate wants to go to the beach."

He heard her mother in the background say, "I can take her."

"Then it's settled?"

"All right," she said, a smile in her voice. "Give me an hour to make myself presentable."

"I've never seen you otherwise," he said, truthfully.

Hanging up, he took a shower, put on shorts and his favorite T-shirt and got everything ready to make breakfast. Punctual as always, Taylor arrived right on time.

She put her bag down and seemed not to know what to do with herself. He tried not to grin. She walked over to the coffee and poured two cups. "Just milk, right?"

He nodded. "Thanks." And he took the proffered brew from her hand, touching her fingers. The same bolt of electricity he'd felt before raced through him. He smiled and she smiled back. Time stood still for a second, hitched and continued on.

She turned toward the stove. "How do you like your eggs? After last night, it's my turn to do something nice for you."

"I don't know about that. I still haven't gotten out of the doghouse yet."

She swatted him on the shoulder and grinned. A vision filled his head of Taylor standing in this kitchen every morning. His heart leaped. Normally, this was the point when he broke things off, not wanting any confusion or false expectations. Except once, which turned out to be a huge mistake.

No, he wasn't stopping anything this time. In fact, he couldn't wait to go full steam ahead.

He watched as Taylor jumped into action. Intent on her task, she didn't see him react, couldn't know the canvas she made, with the tip of her tongue sticking out just so. Nick's heart swelled at her kindness and generosity.

"I'm not Jax," she declared, looking up and flashing him a brilliant smile. "But I make a decent omelet. I hope you're hungry."

"Ravenous," he answered. "I can't wait, but you really don't need to do that."

"Really. I want to."

So, he sat down on a high stool at the breakfast bar that separated the kitchen from the dining area. She poured flour and other ingredients into a bowl and, in no time, had biscuits baking in the oven. While that was happening, she fried up bacon and whisked four eggs.

Watching her work was like watching the same kind of ballet he'd seen other chefs perform. He enjoyed every moment.

She poured him another cup of coffee and sipped her own. Putting the cup down, she transferred the eggs into another pan. While the eggs cooked, she pulled out the tray of biscuits from the oven, and placed them in a breadbasket on the counter. Then she cut the omelet in half—not quite, he got the bigger piece—and they sat down to eat.

The conversation was as good as the meal and Nick knew what he'd missed all those years of traveling—someone to share his stories with.

He bit into a biscuit and sighed with pleasure. "Delicious."

"Easy to make and pretty economical."

Her words made him wonder. "Was your life very hard?" he asked.

By the look on her face, she took his question seriously. "No harder than anyone else's, I guess. Funny, but as I look back, I don't remember the difficult times. I remember snuggles with Kate on Saturday morning, watching cartoons. I remember pre-rush meals with my staff, the teasing, the laughter, the joy."

Nick stopped his hand from bringing what was left of a biscuit to his mouth. "Pre-rush meals?"

"I stole your practice. Most of the kids working for me really appreciated being able to eat first before their shift. They didn't know we used every leftover in the restaurant to create those meals. They didn't know there were times I didn't take home a full paycheck just so they could get theirs. I made it work."

Heart and soul.

Nick stopped chewing and swallowed. His gaze caught hers. He dove inside, swimming in her goodness, her caring.

"What about you?" she asked. "Was yours hard?"

He shook his head. "Cold. The dream may have been exciting, but the reality? You'd have hated it. No family. Just a bunch of prima donnas stabbing each other in the back to get ahead."

"I'm sorry." There was compassion in her eyes.

He frowned. "What for?"

"You deserved nothing but happiness in your life."

"Did I?" he asked, his tone unsure. He sipped his coffee, the brew sweeter than the taste on his tongue. "After the way I used you?"

She reared back and stared. "Used me?"

"Didn't I? All those extra hours I got you to work?"

"Got me?" She laughed. "My choice. I'd have done anything—"

"Exactly. And I took advantage."

"You didn't let me finish. I wasn't going to say, do anything for you. I was going to say, do anything to learn. *Symbiosis*. Mandatory science class in school."

"I know what it means," he said, appreciating her words. "Doesn't justify what I did. I was wrong. I'm sorry."

She shook her head. "You have nothing to be sorry for. Do you have any idea how much I picked up, figured out, being by your side? I knew the best of restaurant management way before I ever went to college. What you, what Diamante's taught me helped me keep Foster's afloat for years."

He hated what he'd done. "Doesn't justify my actions, Tay."

"Well, I'm not sorry. I'm thanking you for them."

Her understanding meant everything to him, and when he looked at her, her gaze sparkled.

"Nick, listen to me. Right or wrong, the past is the past. For whatever reason, your wrong became my right. Let it go."

"Okay, I will."

She finished her eggs. "Look. If you feel the need to make something up to me, search for the coin."

"Right. The coin…" He stiffened. His breakfast became a lump in his gut.

"Nick?"

"I'm sorry about the coin. I wished I could have found it."

"I—"

"I'm wondering, Tay, are you bringing up the coin because you are afraid of this—of us—Tay? Maybe you don't even realize you're doing it. Is that what you really want? For us to stay just friends?"

She stilled, got up from her seat and began cleaning her plate. "I didn't realize I was doing that. I'm sorry. I guess Greg hurt me more than I've even known."

Nick rose and tugged Taylor into his arms and held her. "You're the best, Tay. Whatever you want."

After a long while, she stepped back. "Two admissions in one day," she tried to joke. "Anyone want to go for three?"

"I think I'm good." Nick smiled gently. "You?"

She nodded.

"Sometimes the best way to heal a wound is to talk about it. Want to? I'll always be your friend." Friend. Yes. He'd always be her friend.

She offered a grin but couldn't quite manage it. "And the Island will always be my home," she said. "Let's take a walk on the beach."

Her inflection on the word *home* hit him right between the ribs. He wanted her to think of Can-

tecaw as her home more than anything. *Anything?*
"Deal."

Once they were heading north and away from
where Kate and Cynthia would be sitting, Taylor
began speaking. "Greg was—great, at the start.
And I so wanted to love someone. I wanted a
home and family. I wanted to belong."

"You wanted Cantecaw. Diamante's," he
breathed, understanding her.

"In a sense, yes. Don't get me wrong. I grew up
in a very loving household. But there's something
about your family. You can argue about things
until you're ready to come to blows, then hug
each other and it's all forgotten."

He smiled. "Yeah. We do."

"Heaven help anyone who wrongly accuses a
Diamante of something. There'd be twenty people
backing you up whoever it was, without a doubt."

He shrugged. "Lots of cousins."

"Yes." Taylor sighed. Then her voice dropped
to a whisper. "How could I know he wasn't in-
terested in love, in being in love? That's how he
acted, what he said. But he just wanted the excitement of the chase." She slowed and turned toward
the water. "When I found out he was cheating
on me, when I called him on it, he didn't even
bother trying to deny it. I think he was proud of
his behavior.

"I let him back in the house for Kate's sake. But

the rest of our marriage was dead. Greg didn't seem to care, though. He kept—he kept chasing."

Nick looked into her eyes. "What a fool."

"I tried to feel better by telling myself I was better off without him. And I am. But it still hurts."

Nick clasped her hand and squeezed hard. "Tay, I'm so sorry."

"No. Don't. I made a mistake. My responsibility. Though some mistakes are easier to rectify than others."

Nick shook his head. "He really hurt you bad."

"Yes." Her voice wobbled as she said, "You have to understand. If I don't jump all in right away, this is why. I've got good reason. I don't think I'm doing it on purpose. Maybe I am. I'm not trying to."

"Trust."

"Yes."

He realized then that they'd walked quite far along the shore. "Do you trust me at all, Tay?"

She didn't hesitate. "Yes. Yes, I do."

"Then let's build from there. Think of it like a bridge. One plank, one girder, one step at a time. All right?

"All right."

He put his hands on his hips. "Well, then keeping with this new spirit of bridge building, I say we go back to my place and look for that coin."

A grin appeared instantly on her face. "I'll race you there."

CHAPTER TWENTY

TAYLOR ACCEPTED NICK'S offer to drive her home after their search for the coin. Unfortunately, they'd come up empty. As they turned onto Tenth Street, Taylor's heart started beating faster. She wasn't sure why seeing the little cottage that had become her home caused that to happen. In her excitement, she missed that there was an extra car parked nearby.

Seconds later, as Nick shut off the engine, Taylor muttered, "Speak of the devil."

"Greg?" Nick asked with a frown.

Taylor nodded, her heart lodged high in her throat. What was her ex doing here on Cantecaw without calling? His visits to Kate were few at home—why had he decided to come all this way now?

"Mommy! Mommy!" Kate threw the screen door open with a bang and ran full speed down the path and jumped into Taylor's arms, nearly knocking her off her feet. "Look. Daddy's here."

Greg stepped down onto the walkway and drew closer.

"Yes, sweetheart. I can see him."

Taylor gave Kate a big squeeze and let go. As she rose, Nick walked up to stand behind her. Her pillar. Her rock.

"Invite me in," he whispered in her ear.

"You need to promise me you'll behave."

Kate ran back to stand next to Greg.

Taylor caught Greg's gaze. For an instant, his brows drew together in a single line and his eyes narrowed. Then his face cleared, and he put his hand on Kate's shoulder. Battle lines drawn. "What are you doing here, Greg?" Taylor asked, when they were all inside the cottage. "Why didn't you phone?"

"I did." He smiled. "I called Kate and she told me all about the Island. So, of course, I had to see for myself. Besides, you told me to come and visit, didn't you?"

Taylor bit back the thousand or so words dancing on the tip of her tongue. "Yes."

"And my little scrunchie here," he said, mussing up Kate's hair with his hand, "was thrilled when I told her I'd decided to see the place for myself. In fact, so was your mother. 'Long overdue,' I think she said."

She knew it was all her mother could do to keep a civil tongue and get him off the phone. No love lost between those two at all. "Hi, Mom."

Her mom popped out of the bathroom, looking like she'd had enough drama to last her a lifetime in one afternoon. To Nick, she said, "Thanks for everything, sweetie."

He bussed both her cheeks. Then her mom marched over to Kate, gave her a hug and kiss and headed outside.

Taylor followed and caught up with her mother on the porch. "You didn't say anything to Greg."

"My way of being polite. Did you have a nice time last night? We didn't have a chance to talk before you left this morning."

Taylor didn't know whether to laugh or feel like a teenager again. "Yes," she said.

"We'll catch up when I get back. I'm going shopping."

Taylor knew her mother wouldn't stay at the cottage. Not with her ex there. Then she and her mom hugged and she held on a beat longer before letting her go. "I'll call you when…"

Her mom kept moving. No need to say more.

Meanwhile, Taylor walked into a strained silence. "Kate, honey? Could you go outside and play for a moment? Mom and Dad need to talk."

Her daughter hesitated. "Are you two going to fight again?"

Taylor shook her head. "No."

Once Kate was gone, Greg started to smirk. Taylor wasn't having it. "We're divorced. What I do with my own time is my business."

Greg took a seat on the couch. "So defensive.

Maybe I can call a lawyer. Stop the alimony payments altogether. Seeing as how you're…"

"Be careful," Nick warned.

She needed to figure Greg out and quickly. "You don't pay them now. What are you really doing here?"

Greg said, "Kate kept babbling on about the ocean and the Island. All these wonderful people." His gaze lifted to stare at Nick. "You seem to have landed on your feet while I've had a turn of bad luck."

Why was she not surprised? "How much?"

He didn't answer at first. Was he deciding whether or not to lie? She wouldn't put it past him. "Two grand. But I'll take a thousand now."

Taylor laughed. "You know I don't have that kind of money."

"Your boyfriend here does."

Taylor turned to watch Nick, a little tic started fluttering in his cheek.

"Careful," Nick warned again, his tone low.

Greg grinned like a Cheshire cat. "I can always take you to family court. Tell them how you lost your job, how you're barely holding on. They'll give Kate to me in a heartbeat once I'm done."

"Why?" Taylor asked, angry but much more confused. "You don't even want her."

Greg didn't like the truth. In a very cold tone, he said, "You have until noon tomorrow." Then he rose and swept past them. The screen door flew open just as he got there and Kate ran up to him, throwing her arms around him. "Don't leave, Daddy. Please."

Greg slipped away from her and got into his car. Kate followed him to the sidewalk, and Taylor followed her. He lowered the passenger window. "I'll be back tomorrow."

Greg stomped on the gas, peeling away in his haste to leave. Kate stared after the car, and the hurt on her daughter's face was almost more than Taylor could bear.

"This is your fault. You hate him. You always fight. Now I hate you."

Every word became a dagger. She couldn't breathe. Kate ran up the path and into the house. Taylor waited, hoping it would be easier to talk to Kate once she calmed down.

Nick came along beside her. "I'm calling Rocco. Diamantes stick together."

"So, I'm a Diamante now?"

His gaze turned soft. "Yes, you are. Also, whatever you need, it's yours. I don't like blackmail but if you decide you want to give him the money, I'll give you whatever you need."

Guilt shot through her. "I knew you'd make the offer, but I don't want your money. I'd rather go to court." Taylor stepped into his open arms. "Oh, Nick, I can't lose her. But I'm not giving in to him again. No more."

Nick's arms tightened around her and for the

first time in a very long time, Taylor felt safe. Really safe. They stayed that way for a long while.

"Kate needs to know the truth," he told her, gently pushing the hair back from her face.

"She won't believe me."

"Do you think it would be okay if I helped?"

"I'm not sure she'll believe you, either."

"Together?"

The word. So right. And another truss added, spanning the bridge of trust. "Thank you."

They walked into the house arm in arm. Taylor knocked on Kate's door.

"Go away. This is all your fault."

Taylor opened the door. "Well, how far back do you want to go? Don't forget, if I didn't fall in love with your father, you wouldn't be here. So, yes, technically, this is my fault."

Kate sat up, her tearstained face eviscerating Taylor's insides. But Taylor didn't immediately go over to the bed. She sat on the edge of the other single. Nick followed her into the room. Just the person she needed.

"You know I love you with all my heart, don't you?"

Kate nodded, wiping at her face. "Yes."

"Then you know your father's actions aren't my doing, right?"

"Yes," Kate said, heaving a sigh.

"So blaming me isn't going to make your world right."

"Nothing is."

"Not true," Nick added. "You've found a great world here. Your mom's making a great world for you wherever you go. It's your parents being together that's wrong in the world."

"He drove away. He just drove away. Why did he do that?" Oh, the misery in her daughter's voice. "You made him mad. Both of you." Kate turned to bury her face in her pillow.

Nick jumped in, thankfully, because she couldn't utter a word. "Did we?"

Kate didn't answer.

"C'mon, Kate," he said, his voice soft but firm. "Don't you think your father's the one being selfish?"

"What do you mean?" her daughter asked, raising herself up on one elbow.

"He came to ask me for money, sweetie," Taylor replied. "If I don't give it to him, he says he'll take you away from me."

"No! He wouldn't. He couldn't." Horror filled her gaze.

Taylor wanted to give in, offer hugs and reassurance, but she dared not. Too much was at stake here. "He did. And I'm sorry, but he'll do anything to get what he needs."

She and Nick waited, while Kate wiped away her tears.

"Your mom and I are going to talk to my brother. Now. He's a lawyer. A good one."

Taylor looked at Nick.

He said to Kate, "Do you mind staying with Beth until your grandmother comes back?"

Kate gulped, sniffed and blew her nose into a tissue. A beat passed, then... "Mom?"

"Yes, Katydid?"

"I know you and Dad aren't ever going to get back together again. I shouldn't have hoped so hard."

"You understand why? I hate what your father just did to you, but he's going to do it again."

Kate's shoulders rose and fell. "Sometimes people aren't nice."

"Exactly. I'm so sorry you had to find out like this. Perhaps it's better now than later."

Kate didn't say anything for a long moment, then asked, "Mom? Did you really love Dad?"

"Once. A long time ago. But love has to go both ways, sweetheart, and your dad? He never understood love is a two-way street. He couldn't love me enough because he loves himself more." Taylor's gaze landed on Nick.

"I guess that means he doesn't love me, either, does he?" Kate curled into herself.

"Oh, Kate." Taylor reached out and Kate crawled onto her lap. "Your father loves you very much. But in his own way." *I pray every day it will be enough.*

"Kate?" Nick sat next to Taylor on the bed. "I come from a place where family is everything. I don't think your father did. Your father is in trouble, and he has no one to turn to. He's scared. And he's lashing out at you and your mom."

Kate snuffled and sighed. "Can you help him?"

"Your mom and I are going to try and figure out what's the best thing to do," Nick said. "You have my word."

Nick lifted Taylor's free hand and kissed it, then closed his fingers around hers. "Together."

For several minutes, the three of them sat close, and in Taylor's mind, she could see more of that bridge being built.

Taylor's phone buzzed and Kate excused herself and went into the bathroom. Taylor answered on the third ring, and she and Nick regrouped in the living room. "Mom? Is everything okay?"

"Yes and no. I'm fine but the car isn't. Stalled on me, so I'm at the garage now. I really am sorry, sweetheart. I don't know when I'll get back to the cottage. The mechanic's looking at it. I think you should consider keeping Kate an extra day. I'll call my boss and take another vacation day. And when we get home, I'll explain to the powers that be at school."

"It's okay, Mom. Honest." Taylor paused. "And you're right. I'll call Mrs. Daniels first thing tomorrow morning."

Noise at the garage ramped up, so her mother's voice rose. "You're still at the cottage?" she asked.

"Yes. Greg's gone. We're going to drop Kate

off with Beth. Could you pick her up?" Taylor put her mom on Speaker.

"I can do that. I'll get a rental or an Uber or whatever, but are you all right?"

Taylor looked over at Nick, grateful for his support. "As well as can be expected. He needs money. Quite a bit. He's threatening family court again."

Nick put a gentle hand on her shoulder.

"He doesn't have the money for a lawyer," her mom scoffed.

"That's no guarantee. He might just show up this time. He thinks Nick can give me the cash."

"Goodness, Tay. I don't know what to say. He'll do anything, say anything, to get what he wants."

"I know, Mom. I know. But I told him I'm not covering for him. Let him take me to court. I'm done. He's not my responsibility any longer."

"Not even for Kate?"

Taylor was certain. "Not even for Kate."

"Thank goodness." Her mother exhaled. "I've been waiting for you to say those words for a very long time."

"You have?"

"Yes. Greg needs to grow up. Handle his own messes."

"Kate's heartbroken."

"She'll understand. She's smart. And she loves you. So do I—I love you. You'll both get through this. I'll see you soon."

"Bye, Mom. I love you, too."

Stunned, Taylor couldn't collect her thoughts. In the past, she'd been willing to sacrifice anything for Kate. But that hadn't helped them, not really. And in truth, it hadn't even helped Greg.

Well, not anymore.

Nick smiled. "I'm guessing, by the look on your face, you've finally realized something important."

"Yes."

"When you're strong for yourself, that's when you can be strong for those around you."

"I think I'm catching on." Taylor offered a small smile. "What would you do if Rocco had done this?"

"I don't know. Figure something out. Make a deal maybe."

"And if none of that worked?"

"I don't know. Are you asking if I could walk away?"

"I am."

"It would be the last of the last resorts. But then, if he'd done what Greg had, he wouldn't be my brother by that point, either."

Talk about a truth. "Love has to go both ways."

"And add up equally. Can't just be ninety-ten all the time."

She sighed. "Any idea how to explain that concept to a seven-year-old?"

"We'll come up with something."

"I hope so."

He smiled. "You know, there's a certain stuffed animal you forgot in my car last night that might help."

Taylor smiled back, went to retrieve the stuffie and returned. "Katydid?" she called to her daughter.

"I'm coming, Mom."

Her daughter appeared and tried to peek around Taylor to see what was behind her back. "We stopped at the Village last night. And I promise, we'll take you soon. It seems Nick is very good with darts." Taylor held out the dragon.

"He's adorable!" Kate took him and squeezed him, then looked at him again.

"You'll need to give him a name. But maybe wait a while, until you're sure."

She turned to Nick and threw her arms around him. "Thank you."

Taylor thought her heart would burst with love.

They ushered Kate into the car and set off for Rocco and Beth's house. Beth didn't say a word when Kate ran inside, she simply hugged Taylor.

"My mother's coming," Taylor explained. "One way or another she'll be here to pick up Kate later."

Beth seemed to understand. "Good thing that Roc's an attorney."

She and Nick left, and he drove them to Rocco's office. "Don't argue, Tay. You should stay home

with Kate tonight. She needs you more than Diamante's."

"I can't, Nick. You and I were both gone yes-
terday."

"And nothing happened. Please. For me."

Taylor appreciated his thoughtfulness. "Thank
you."

Two men, she thought, comparing the images
of Nick and her ex. One, a shining example, the
other, not so much. Hard for her to miss, not so
hard for her to embrace.

Rocco promised to help in any way he could.
"I'm not a family court specialist, but I'll make
enquiries. I'll find the best lawyer for you that I
can. In the meantime, no fighting, no antagonism,
nothing he can use as fuel in court. Did you have
a lawyer back in Pennsylvania?"

Taylor nodded. "Scott Devlin." She gave Scott's
number to Rocco.

"Good. I'll call and start figuring out what we
can do."

"Thank you. Thank you both," she said.

Nick was the first to answer. "You're family.
No thanks necessary."

CHAPTER TWENTY-ONE

WHEN NICK DROPPED her off back at the cottage, the house was empty, but her mother's car was out front. Taylor called her mom. "Hi. Where are you?"

"Kate and I decided to take a walk on the beach. Seems to be helping."

Bless her mother for understanding. Taylor needed to be alone for a moment. Strong, Nick said. Be strong for herself. Strong enough not to give in. To her ex or her daughter. Taylor had forgotten to protect herself.

"Luckily, the car was an easy fix. Didn't take long at all. I picked Kate up in no time."

"That's good. Thanks, Mom." Tayler said her goodbyes and tucked the phone in her pocket. Right now, though, she had pieces to pick up. The weather had turned. She looked at the cloudy, gray-black sky knowing it represented the turmoil in her life, turmoil only she could quell. To do so, things and people were going to have to change.

Taylor was just about to go join her mother and

daughter when she spotted them coming down the street. Kate didn't say a word to her. Her daughter brushed past her and went into her bedroom. Her mother offered a small smile and shrugged.

So Taylor waited, running a load of wash and preparing dinner.

Her mother squeezed her hand and let go, picking up a knife and chopping vegetables for the salad. "What are you going to do? With Kate?"

"I don't know. I should fight for sole custody. Every cell inside me wants to protect her. He's only going to let her down again and again and again."

"Then all you can do is be there for her and pick up the pieces, I guess. Just the way you do now. Make sure she knows she's loved. I think I can help you with that."

Taylor tried to put up a ghost of a smile. "I also think Kate needs to spend more time with Nick, with the Diamantes. She needs to see what a larger, loving family is all about."

Her mother laughed. "You or Kate?"

Taylor smiled and told her mom all about the evening, starting with the amusement park, but not about 1821. She wanted the restaurant to be more of a reality before she shared the news. "Can you believe it? Skee-Ball of all things?"

"Sounds like you had a wonderful time. You deserve more of them."

"Oh, Mom. Stop."

Her mother snagged her gaze. "There's always the coin, you know."

Taylor shook her head. "No, there isn't. And even if we found it, Greg needs to get himself out of his own trouble."

Her mom nodded. "He needs a steady income. A decent job."

"He's had those. He gets bored."

"This time he'll have no choice. He'll have to pay up himself."

Taylor wanted to sound positive. "I'm going to have to make him understand. Well, at least, try."

Her mother looked at her warmly, then went back to chopping. "All right. Try."

Later, after the three of them ate dinner and her mother and Kate went to bed, Taylor sat on the stoop and called Greg.

"To what do I owe this very expected phone call? Are you going to yell at me for leaving Kate today?"

"Would it do any good?" she asked. "You've already twisted things in your mind so you're not to blame. But I do have a question. Why? Your behavior doesn't hurt me. But what about Kate?"

"I didn't mean to. Just give me five hundred so I can get things straight for a little while. I'll find a job. I'll make it back. I swear I will."

"Sorry, Greg, no. Not this time. You have to figure out your own finances. But I will try to help you find a job so you can pay the money back to your creditors."

"You don't understand. These aren't the kind of people who do installment plans."

Her stomach hollowed. "You need to get a job and get a loan from the bank and then pay back the bank. But you don't use your daughter as part of a threat. And you don't ever, I mean ever, hurt her the way you did today."

Silence. Was he listening? "Look, if I didn't know you love her, we wouldn't even be having this conversation."

"I need money now!"

Steeling her spine, Taylor retorted, "Then sell your sixty-inch, flat-screen television and your mega sound system."

More silence. Obviously, Greg didn't like hearing the truth. "I'll take her away from you. I swear I will."

Determination threaded through her bones. "You can't. You don't have a steady job and—"

"Neither do you," he sneered.

"Ah, but at least I'm employed. And when this job is over, I'll find another. You won't try nearly as hard. And let's not forget that I've been the one providing a stable home for Kate this whole time. You visit when you want, and you don't pay child support."

"Yes, I do," he blurted.

"How many months, Greg? When was your last

payment? I'll bet you don't even know." Taylor kept a tight hold on her temper. "I had to downsize my apartment to a studio to make ends meet partly because of you. I'm pretty sure your behavior won't endear you to any judge. Stop threatening me."

"Or what?"

"First, any help you think you might get from me goes out the window. Second, I can turn the tables on you and apply for full custody."

"You wouldn't. You'd hurt Kate."

Taylor closed her eyes, summoning all her strength. "Yes, I would. But it'd hurt less than where you're taking things. You know where all this is headed, don't you?"

He backtracked. "Hey. C'mon. It's not that bad."

"It will be. You've disappointed your daughter for the last time. Make up your mind. Be Kate's father or don't. If you want a last chance, be here at nine tomorrow morning for breakfast. Take her to the beach. If you don't show up, that's it. We're done. Through." Taylor didn't wait for him to answer. She hung up. It was his choice.

She kept seeing Kate's face as Greg drove away. Tears streaming down her cheeks.

How long she sat there, Taylor didn't know. She had to keep believing. She had to keep telling Kate the truth. For Kate's sake.

Taylor heard a car drive down the block and

lifted her head. Bessie. What a welcome sight. She rose and waited for Nick. He walked up to her smelling of cologne and spaghetti sauce. She drew him into a tight hug. "Hold me. Please. Just hold me."

He pulled her close.

"I stood up to him," she continued. "About Kate. Gave him an ultimatum, told him I'd turn the tables on him. I had to. He needs to decide to be her father."

Nick tucked her into his chest.

"I told him, no money. And to be here at nine for breakfast and the beach." She leaned back.

She knew his smile was for her and her alone. He gave them a bit of space and asked, "You think he'll show?"

Taylor wasn't sure. "Forty-sixty he turns up. I'm so tired of fighting."

"Then lean on me, Tay." His gaze warm. "I'll always be here for you."

He hugged her once more and all of a sudden, Taylor realized something else important. She smiled and let go. "I don't need the coin, Nick. I have you."

He smiled back. "Yes, you do." Then concern covered his face. "Will you leave? In August?"

"I don't know," Taylor answered honestly. "Kate's entire life is in Pennsylvania. It's unclear if she'll want to move here."

"Fair enough," he said and nodded. "We have the rest of the summer to find out."

"And us?" Taylor asked.

The corner of Nick's mouth lifted. "Is there an 'us'?"

More certain of this than anything else in her life, Taylor answered, "I'd like to try and find out."

"Me, too."

CHAPTER TWENTY-TWO

NICK PARKED BESSIE in front of the cottage promptly at nine the next morning. He noted only Cynthia's car and Taylor's in the driveway. Sadness filled him that Greg was going to let Kate down again.

He knocked on the door and Taylor answered. She looked tired—no, weary—and gave him a quick shake of her head. Obviously, to spare Kate, she hadn't said anything. Neither should he.

"You can count on me," he whispered as they hugged.

Nick entered the living room. Kate was sitting on the couch, playing with her dragon and watching something on a phone. "Hello, Kate."

She looked up. Like her mother, Kate looked a bit weary. "Hi, Nick."

Mother and daughter nearly broke his heart. All because of one very selfish man.

"Kate, are you doing anything today before you go home?" The girl shook her head. He looked over to Taylor, who winked at him. That was the all clear he was hoping for.

"Well, now. I heard the weather report and it's going to be kind of cool for the beach today. And I'm pretty sure you'd like to have a little bit of fun before you leave. So, I have an idea."

Kate sat up a bit straighter and put the phone down.

"How would you like to go crabbing off the dock at the restaurant?"

"Crabbing?" Kate asked, her curiosity obviously piqued.

"You take a small metal cage, put in some bait, the crab comes in for a free meal, and the cage closes. Most of the critters in the lagoon are too small to eat, so we throw them back, but it's kinda fun."

Kate perked up a little and nodded. "I'd like to try."

"Good."

Taylor silently said a thank-you from across the room.

He continued. "And next weekend, for Memorial Day, you're all coming to my house for a barbecue. I finally convinced Mama to close the restaurant for the holiday. Always a slow day."

Kate started bouncing. "Hamburgers and hot dogs?"

"You bet."

"Oh, c'mon, Nick. Do you really mean to say Bella won't cook?" Taylor asked, her tone skeptical.

He grinned. "Roc stamped his foot and so did I. One dish. No more."

Cynthia came out of the bedroom. "Good morning," she said, smiling.

"Good morning," they all replied, chiming in together as if they'd rehearsed it.

"Nana!" Kate exclaimed. "Nick's having a barbecue next weekend for Memorial Day. Can we bring something?"

Nick watched Taylor and her mother share a look.

"Cheesecake," Cynthia announced.

As if buoyed by the conversation, Kate jumped off the couch. "We're good at making cheesecake."

"Done," Nick said. "All this talk of food's made me hungry. I hope there are pancakes."

"Of course," Kate said, dancing around the room.

Nick told Cynthia about his trip to New York and how Jax was the find of the century. But he didn't say anything about the property. Then he talked about the evening along the boardwalk. He glanced over at Taylor for confirmation a few times, and though she added her thoughts, she didn't seem very happy. He'd been able to cheer up Kate, and he wanted to do the same for her mother.

"Nick?"

"Yes, Kate?"

"Did your dad leave you, too?"

His last bite of pancake got stuck in his throat. "Not exactly, Kate. My father passed away a long time ago."

Kate looked down at her plate. "I'm sorry. I shouldn't have asked. I was just wondering why I never met him."

Nick smiled. "I understand. My family talks about him a lot. When you remember someone, they're never truly gone."

"So, if I try to think about my dad, he won't leave me."

Taylor drew in a harsh breath. "Kate, your father made a mistake. But he loves you. He's not out of reach. He'll figure out what's important. You'll see. In the meantime, you have Cantecaw and the Diamantes and the beach and a bunch of new things to try."

"Like crabbing." Kate smiled.

"Exactly."

Nick rose. "Breakfast was delicious. Thank you. Now, unless you want to pick up ice and some bait," he teased Taylor, "I need to make tracks."

She made a stop sign with her hand. "Pass. Definitely not."

"Then I'll see you all at noon."

"Thanks, but count me out. I'd rather go shopping or read my book," Cynthia said. "Am I invited to your pre-rush meal, though?"

"Always."

"I'll bring Kate home after. See you, then."

Nick left and went directly to pick up the ice and bait, which he dropped off at the old freezer on the dock. Then he headed to Rocco's office. Even the fresh ocean breeze couldn't quell the surge of anger still sitting in his gut. "Hey, bro," he said, hugging Rocco.

"Hey."

Roc motioned for him to sit and stared at him until Nick quirked his mouth. "Where do we stand?"

"We?"

"News travels fast in our family. I heard you spent an evening on the boardwalk with Taylor."

Nick heaved a huge breath. "Someone saw us?"

Roc laughed. "Of course."

"It was business, sort of. And, yes, there was some hand-holding." Nick refused to mention the kiss. If his mother heard about that, she'd be printing wedding invitations. "So?"

Rocco sobered. "Judges in family court tend to want the parents to work things out on their own if they can."

"Kind of hard to do," Nick replied, "when one of them is being a jerk."

"Agreed. So I asked around as I said I would. Charles Kelsey came highly recommended. I asked him to take a look. Even though it was a Sunday, he was able to get in touch with Taylor's lawyer, Scott, in Pennsylvania. So far, things seem to be in Taylor's favor. She hasn't pressed her ex, but he's in arrears for this entire year. Hasn't paid her a dime of child support."

"She said she knew she was going to lose her job, so she downsized to a studio apartment. How could she go on— Wow."

"Charles says she's making automatic payments on the rent even though she's here on Cantecaw."

"So Taylor gets a ten and her ex gets a zero."

"For now. Until he can prove he's capable of holding up his end. I'm sure any lawyer he talks to will tell him he needs steady work and to at least pay what he owes this year. Or make an attempt to."

"So she's got this? I mean, custody of Kate."

"Judges tend to lean toward the mother for residential custody and her ex gave his consent for them to come here for the summer, right?"

"Yes," Nick replied with caution. "Is there a problem?"

"Possibly. He'd have to agree to a move of full-time residence if they want to stay here on the Island."

"And we both probably know what he'll want in return."

Rocco sighed. "Not the end of the world. And not a problem for the summer. Hey, bro, things can change."

Nick knew that was true. "I feel so bad for

Kate. She's a good kid. You should've seen how hurt she was." He shook his head. "She asked about Dad today. Didn't know he was dead. Kind of like she was asking how I felt without him."

"And you told her he isn't gone, didn't you?" Rocco knew him so well. "All you can do, bro."

"Yeah." Nick straightened and rose. "We're going to go crabbing off the dock this afternoon if you and the family want to stop by."

"I have extra work now, remember? And you have your hands full. Also, we're planning a barbecue, as well."

"How could I forget? It's at my house," he deadpanned.

Roc laughed and they hugged. "Hey! I'm trying to find one. It's really tough. We went to look at a cape the other day in our price range but it's too small. Soon, bro. I promise."

"For you guys, I hope so."

Nick left the office. Taylor didn't want him to look for the coin any longer. Funny, now that she didn't, he did. She'd been right all along. If it was the coin in the news and they cashed in, he could do quite a bit of good with his share of the money. Yes, there was sure to be a mess with her ex. But they could work out a way for Kate to stay here. Roc could have the house he needed. Mama could travel. Well, at least not work so hard. And Taylor? Wouldn't relieving the stress in her face be priceless?

All along, Nick had been terrified that the coin would mean she'd leave. After their evening on the boardwalk, he felt better about her chances of staying.

Cantecaw and Diamante's caused roots to grow. But love was the lifeblood of the tree. He was falling in love with Taylor. His greatest hope was that she was falling in love with him, too. But if she felt the need to go, Nick knew now he'd have to find a way to cope. Even if it broke his heart.

Nick drove to the restaurant, settled within himself. They had a plan of action. All they had to do? Carry it through. So, when Taylor and Kate arrived, he pulled Tay close. "It's going to be all right. I promise."

Kate became an expert crabber in no time, not even minding the smell or handling the bait. Waiting for the hungry crabs became the hardest part, so Nick went inside and prepared a snack of mozzarella and tomatoes on homemade crostini.

Soon the rope holding the trap started to move. Kate helped him pull it up, and sure enough, there was a small crab inside. Too small to keep. Nick opened the cage and the crab bolted onto the dock. Kate screeched. Nick tried to head the thing back to the edge of the dock and into the lagoon. It skirted around him, and the next thing he knew, the crab had a hold of Taylor's pant leg. She screamed. Kate started laughing. She ran to get her mother's phone and make a video.

Nick couldn't move. Taylor was shaking her leg trying to get the crab to let go and all he could do was laugh, too. Gut-shaking, knee-buckling laughter came out of him.

"Get him off me! Please!"

Nick tried to sober. He managed just enough to get his hand around the crab and pull. The critter came loose, and he chucked it back into the water.

In between gulps of laughter, Kate said, "Oh, wow, I can't wait to share this with Rachel and Terri."

"No, you don't, young lady," Taylor warned.

"C'mon, Mom. Please? It's funny."

Even Taylor could see the humor. And after everything Kate had been through? "Thanks a lot."

Kate took the phone over to a bench to talk to her friends.

Nick sent Taylor a sheepish grin. "Sorry. I didn't mean to laugh so hard."

"I guess I'm the butt of everyone's jokes these days."

"Oh, Tay. No. Never. And about your ex? I went to talk to Roc this morning. He says you have all the pluses on your side. The lawyer's going to contact you. Greg will have to straighten out his act if he wants to take any kind of legal action."

Relief filled her gaze. "Thank you."

"For you? I'd do anything."

The spark between them popped when their eyes met. Oh, how he wanted to kiss her sweet lips. Hearing Kate's laugh again, he knew this wasn't the time or place.

Instead, he planted a quick kiss on the tip of Taylor's nose. Stepping aside, he bit back a grin at her suspicious look. Soon, though. Very soon.

In the meantime, there was that coin.

For her, he'd tear apart the universe. Instead, he'd settle for his house again and the restaurant. His instincts told him he'd find it. One very old, very expensive coin coming up.

CHAPTER TWENTY-THREE

"Mom, wake up. C'mon, Mom. Wake up. Or we'll miss the parade."

Taylor groaned. She rolled over, burying her head beneath a pillow. The week had passed by quickly with managing the front of the busy restaurant, meeting with Jax about menus and seatings for the back area and figuring out how to manage the flow between the old and the new. She also worked with Nick on scaling up the decor and table settings, not to mention lending a hand with a thousand other details. Nick did say he needed her, and she was happy to do it. Diamante's meant so much to her.

There were innocent glances and touches at first, followed by impish grins, and knowing looks, and her dreams were beginning to take on a very specific direction. Especially the one last night where she and Nick were walking on the beach in the moonlight.

"Mo-ooo-mmmm."

Coffee. Taylor smelled coffee. Had to be coffee.

She popped one eye open, then the other. Blurry. But she'd known worse. Rubbing her fingertips over her eyelids, Taylor tried to focus. What came into view was a mug of necessity.

After three heavenly sips, she almost spilled the hot brew as Kate bounced onto the bed. "Kate!"

After one sheepish shrug and a devilish smile from her daughter, Taylor knew that Kate had rebounded in spite of Greg. Still, they would have to talk. "Is Nana up?"

"Yup! The parade starts at ten."

"All right, we have plenty of time. Why don't you go help Nana while I get dressed?"

Kate saluted and left. Sassy girl.

Fortified by half a mug of coffee, Taylor showered and started dressing. She chose capri pants but a long-sleeved blouse because it would be cool. She walked into the kitchen to buss her mother's cheek. "Good morning."

"Well, yes, it is a good morning." Her mother looked deep into her eyes before letting her go. "Do you want some eggs?"

"No, thanks, Mom. Just some toast. I can't imagine how much food and how many people are going to be at this barbecue."

Kate asked, "Mom. Can I bring my bike?"

"Sorry, sweetie, not this time. I think there'll be too many people. You can ride it when we get back."

They walked up to Main Street, and right on

the dot of ten, Taylor could hear the faint sounds of a band playing. The parade reached them not too long afterward.

A shiny, straight-out-of-the-seventies convertible led off the parade. The fancy car was big enough to hold six people comfortably. A lone gentleman sat on the top of the back seat, waving to the crowd.

"The guy in the suit there is Bob Burke, the mayor."

Taylor turned to find Cheryl standing next to her. "Oh, hi. Glad you're here."

"Me, too," Cheryl smiled. They hugged.

"Kate? This is Cheryl. She's an old friend of mine. Her family owns McGinty's."

"Hi." Kate gave Cheryl a quick smile. "Nice to meet you."

Taylor began to introduce her mother, but Cheryl put a hand on her arm. "We've already met at the store. Nice to see you again, Cynthia."

"Likewise."

The rest of the conversation was soon drowned out by the sounds of the high school marching band.

Kate jumped up and down beside her as the musicians passed by, their teal-and-gold uniforms glinting in the sun.

"I love the colors!" Taylor shouted to Cheryl.

"Hampton High. I was a cheerleader for the Terrapins."

Hampton Terrapins. The Island only had one school, kindergarten through grade eight, then students went to Hampton. She'd heard some of the waitstaff chatting as they'd set up the tables.

The decibel level returned to almost normal and she was able to tell Cheryl, "This is fun," in a normal voice.

"Yeah. It is."

Cheerleaders and baton twirlers followed the band, their pom-poms and batons flashing. For a moment, Taylor pictured Kate wearing one of those uniforms, a huge smile on her face.

A tug on her shirt brought her back to the present. She leaned down to Kate. "I'd like to be a cheerleader someday."

"Then I'm sure you will." She smiled. "All it takes is—"

"Hard work," Kate finished for her.

Three riders on horseback came into view, their saddle pads bearing a familiar green four-leaf clover with a gold-and-white *H*.

Next came the military veterans, marching proudly, their heads held high, followed by the Boy Scouts and the Girl Scouts, their sashes brimming with the badges they'd earned.

There was a drum corps, too. How they managed to be in sync, Taylor would never know, but the members all threw one of their drumsticks in the air, and caught them in unison.

"They're great, aren't they?" Cheryl nudged Taylor's arm.

Law enforcement and first responders came next, sharp in their uniforms. "That's Ethan Cramer, the chief of police," Cheryl told her, pointing to the really tall, burly man leading them.

Two bright red fire trucks, one large and one small, drove up the street. The trucks had ribbons tied to the sides that floated in the wind; their chrome gleamed. One of the drivers blew the horn and Taylor winced. But not Kate, she noticed. Kate only cheered.

The volunteer ambulance corp appeared. The EMTs waving as they walked behind their ambulance.

Last, but not least, were several clubs. Taylor smiled and waved to Jason at the head of the Surfing Club. They wore yellow surf shirts and navy blue shorts, and their boards were all different colors. He smiled back. Other clubs followed, fishing and boating, with nautical crests printed on the backs of their shirts.

Soon, the last club arrived—the Aquas, an ocean-swimming group of retirees—and the parade was over.

Kate seemed disappointed. "Not as big as the one at home, eh?" Taylor said.

"No, but it was all right. It's just, well, they didn't have as many horses like the 4H at home brings every year."

LINDA J. PARISI   271

"I know."

Cheryl said, "I have to get back to the store. I'll see you all at the barbecue later."

They hugged and Cheryl was off.

She and her mom, plus Kate, began to stroll back toward the cottage. "The 4H Club might not have lots of animals to parade, but the surfers have really colorful boards, don't they?" she pointed out.

"Yeah. Lots of crazy patterns, too." Kate alternated between jumping and skipping along the sidewalk.

"You know, I think I remember Nick talking about a surfing competition next weekend." Taylor moved out of the way of a couple pushing a double baby carrier.

"Yes," her mother said. "I read about it in the paper. Why don't we try to go?"

Kate brightened. "Cool! I'd like that."

It didn't take long to get back to the house, and so Taylor asked Kate, "Do you want to ride your bike or help us make cheesecake?"

"Cheesecake!"

"Then let's get started."

No matter how careful Taylor tried to be, the kitchen always looked like a disaster area after baking cheesecake. She shooed her mother and Kate away and cleaned up while the dessert chilled in the fridge.

Kate managed to wear quite a bit of batter, so

Taylor had her change. Nick had said to come at one o'clock, but Taylor didn't want to be the first to arrive at the barbecue. She needn't have worried. But she was glad they'd walked. There wasn't a parking space to be had anywhere nearby.

The Diamantes' backyard was crowded, with several tables placed end to end already filled with dishes, and delightful aromas. Mama Bella grabbed her by the hand, hugged her and introduced her to way too many people for her to remember names. Some folks were family, and others were close friends.

Nick saved his hug for last and lingered a moment by her side. "Kate seems to be hanging in there. Have you heard anything from your ex?"

"No. I know we haven't had a chance to talk about anything but the restaurant recently, but let's not ruin the day."

"All right. How are you at meeting a few more people?"

"More?" she exclaimed on a laugh.

He shook his head slowly, his mouth curving upward. "This is just the first wave. Word got out. We know almost everyone on the Island who lives here year-round."

Taylor glanced at the growing numbers. "You should've had this at the restaurant. More room."

"More public, although I have a feeling a few

renters in the neighborhood are going to wander in. It's all right. We don't mind."

"Generous to a fault," Taylor said, the words deeper in meaning than just about hosting a barbecue.

He grinned. "Can I get you anything? You need to keep hydrated. It's going to get hot later."

Rocco called Nick to come back to his station at the grill. So, Taylor found a lemonade, spotted Beth and pulled up a chair. Her mom was deep in conversation with Bella, while Kate had already joined in with the other kids, playing games.

Beth shifted in her chair and smiled at Taylor. "I thought you guys were going to kiss there for a moment. And in front of everyone."

"Not the time and place."

Beth's smile grew. "If you had, it would have been tantamount to a public declaration."

Horrified and yet pleased at the same time, Taylor exclaimed, "You mean like heading-down-the-aisle declaration?"

"In front of the whole family? You betcha." Beth turned serious. "You love a Diamante, they love you for life."

The words settled in her brain. Taylor hadn't really understood it until now. But, after Greg, wasn't a true lifetime commitment the exact kind of love she was looking for?

Beth seemed to understand. She changed the

subject. "You do know your daughter is a gem, don't you?"

"I do, but I can't always let her have her own way. It's been tough, but I hope she's a strong kid because of it, at least."

Taylor looked at the kids, and then the toddler in Rocco's arms. "Roc Junior is adorable."

Beth beamed. "Thanks. You know, in spite of what's happened, Kate seems to be all right."

"Rocco told you?"

"No. That's attorney-client privilege. But it wasn't hard to guess. And I overheard Kate talking to little Roc."

Ah. Someone to talk to who wouldn't tell her what to do. "I guess toddlers don't answer, do they?"

"We all make mistakes. You have nothing to be ashamed of."

"I've asked myself too many times why I never saw the real Greg until it was too late."

"You'll probably never have a really good answer, either. But you have your daughter."

Taylor nodded. "She needs her father."

"I don't know," Beth answered, sounding genuine. "She needs *a* father."

Taylor spotted Nick. She smiled. Was Beth right? She turned to her friend who was still smiling at her.

"I understand. I took my time, too. Falling in

love with a Diamante comes with its own particular challenges."

She and Beth sat in silence for a while, before she asked, "How's the house hunting going?"

"Not as well as I'd hoped," Beth answered. "We'll find something eventually."

"The Island is expensive."

"And we can move off the Island, if the right place comes along. But Rocco's office is here and we're closer to everyone."

"And Bella may need help in the future. It makes sense."

They chatted about the kids and having babies and each time Beth shifted, she knew her friend was uncomfortable. "This one is a soccer player."

"Should I get Rocco?"

"No. I'm fine. Just not used to so much activity, Roc never kicked like this."

Taylor could relate. "Kate did. Amazed me."

Nick announced the food was ready. Taylor didn't plan it but somehow Kate found her way into a group of Diamante cousins. Her mother sat with Mama Bella and some of the aunts and uncles. That left Nick and Rocco to sit with her and Beth, reminding her of the same sense of belonging she'd felt ten years ago. Luis and his wife, Rosa, joined them.

"Not much expertise in making a burger," Luis teased Nick.

Nick drew back, pretending to look affronted.

"Says who? I'll have you know there are special spices that go into the meat."

Rocco guffawed. "Yeah. Montreal mix." They all joined in talking and swapping stories.

Nick lifted his voice, saying, "All right, all right. You've got me this time. And the potato salad is very good."

Luis smiled. "You should know, bro. Restaurant recipe."

Taylor listened to the familiar teasing, realizing Luis was really part of the family. Actually, everyone at the barbecue was. Diamante love was as widespread as it was fierce.

Suddenly, Taylor realized it wasn't Cantecaw or the restaurant she'd been seeking, it was this, the sense of big love and the loyalty that came with it. Diamante love was intimate and yet all-encompassing, layered and ready to protect everyone like a dome. Diamante love looked past outer shells and focused on what was inside. Goodness, respect, truth, honesty, these were the ideals they sought. And once found? A bond formed that couldn't be broken. Taylor reveled in their camaraderie.

Nick got called back to his grilling station. A second wave of guests mixed with the first and more food got served. In time, Taylor rose and began cleaning up. Soon, tiki torches were lit and zappers got busy. Mosquitoes didn't care who you were related to.

Later, leftovers were packaged and put off to the side and dessert was served. Nick came over and slid an arm around her waist, hugging her once, then letting go. "Hey," he said warmly.

Was it only a few weeks ago that Taylor had returned to Cantecaw? And now she felt completely at home. "Are you off duty finally?"

He nodded. In his other hand, Nick had been balancing a plate of cheesecake and two forks. "I had to push in front of a couple of cousins to get this. Come sit with me."

Taylor found chairs for them in a mostly quiet corner of the backyard. They sat and he fed her a dollop of the dessert, swiping a leftover bit from her mouth with his fingertip.

Taylor forgot to swallow. She filched a corner of the cheesecake with her finger and his lips parted. The flick of his tongue caught the delectable morsel.

"Mom! Mom!" Kate came running up to them.

Taylor quickly dropped her hand to her lap and smiled. Kate began tugging on the sleeve of her shirt. "Come play with me. Come play with me."

The moment with Nick had broken but the promise remained. Taylor threw him a sheepish grin. He smiled back and gestured for her to join Kate and the others.

She played ladder toss with the kids and lost two times. Kate gloated with glee. Then she noticed her mother started saying her goodbyes.

Although it wasn't a long drive back to Pennsylvania, her mom and Kate did have to go home, and holiday traffic was holiday traffic. Taylor felt tempted to let Kate stay another day. And if Kate hadn't been here the previous weekend, Taylor would have tried to bend the rules. But the school was being, had been, more than generous. So, it was time for Kate and her mother to be on their way.

Taylor took Kate over to say good-night and thank-you to Bella and the rest of the family.

Nick said, "Let me walk you out."

She turned and Jax, looking absolutely stunning in linen pants and a midriff blouse, walked up to them.

"Hi. Sorry, I'm late. We had a small get-together at my dad's house."

"No worries," Nick replied. "Glad you could make it," he added.

"Hi, Jax. You look…great." Taylor tried to squash a sudden jolt of jealousy.

"Beats a chef's coat, no?"

"We were just leaving," Taylor remarked, trying to gather her wits. "Kate's got to get home. Mom? You met Jax at the restaurant, didn't you?"

Her mother stepped forward to greet the young woman. "Sorry, I don't think so. I'm Cynthia. It's nice to put a name to a face."

Jax smiled. "So glad to meet you." They shook hands. "And a big hello to you, too, Kate."

Kate nodded and reached for Taylor's hand. "Thank you again for a wonderful day," she told Nick.

"Yes," her mom agreed. "Wonderful."

Kate kept tugging, so Taylor rolled with the flow. She turned back once and watched Nick laugh at something Jax had said.

"Hmm," her mother teased as they moved in the direction of the cottage. "Is that green you're wearing?"

Kate, ever innocent, piped up, "Nana, that's blue. Mom's shirt is blue, not green."

Her mom smiled. "Oh, yes, you're right. How silly of me to make that mistake."

"Very funny," Taylor admonished.

Kate wisely ignored them both and started chattering about her day and all the things she would tell her besties when she got home.

The two of them didn't have much to pack, since most of their clothes and other items could all stay at the cottage for future use. Taylor hugged her mother again. "Be careful, please." Then she kissed Kate three times and told her, "Best behavior or no beach when you get back. You hear me, young lady?"

Kate promised.

Taylor watched them drive off and even the thought of pretty, talented Jax couldn't interfere with her good mood. Not until later, after her mother's call, telling Taylor they were safe and sound and that Kate was already in bed.

Once she'd hung up, Taylor began to wonder. She'd never been jealous before. Never thought of the emotion. Hadn't had to. Greg's pursuing other women meant she hadn't given him a second thought. Besides, she and Nick were just friends.

Weren't they? Taylor marched right up to that line, that line of no return. She peered at the other side, trying to imagine the two of them together as a proper couple, bits and pieces of her dreams coming to the fore. She wanted to take that last step, but the debris from her relationship with Greg couldn't be cleared so easily.

Still, the notion no longer remained buried. Love. Was the dream of a forever love possible? Could she have a future with Nick? Could there be mornings in the kitchen making breakfast together? And days in the sand playing with Kate? And nights working side by side with the satisfaction of knowing they were building a future? She wasn't sure. But she was willing to find out.

CHAPTER TWENTY-FOUR

THE NEXT SEVERAL days sped by. With Kate coming back for good this weekend, Taylor had insisted her mother should stay home and rest, and she'd pick Kate up Saturday morning. She also wanted to collect some items she hadn't thought to bring before, but her mom kept saying she was fine with the commuting and to tell her what items she needed from the studio apartment. Her mom was looking forward to spending time with Bella and taking Kate to the beach.

In the meantime, Taylor wanted to escape. Bella and Jax had already started carving up territory in the kitchen. Jax was good about it but even she had limits. One afternoon things boiled over as Taylor had known they would.

She'd walked into the restaurant to set up for pre-rush and ran into a war zone. Nick and his mother were going back and forth in Italian, while Jax looked ready to scream but had tears in her eyes. And Luis? Bless his soul. He was hiding. Smart man.

Taylor motioned to Nick and nodded in the direction of Jax. Drawing in a deep breath and letting go, Taylor steered Bella into the dining room to sit and rest. Bella continued stating her case, half in English, half in Italian. Taylor didn't need to understand every word. She already knew.

Finally, she asked, "Mama, do you feel better now?"

"Si. Si."

Taylor had been surprised a flare-up hadn't happened sooner. "And you realize you can't get yourself all knotted up because of your blood pressure, right?"

"Humph. She takes up half the kitchen. Brings her own knives. What's wrong with the knives I got, eh?"

"Mama, you know chefs decide upon a set of knives that are theirs alone. They don't cook without them. Like that old spaghetti pot you use."

"Luis. Me. We work together fine. No problem. *Armonia.*"

Taylor gave Bella a sharp look. "And how long, exactly, did this 'harmony' take to develop?"

Bella didn't answer.

"My point exactly. You need to give Jax a chance. Have you tasted her food?"

Bella shrugged. "Is okay."

Taylor nearly laughed. Jax was producing dishes that were better than okay and Mama knew it. "We understand how you feel, Mama, but Nick is trying really hard to build something here."

Bella nodded. "I stop when you marry my Nico. Okay?"

This time Taylor couldn't help but push back. "No deals. Let's have some understanding. Please?"

Bella cupped her cheek, then pinched it. "For you, I try." She rattled off another comment in Italian under her breath.

Now to report the all clear to Nick and Jax. Only they weren't outside on the deck, or down in the storeroom. Thinking Jax might have quit, Taylor felt a sinking feeling in her stomach.

Just then, the front door opened. Jax seemed calmer. Nick said something Taylor couldn't hear and pulled the new chef into a Diamante hug. Taylor knew it was just a friendly hug, but still she'd turned an unflattering shade of green. *I'm right here.*

All through the rest of the afternoon and the later service, she'd chastised herself. Hadn't she been the one to argue for trust? If she truly trusted Nick, then she needed to act that way. But once the last diner had left, her exasperation boiled over.

Nick raised his arms as if surrendering. "You're mad at me. I mean, I know Mama and Jax were bound to happen, but I didn't intend for you to get caught up in it. I've been wondering all night if I might've bitten off more than I can chew."

"You did. You also forgot who helped."

"You're right. I should have said thank-you to you earlier. Better late than never? *Thank you*."

Taylor cocked her head and felt the tell-tale crease form over her nose. "Aren't you behaving just a tad cavalier? Your mother is upset. And not because of Jax."

"What?"

"Your mother doesn't dislike Jax. She doesn't like the idea that she's growing old. She's unhappy that she can't do what she used to do effortlessly, anymore. Ten years ago, you'd have been disowned if you'd suggested even the idea of a Jax."

His shoulders fell. "I know. It's hard for all of us. I've always thought of her as invincible."

"She probably was at one time. Especially after your father passed. You know, for all your talk about family, sometimes you don't see what's right in front of you. You need to talk to her again. You need to get her to agree to cut back on more hours she spends here."

"I've managed to negotiate a partial victory. She's got really tough armor, though. It's a challenge to get past it."

"Tell her you love her."

"I have. Many times."

Taylor knew that was true. "Kate's tough in that respect, too, I'm afraid."

"You don't say."

"Yeah. But when it's important, I keep trying to get through to her. I'm not always sure I've made my point, but at least I know I've gone above and beyond."

He smiled. "Thanks, Tay. You're right. I'll keep trying." He stopped and turned to face her. "And speaking of trying, I owe you."

The coin. "Yeah, you do."

He winced. "Listen, Tay. I want you to know I tried looking for it some more. I mean, I really tried."

Her stomach clenched. "You can't find it."

"No," he answered with a quick shake of his head. "I'm sorry. I genuinely am. I tore my house apart, I tore Mama's house apart, and even the restaurant."

"The restaurant?"

He sighed. "I thought long and hard. I remember the pier. I remember coming back this way to go home but nothing else. So, I looked here also. I can't find it anywhere. I'm so, so sorry."

It was disappointing to hear this, but the world wasn't lost. She had to have some perspective. "It's okay. We'll survive without it. We already have." She began to go.

He cocked his head. "Does this mean you're going to leave Cantecaw?"

Taken aback, Taylor wasn't sure how to respond. "Leave? Why would I?"

"Because you came here to find the coin."

Oh. A warm feeling spread through her. He really didn't want her to. "I came here for the coin, but I've found more reasons to stick around. Nick, I've put a lot on the line to stay. I've put Kate at risk in a sense. If Greg hadn't agreed to let her come, we might have ended up back in court. My mother has been pitching in, driving in some dicey weather because I'm on the Island. Not to mention, I've been working so hard right by your side to help make these Diamante dreams come true."

"And I'm not sure I'll ever be able to repay you. Or pay you what all this has meant to me." He paused. "So, you're not leaving?" The hope in his tone was palpable.

"I don't quit, Nick. And I never will. So no, I'm not leaving. Not until Kate has to go back to school, at least."

"And then what?"

"We'll have to see. The person who matters most at this point is Kate. She has to want to stay. But honestly, her life is back in Pennsylvania. No promises, I'm afraid."

"Fair enough. But for the record, it would be great if you both would, you know, be full-time on the Island."

"For the record, there's no place on earth I'd rather be."

He smiled and she exited, the door clicking shut behind her.

Outside, Nick caught up to her, calling to her

to wait. Was it just the moonlight or did she see something more, something glowing in his gaze?

"I'm falling for you, Tay. Not the young girl you once were, but the woman you've become. You're a wonderful mother and a great partner. I've always thought of you as beautiful, full of promise. You've matured into, well, my dream of you."

Taylor sucked in a breath and released the air in a rush. "I—I don't know what to say."

"Don't say anything," he replied, with a goofy grin. "You're not ready. Which was why my heart was able to survive the pier all those years ago."

"I thought mine had," she murmured out loud.

"I know. You've built a wall around your heart for protection. But this seems real between us. Maybe it could be more?"

They continued to the parking lot in silence. She unlocked her car door and he opened it for her. He kissed her cheek before she got in and shut the door. Then he went to his car. Taylor watched him drive away.

There came a moment in a person's life when they either looked in the mirror or they looked away. Nick had done nothing but show how much he cared. He'd shared her fear when Kate was lost and done everything he could to assist. He'd understood about her past and helped her see a way forward.

He'd been the partner she'd dreamed of, working his fingers to the bone to make these Diamante dreams a reality. He'd been the friend she'd leaned on when Greg had turned up, going above and beyond to help her sort out her legal troubles. At any time, he could have gone in a different direction and been justified in doing so. But he hadn't. For her sake.

And what about her wall? Ten feet high and nothing but fear. Taylor had let her dread of making a mistake consume her personal life. She'd let the stop sign rule her heart. Did she want to break the wall? Did she want to lay down the sign?

All Taylor could see was the line she dared not cross.

In her mind, Taylor knew what she wanted. She wanted a road she could travel, a straight road, no more twists, no more turns, no more reacting to a terrain she had no control over.

Taylor remembered the love she had for the boy. Now she needed to nurture the love she was beginning to feel for the man.

A seedling must have rich earth, sunlight and water to grow. Well, she'd dug the hole and placed the sprout in the ground. Now, she had to step back and allow the sunlight to shine. Time would tell if the roots were strong enough or not.

CHAPTER TWENTY-FIVE

NICK IMMERSED HIMSELF in opening the new part
of Diamante's. Mama eased up, but there were
times when her keen gaze turned sharper than
one of Jax's knives. Still, the kitchen began to
return to normal.

One of Nick's attributes from his time in
corporate-land was his ability to network and make
friends. Traci became a huge asset. She worked
with Jax on various menu pairings along with pro-
curing some high-end wines. Nick grimaced at the
initial outlay and used some of his savings to pay
the bills. His idea, his risk. All he could hope for
was that people would like his vision.

Nick admitted marketing wasn't his "thing,"
so Taylor put together a social media blitz with
a couple of kids on the waitstaff. They also purchased ads in local newspapers, showcasing their
first menu and pricing. But the champagne flutes
were really the hit. On each one, they'd engraved
a capital D for Diamante's in gold. Nick gave everyone working in the restaurant a pair of glasses

as a present at the pre-rush meal the day they were to open.

As soon as they began taking reservations, the first two weekends were booked solid, including the Fourth of July, forcing him to add Thursday nights to accommodate the demand.

Now he faced the true test. Opening night. A Thursday no less. Taylor walked up to stand by his side. It made him feel like he could achieve anything.

"You look nervous."

"I'm not nervous."

"You look like you are," she teased.

"I'm not."

"Now you're getting testy."

He stared at Taylor and grinned. "Yes."

Taylor slipped her hand into his and squeezed. Oh, so reassuring. "Everything about the new area is perfect. You know it is. Relax. Enjoy the moment. Take a deep breath. Have fun."

Have fun. Very well. He would. And did. From greeting the first wave of customers to maybe hovering a bit too much, to bringing out Jax a couple of times and seeing her appreciate the compliments.

Nearly every Diamante's customer wanted to know what was going on, so he handed out the postcards. He saw some sticker shock, but for the most part, the comments were favorable. Folks saying they'd try it or save the new menu for a special occasion, which he could understand.

Nick knew grand openings brought customers in out of curiosity. The true test would be after the first few weeks. Would they be able to keep the business thanks to steady repeat guests?

Only time would tell. Rather than worry, he decided to revel in their achievement. He went home jazzed and exhausted Thursday night, the same Friday night, more than tired Saturday night, and with Sunday being July third, he wondered what had happened to the entire weekend as it all seemed a big blur.

Sunday night he asked the staff to stay a moment after closing. He and Jax opened several bottles of champagne. "I know you're all tired. I am, too. But I can't thank you enough. Each and every one of you contributed to this weekend's success. But it wouldn't have happened without three very important women. To Mama Bella. Thank you for letting my dream become a reality." He inclined his head to his mother, who waved him away and lifted her glass of champagne. "To Jax, chef extraordinaire. Your food has surpassed my expectations." Jax looked down and scuffed her foot on the floor, then lifted her head to give him a huge smile. He raised his glass again. "And to Taylor. Without you, your belief in me, I would have folded. You are the rock upon which everything we've worked for has been built."

Nick caught her gaze. She seemed a touch embarrassed. No limelight for Taylor, no matter how much she deserved it. He gestured with his glass to her, to all of them, and drank.

Once everyone started leaving, he said to Taylor, "Stay a moment? Please?"

Nick sat down and poured the last of the champagne for them. He settled into the booth. Even with the new part of the restaurant, Diamante's still felt like Diamante's.

Taylor sat down next to him. "They say home is where the heart is."

He wondered how she'd known what he was thinking, then smiled. "Whoever 'they' is, they're right."

"I'm proud of you, Nick. You did everything you set out to do."

"I'm getting there," he replied with a slight shrug. "Thank you." He clasped her hand. "I meant every word I said. I couldn't have created this without you."

Twin spots of color formed high on her cheeks but she simply laughed. "I know."

Nick reached into his pocket and pulled out a box. "I didn't know any other way to say thank you." He set the box in front of her. "I can't tell you how glad I am that you came home. I'm very sorry about the coin but your friendship and more is far more important to me. However, I thought this might make up for it a little."

Curiosity danced in her eyes but she shook her head. "You didn't have to do this."

"I know," he said and smiled. "That's why I did it."

Taylor opened the box. Her breath caught. Resting on a bed of velvet sat a pendant with a gold chain. The pendant was a set of numbers. A date. *1821*.

He watched her mouth form this little O and grinned. "Thank you," she breathed.

"I'm sorry I didn't take your quest as seriously as I took mine."

"Quest? I never thought of it that way. When I saw the news program, when I did the research, things seemed preordained, meant to happen. Now I know I was right. No matter what, my *quest* as you call it, brought me back to the Island, to you. And I'm very glad."

Taylor slipped the chain around her neck. Nick leaned in and placed a soft kiss on her cheek.

"I think I'd better go," she said, standing up.

Nick escorted her out to her car and couldn't wait to see her tomorrow.

THE FOLLOWING EVENING, since Nick had promised Kate they'd enjoy the fireworks off the pier for the holiday, he closed the restaurant an hour early. The last of the diners were gone by nine. Cynthia brought Kate to Diamante's, where Nick set out chairs. He grilled hot dogs, included all the fixings and set out a pot of chili as well. Rocco and Beth came with the toddler because there was a better view of the festivities from the restaurant than their condo.

The fireworks shot out over the bay, flying high in the air and bursting into patterns of red, white and blue, each one more amazing than the last. Kate chose to sit on Taylor's lap and Nick sat next to them, his heart turning over in his chest. With Kate's head resting on her mom's, there could be no doubt of the girl's lineage. But it was their oohs and aahs, so similar in tone and expression, that defined mother and daughter. With each gasp, each exclamation, Nick's heart swelled. The show wasn't in the air, it was right beside him, and he couldn't get enough. No matter what happened, Kate and Taylor were special to him, now and forever.

Once the fireworks were over, he noticed his mom looked tired and Roc Junior started to fuss, so Rocco and Beth took them both home. Nick cleaned up and the three of them, plus Cynthia, sat for a while, listening to the bay lap against the bulkhead, staring at the lights of the mainland.

"How come you bought my mom a gift, Nick?" Kate asked.

"She's worked very hard. I wanted to say thank you."

Kate seemed to process that. "What does 1821 stand for?"

He wasn't sure how much Taylor had shared with Kate, but given the seven-year-old's smartness, he figured honesty was the best policy.

"A long time ago, before you were born, your mom found a coin on the pier with that date on it. Turned out it was both our ages at the time. She was eighteen, I was twenty-one. Anyway, she gave it to me. To remember us and the time we spent together that summer. I gave it back to her. I told her it belonged to both of us. But she insisted I hold on to it for safekeeping. So, as a memento for her and to say thank-you, I had the date made into a necklace."

Taylor stared at him long and hard. Then she grinned. He hadn't given away the secret of the coin but had told the absolute truth. The bright blue of her eyes warmed.

"I wish there were fireworks every night," Kate said. "Then we could be like this. All together."

Nick cleared his throat. He was glad he and Kate had the makings for a solid bond, but so much was still undecided. Would they all still be on the Island once the summer was over?

Taylor looked at odds, too.

Seemed, though, that grandmothers were immune. Cynthia smiled knowingly and said, "C'mon Kate. It's late. I have to leave tomorrow and I want to go to the beach in the morning. Weather permitting."

"Good night." Taylor hugged and squeezed them both. "I'm right behind you."

Once they had left, she turned to him. "Thank you."

"What for?"

"Kate hasn't had a great deal of honesty in her life from her father. You've taken on the role like you own it."

A sear of pleasure ran through him. "I don't lie. But maybe she doesn't need all the details. Yet."

"Yet." Taylor chuckled. Her gaze filled with a mixture of gratitude and something deeper, more intense. "She's growing up so fast."

Nick loved her laugh—its sound was all Tay, full and rich and from the heart. He couldn't get over her beauty, No, not just the outside kind, although there were times when he looked at her and he forgot to breathe. Her true beauty came from inside, from her kindness, her humor, her integrity. These were the reasons he'd given her the present. He couldn't help wanting more. The idea rose again about how the end of the summer was looming, and he pushed the thought away.

"I'm glad you're wearing the necklace."

"I don't ever want to take it off. But I'll have to. No way this—" her fingertips grazed the pendant "—is going near the ocean." She stood.

He looked up to catch a glint in her gaze. Was she leaning toward staying? Toward there being more between them? Hope fired through his veins. "I'm glad. I'll see you at the beach in the morning?"

"We'll be there."

CHAPTER TWENTY-SIX

ONCE THE NEW area of Diamante's had opened, the days seemed to fly by. Kate, having finished with school, reveled in the Island and they established a summer routine. Kate would wake her up by nine, they'd do chores or run errands and be on the beach by eleven. Beach time with Kate was the best time. Taylor learned to swim in the ocean again, and Nick helped Kate to understand when to go into the ocean and when not to. He even bought her a boogie board to ride the waves.

Her mother engineered long weekends, using her company's half-day Friday summer hours and tacking on Mondays as vacation days. Beth never said no to keeping an eye on Kate. In fact, there were times when she asked for Kate to come over. Kate had a special bond with Roc Junior that allowed Beth to rest, or let Rocco and Beth have some quiet time to themselves on their deck.

Taylor managed to have lunch with Cheryl, and afterward they scoured the outlets looking for bargains. Taylor found two outfits for Kate for school, but on the drive back to the Island, the thought of leaving this special place haunted her.

"Cantecaw digs in deep, doesn't it?" Cheryl asked her. "I've never really been able to let go. When Luke decided to join the army, I went with him. But my heart never stopped being here."

"I don't know what I'm going to do," Taylor confessed. "Kate's life is in Pennsylvania. But she loves it here. I know she'll miss her friends, her school and her life there."

"What about you? Anything you can't give up?"

"Besides my tiny studio apartment?" she laughed. "My mother, of course."

"Who seems to be in my store every weekend," Cheryl joined in. "I wouldn't worry too much on that score."

But Taylor couldn't help worrying. Time seemed to be soaring by.

When she first mentioned to Nick that Kate wanted her besties to come to Cantecaw, he didn't hesitate. He suggested they swap houses for the weekend. This way there'd be room for Kate's friends and their mothers, who literally jumped at the chance for a girls' weekend away.

He also insisted she take at least Friday night off, and that they all come to pre-rush dinner on Saturday.

Kate couldn't stop bouncing when the day of her friends' visit finally arrived. Nick helped them bring over a few things from the cottage and packed a suitcase for himself. He made sure the wine fridge was stocked and they had plenty of snacks and breakfast items.

Taylor reminded Kate of Nick's generosity with a pointed look as he got ready to leave. Her daughter had the grace to look a little sheepish.

"Nick?" Kate said.

"Yes?"

"Thank you for letting my friends and their moms stay here. Our house would have been too small."

Our house. Taylor wished it could be true.

"My pleasure, Kate. We're family. And family helps family. Always."

Kate nodded, turning thoughtful. "I'm a Diamante?"

"For as long as you want," Nick answered. Taylor sent him a look of pure gratitude.

Of course, just as Nick was heading out the door, the guests of honor turned up. Kate squealed and ran out the door, and the girls started jumping in place, then hugging. Taylor followed her daughter outside and hugged Lisa and Shannon.

Nick stood there, looking at her expectantly. Taylor groaned inside, more of her worlds colliding.

"Nick? This is Lisa Baines and Shannon Mc-Guire. Ladies, this is Nick Diamante. He owns the restaurant where I work. He's also the gentleman giving up his house for the weekend."

"Much appreciated, Nick," Lisa said, holding out her hand.

"Ditto," Shannon added, doing the same.

Nick shrugged. "My pleasure. Enjoy."

He gave Taylor a quick squeeze and waved before getting into his car. The man's grin was to die for.

"OMG, Tay. You have got to spill. He's hot," Shannon said, following the girls into the house. The kids ran up to "their" bedroom for the weekend and slammed the door shut.

"We'll break that up in a moment," Lisa said. "Let's get back to Mr. Chili Pepper, please."

Taylor explained a bit of her past and her need to see the Island and Nick's offer for the summer.

"I can't believe how lucky you are," Shannon said. "This is a great setup."

Taylor laughed. "The cottage we're staying in is quite a bit smaller. This is Nick's house. Don't forget he's letting us borrow it for the weekend."

Her friends understood. "Then we'd better make sure the girls behave," Lisa replied. "And thank him again the next time we see him."

"You can do that tomorrow. We're invited to a late lunch or early dinner at the restaurant. Tonight, I thought we'd grill something easy. The girls have their room, each of you will take a bedroom, and the living room has a pullout couch for me."

"No. We couldn't."

"You can and you will," Taylor insisted. "Now, I don't get many nights off. So let's get these young ladies to the beach. And when we're back, you're going to love the outdoor shower. The sand will stay outside."

An hour later, they'd wrangled the girls and made it to the shore. Terri wasn't as good a swimmer as Kate and Rachel so the kids stayed close to the beach. When they were in the water, at least one mother was there with them. And Taylor wasn't surprised when Jason drove up in his lifeguard Jeep to make sure they were all okay.

"Hey, Tay. You all good?" he asked.

She nodded. "We're fine, Jason. Tell Nick thank-you for the extra security."

"Will do." He grinned. "Just looking out for my bud is all."

"I know. But the possibility of a tray of lasagna doesn't hurt, either," she teased.

Jason hung his head. "You caught me." He straightened. "Ladies, enjoy the beach."

As soon as Jason was out of earshot. Both of the moms started. "Oh my goodness, things just keep getting better and better. Did you see the abs on him?" Shannon exclaimed.

"I have got to get hubby to start going back to the gym," Lisa added.

How long had it been since Taylor lounged at the beach and enjoyed some fun female companionship? They talked about nothing and everything all day.

"You have both got to stop joking. Please. My mouth hurts from smiling so much. Plus, the girls are probably listening in."

"Doubtful," Lisa replied. "But I'll go check on them. It's getting kind of late."

"Thanks for the invite. I needed this," Shannon said, blowing out a huge sigh of contentment.

"So did I," Taylor replied.

THE NEXT DAY the girls had them up pretty early. And they got in a really good beach morning. But Taylor knew, as any beachgoer did, that the winds could shift and the clouds could roll in at any time. So they went back to the house, cleaned up and had a light snack. The girls played a card game and Shannon joined in to make a foursome.

"You want to stay here on the Island," Lisa remarked, joining Taylor on the deck.

The ocean breeze kicked up and Taylor shivered. "Yes."

"More than one reason, I bet."

"Don't know."

Lisa smiled. "You will. And the girls will be friends no matter where you and Kate end up. They're besties. They know how to use Face-Time."

"Thanks. I know they do. And I can always go back and stay with my mother so the girls can see each other. I guess I've been beating myself up. I don't want Kate to be unhappy here. Summers are one thing, but year-round? Different life."

"Don't sell it short. Lots of pluses. Plenty of workarounds, too."

Taylor knew exactly what or rather who Lisa had referred to. She grinned. "Indeed. And I'm not. But—"

Lisa shook her head. "No. No excuses. You need to figure out what Taylor wants, what's best for her, too."

Taylor nodded, knowing what had been missing. A little extra reinforcement. "Thank you."

"My pleasure."

Pleasure, it seemed, ended up wrapped in tomato sauce and noodles and meatballs and all kinds of food as they went to Diamante's for prerush dinner. Jax joined the fray with a light summer salad and flan for dessert.

Taylor lost count of the introductions, and the noise level reached powerful decibels, but nothing could match the intensity of Nick's gaze. Her heart fluttered. The world fell away every time he looked at her. When she finally broke the spell and dragged her gaze away, she ran headlong into Lisa's grin.

She shrugged. What else could she do? Besides, Lisa was right. She had to do what was right for her, for them all. And Cantecaw—no, Nick—well, both were more than right.

There would always be storm clouds and rough seas, for the world was both beautiful and ugly. But facing it all with someone she trusted was the type of future she could finally admit that she wanted.

The noise faded and nothing existed but Nick and what she believed was the love shining in his eyes. Greg's infidelity always hurt, since Taylor thought it had happened because she wasn't enough, that she didn't measure up. Now she knew with every spark she felt that she'd been more than enough. Nick thought so. Greg was the fool for not wanting to hold on to what had been right in front of him the whole time.

Taylor understood that sometimes a person needed to learn wrong so they'd recognize right when it came along. Well, right stared at her with a slight smile on his lips, as if he'd been waiting for her to come to this very conclusion.

CHAPTER TWENTY-SEVEN

WITH HER NEW frame of mind toward Nick, each smile and kind word from him chipped away at her plan to return to Pennsylvania. She still had a lot to think about, though, and weigh up.

Kate seemed subdued after her friends left for home. Taylor chalked it up to her missing them. So on the beach one day, she asked, "You miss Rachel and Terri, don't you?"

Her daughter tried to hide her feelings but clearly couldn't. With a heavy sigh, she answered, "Yes."

Taylor wanted to be happy, but she wanted Kate to be happy, too. "Do you hate it here? On the Island?"

"Oh, no," Kate replied instantly. "I love the beach. And Jessica is fun. Little Roc is adorable."

Taylor braced herself. "Do you dislike Nick?"

"No." Kate turned thoughtful. "Sometimes he makes me do stuff, like clean up my stuff."

It's called good parenting.

Kate deepened her voice and spoke firmly. *"A Diamante pulls his weight."*

Taylor laughed at the excellent impression. "Do you really dislike it when he says things like that to you?"

"Sometimes. Sometimes I don't like it when you tell me what to do, either." She paused and frowned. "What's going on, Mom?"

"Kate, Nick needs me to help him with the restaurant. It's a good job with a nice place to live."

Comprehension dawned slowly and then complete shock filled Kate's face. "You mean, stay here when school starts? Live here?"

"Yes."

"No!" Kate started shaking her head. "No. I can't. I have to go home. I have to go to school with Rachel and Terri, and I... We're all supposed to go into Mrs. Peterson's class. We're supposed to have my birthday in Nana's backyard just like we always do. I owe— I owe Peter Davis a mean look. He hasn't been so nice to Rachel and Terri."

A wave of sadness filled Taylor. Never had she thought Kate would be this upset about staying on the Island. For a quick moment, the thought of commuting crossed her mind. Having Kate stay with her mother, Taylor would still be able to visit them during the week. Could it work?

"I hardly know anybody, Mom." Kate's voice was raised. "When the bad weather comes, I won't be able to go to the beach. I won't—"

"I understand, Kate. I get it."

Kate's eyes were red. And to be honest, Taylor was also trying not to cry. It felt like her own dream was slipping away.

"Kate, I have a job here. A good job. You know, before we left, I sent out a ton of résumés. I haven't gotten back one request for an interview. What do you expect us to live on?"

Kate looked hopeless and Taylor's heart felt as it was tearing apart. She reached out to hug Kate, but Kate jumped up and ran down to the water's edge, where she sat with her knees drawn up under her chin. Taylor started to go after her, then changed her mind. Giving her daughter a few minutes to collect her emotions would definitely help.

A beat later, Nick came running up from the beach. "Kate won't say hello to me. And you're sitting here with tears in your eyes. What's going on?"

"I started the conversation. About maybe staying."

Nick nodded and sat down on the sand next to her chair. Taylor turned to him. "You're not saying anything? *You* have an opinion on everything." Her attempt at levity did lighten her load for a moment.

His gaze warmed though he didn't smile. He knew how difficult her decision would be. "And what about you? What are your thoughts on staying?"

Taylor knew in her heart what she wanted, but

it wasn't that simple. "What you've done, what you've put together, is fantastic. I really like working with you."

He looked disappointed. "Just working?"

She cocked her head. "Right now, yes. But I could use a hug."

"Oh, really?" he asked, his voice sweet.

"Yes," she answered. "But you're all sweaty from your run."

He nodded, grinning. "So, no hug, then, fine. I see how this is going."

"Hey, I can only handle one meltdown in a day. But a hug tomorrow or in the future? I'm all in." She stared at him for a moment and sparks flew.

"There's still hope, Tay. We're good together. And I think we're both at the point where we want more. We can help Kate. Together. Show her what we see that makes this place so great."

Taylor tensed. "What about Greg? I need his permission to relocate. He can raise an objection and take me to court if Kate insists she doesn't want to move."

Nick frowned. "All right. Not so easy. Let's start by really introducing her to the Island. We'll take her to the lighthouse. The marina. Make sure she knows there's a *real* mall not too far away. Let's see if she likes fishing. We'll find out who's going into the third grade and have a get-together."

Nick continued with more good suggestions

and Taylor fell into his strength like a parched woman leaving the desert. "You know what's so great about this Island? You.'

Nick rose and squeezed her hand. "I'm here for you, Tay." He peered at the ocean and Taylor knew he was looking for Kate. Taylor hadn't really let her out of her sight, noting her daughter had still looked forlorn with her shoulders slumped. "No one can survive a Diamante with a purpose," he teased.

Diamante bulldozer was more like it.

Nick suggested that they take Kate over to the lifeguard station. Kate couldn't wait to go. She seemed entranced with the explanation of all the different equipment and how various techniques worked best for swimming in the ocean. There was a pool where lifeguards in training practiced lifesaving procedures. Kate studied them for a long time and Taylor just knew that Kate had made up her mind to become a lifeguard one day.

Then Jason took her over to a rack with all kinds of surfboards. He showed Kate how to balance herself on one, promising to teach her how to surf before the summer was over. Kate talked about nothing else all afternoon.

The following day, Nick packed a picnic breakfast for them, and even though it was a cloudy day, they drove up to the lighthouse. Kate and Nick set out to walk all the way to the top. Taylor passed, not comfortable with tight spaces.

"So, there really is a chink in your armor," he joked. "You're *not* a superhero, able to accomplish everything?"

Taylor grinned and nudged him away.

Not long after, Nick and Kate returned from the top of the lighthouse. Kate was giggling. Then she seemed to catch herself and stopped. Taylor knew. Kate wanted to like Nick but didn't want to be disloyal to Greg. Small steps, she thought.

Taylor spread out a blanket in a grassy meadow next to the pathway. She unpacked drinks and breakfast sandwiches. Kate and Nick joined her. She looked her daughter over, from her toes to the top of her head. "So, you made it down okay?"

"Sure. What's up, Mom?" Kate asked, casually taking a huge bite of her sandwich.

Time to face a fear. "I was just making sure you're all right. I couldn't stand it if something happened to you."

"Oh." Kate bit into her sandwich and chewed, her features falling. After a moment or two, Kate swallowed and brightened. "I know I gotta be careful, Mom. Nothing's going to happen to me, so you don't have to worry." Said with a seven-year-old's look of complete innocence.

"Parents have a duty to worry about their offspring," Taylor replied. "It's on page three hundred and twenty-four of the parenting handbook.'

Kate giggled. "Oh, Mom. Stop being silly. You know there's no such thing."

Did she? Taylor wondered. She looked over to find Nick staring at her, approval shining in his gaze. The tightness in her throat eased and she managed a few bites of her sandwich.

Kate finished hers and wiped her fingers on a napkin. Her daughter jumped to her feet. "May I please be excused? I want to look for shells."

"Stay where I can see you."

Taylor put her half-eaten sandwich down and watched for a minute to make sure her directions were followed. When she was satisfied, she sipped some coffee and found Nick still looking at her. "What?"

"I'm trying to figure out how to put my 'two cents' in," he said.

Taylor gestured for him to explain.

"Well, if Mama were here, she'd tell you not to invite trouble because trouble has a way of finding you no matter what you do. I'm saying the same. Because I care."

Taylor reached out and gave his hand a quick squeeze. She got lost for a long moment in his kind gaze. She broke away and sought out Kate, who was busy picking up shells to keep and discarding the ones she didn't want.

When she was satisfied that Kate was in no danger, she said, "I guess I can be a bit hard on myself. I keep asking if I would be strong enough to endure."

He answered for her. "You would. I know you would."

"You're just trying to be nice."

"Am I?" He turned serious. "I'm not trying to pander here."

Taylor lifted a brow, but couldn't help smiling.

He let out a big laugh. A second later, he sobered. "Look," he said.

Kate had left the sand and walked up to a younger girl in a wheelchair. A woman was with her. The two kids talked for a few minutes, then Kate held out her hand, giving the girl what was inside her palm. Kate continued to chat, and Taylor watched the tall, slender woman with auburn hair speak to the girls.

About to get up and introduce herself, Taylor paused when Kate came running back to her and Nick. The woman inclined her head and smiled, then she and the young girl left, heading for the pathway.

A touch breathless, Kate said, "I went over to say hello. Her name's Amanda and she's seven just like me. She said it doesn't hurt. Most of the time."

Taylor nodded, realizing what Kate was talking about.

"She said she has a problem with her back. She said scoli—scoli…"

"Scoliosis," Taylor finished for her daughter.

Kate nodded. "She was cool. I gave her the piece of sea glass I found. She liked it.'

The friendly gesture made Taylor want to hug her daughter and never let go. "That was very thoughtful of you."

Nick chimed in. "Well, now. I would say you deserve a treat."

Kate shook her head. "No. I liked giving the sea glass to her. I don't need a prize for doing it."

Wow. How grown-up Kate sounded.

"Still," Nick continued, "I think we can go pick up vanilla ice cream and sprinkles for later on. It's too early to have ice cream now."

"Huh?" Kate said, smiling. "It's never too early to have ice cream!"

Taylor smiled and started gathering their things. Nick and Kate pitched in. But she couldn't get the worry over Kate wanting to be in Pennsylvania at the end of summer out of her mind.

Taylor's concern only increased later that night when she found out that Kate had called Greg after she'd left for her evening shift at Diamante's. Kate seemed tense when she tucked her in and Taylor tried, but her daughter didn't want to talk about it. Beth had let her know about the call and Taylor was grateful. She wanted to press Kate, but didn't have the heart.

Sometimes, she figured, it was best to wait and find out all in good time. She never expected it would come in the form of an explosion.

CHAPTER TWENTY-EIGHT

THE FOLLOWING SATURDAY, the front door of the restaurant opened. Bright sunlight poured in briefly. Mildly concerned, Nick cocked his head to see who was there. He should have locked the thing.

"Hey, jerkface! Where's my wife?" Greg hollered.

Nick stiffened. He remembered the day Taylor had walked into the restaurant and into his life for the first time. How beautiful she was. His beauty, he hoped, one day.

Standing before him now, the beast.

He stopped racking wineglasses and placed his hands on the bar. "You're not married anymore."

Greg waved his statement away. "Semantics."

Concern turned to mild alarm. Why would Greg call Taylor his wife when they'd been divorced for all these years? "What do you want?"

He heard his mother before he saw her. "Nico?"

"It's okay, Mama. This gentleman was just leaving."

She nodded. "We serve lunch soon, eh?"

"He'll be gone soon, Mama. Don't worry."

Once his mother was in the back, Nick turned his full attention on Taylor's ex. "You should leave. I won't ask again."

"What're you going to do about it?"

Nick came out from behind the bar, threw an arm around Greg's shoulders and led him outside. Greg shoved him away and faced him.

"Talk. What do you want?"

"I don't have to explain anything to you. I need to speak to Taylor."

"They're probably down at the beach. Did you call? Say you were coming?"

"No," Greg spat out. "Why should I?"

"I don't know. Kate, maybe? Nice of you to ask about her, by the way."

"How dare you!" Greg shouted. "You have no right to judge me. She's *my* daughter."

"She is. And you owe her an explanation. You broke her heart."

All of a sudden, Rocco's truck screeched to a halt nearby.

"Hey, bro."

"Hey, Roc."

"Coward." Greg sneered.

Rocco laughed, shaking his head. He leaned against the hood of his car and crossed his arms over his chest. "I just came to watch."

Greg did look a bit confused. "Watch what? We're just talking."

Rocco nodded. "Talking is good, sure."

Greg blanched. Once he was behind the steering wheel, he called out to them. "You tell Taylor I know all about her secret. You tell her she can't cut me out. You hear me?"

Greg took off, narrowly missing the rear fender of Rocco's truck.

His brother frowned and looked at him. "What's he talking about?"

Nick's stomach hollowed. He punched Rocco lightly in the shoulder and his brother punched back. They turned and walked back up the steps and into the restaurant. "It's complicated."

"When has that ever stopped you before?" Rocco grinned. "I've known about your complications all my life, bro," he teased. "So, what's he want?"

Nick claimed a seat at the first table. "Mama called you?"

"Of course."

Once they were both settled, Nick started explaining. He went all the way back to the pier ten years ago and told Rocco about the coin.

"I can't find it anywhere, Roc. I lost it. And every time I think of it, my stomach goes south. The money would've done so much good. I can't believe I've been so foolish. But I didn't know. It was just a memento, a memory of a beautiful summer."

Rocco reached out and squeezed Nick's shoulder. "You're right. You didn't know. But now, Taylor's ex does know and look what it's doing to him."

"Yeah. About that. I can't imagine how he found out." Nick couldn't help feeling as though he'd failed everyone. "I've looked all over for that coin. The garage, the attic…"

Rocco rubbed his jaw. "I kind of remember we were all celebrating that night. Except Taylor. She didn't want anything to drink."

"I walked her to her apartment. Then I stopped here to make sure Mama had gone home. I thought I had the coin with me. Put it somewhere for safekeeping."

"And what about you and Taylor?"

"She came out here to tell me about the coin. As soon as I saw her, Roc, all I wanted was for her to stay on Cantecaw. I love her."

Rocco grinned and Nick grinned back. "Does she know that?" Rocco asked.

"I've tried to tell her. But we've been so busy, and then the custody problems, there hasn't been a good time to talk. I mean, really talk."

"Don't you think you should make time?" Roc's gentle smile reminded Nick of his father.

"I was going to. But now, with all this, Taylor's priorities will have shifted. I can't believe what a jerk that guy is."

Rocco lifted his head, cocked an ear toward the

back. So did Nick. Silence. "You do realize Mama's probably been hanging on our every word."

Nick smiled. "I know." He instantly sobered. "I've let everyone down, Roc. I keep thinking, *what if?*"

"Don't," Rocco insisted. "What's meant to be is meant to be. Stop beating yourself up."

"Can't help it." Nick shrugged.

"Look, you and Taylor will figure things out. And as for the business, every Diamante has to build from the ground up. Seems to be one of our traits. Papa did. Mama did. I did. You are. Focus on what you *can* change, not what you can't. I bet, as soon as you do, that coin turns up. And not the way you expect, either."

TAYLOR WALKED DOWN the street with Kate, carrying their canvas chairs and a large tote bag. They'd had a good day together at the beach. Kate swung her sand pail with a pair of shovels sticking out of the top. They'd made an awesome castle with a moat.

But Taylor frowned as soon as she saw the cars. Greg immediately left his car and approached them. Nick and Rocco followed him.

When Kate spotted her father, she jumped with delight and ran to him, hugging him tight. "Daddy! Daddy!"

Greg extricated himself without even saying hello to Kate and instead, spoke directly to Taylor. "I know the truth," he hissed. "You're not cutting me out, Taylor. You hear me?"

Caught off guard, Taylor was confused. "What?"

Greg pointed to Kate. "My little pumpkin, here. You helped Daddy, didn't you?"

Taylor looked at Kate.

Her daughter's face fell and her whole body tensed. She must have realized she may have made a mistake. "I heard you talking, Mom. I'm sorry."

Kate ran to Taylor and put her arms around her. "It's okay, baby. Not your fault."

"Hey, look. We can all be friends here, right? Kate," Greg said, stepping toward them. "You didn't do anything wrong. You told Daddy something very important. To help me. You said if I had the coin, I wouldn't be in trouble anymore. And I won't."

Taylor sighed and Kate turned away from Greg. Even the seven-year-old knew Greg's attitude and actions were wrong.

"I don't have the coin, Greg," Taylor confessed.

"I don't have it, either," Nick added.

Looking baffled, Greg cried, "What? Wait. I don't understand. Where is it? Did you turn it in already? Where's the money?"

"It's lost," Taylor told him. "Gone. We can't find it."

Greg roared with laughter. He didn't stop for a long time. Wiping the tears from his eyes, he said, "You really expect me to believe you? How lame. You just want it all for yourselves. I won't let you."

"She's telling the truth," Nick said. "You should believe her. She's the best, she's—"

Greg scoffed and then began laughing again.

Rocco ended the laughter with a stern look. "Listen to him."

"No one hurts a Diamante," Nick continued. "Not on my watch. So, you need to believe her. Believe us."

"Really?" Greg snickered. "You going to make me if I don't? Touch me and I'll call the police."

Almost in unison, Nick and Rocco recited a phone number.

"That's the cell for the chief of police. We grew up together." Nick glanced over at Rocco and smiled.

"I'll take Kate away from you, Taylor. I swear I will." Greg looked defiant.

Taylor knelt down, speaking softly but firmly. "I know why you did what you did. I've been making excuses for your father, making him out to be what he really isn't. I'm so sorry."

"Oh, Mommy." Kate threw her arms around Taylor.

Taylor rose and turned to her ex. "Tell her. Tell her the truth. She needs to hear it from you."

"What truth? That I'm in a little trouble? Okay. You knew that, right, Katydid?"

Kate only stared at her father.

"I just need some money. To cover a few expenses. Things got out of hand. The coin will make things better. Like it was before. You'll see."

YES, NICK THOUGHT. Kate could see. Her expression full of sadness and disappointment.

"You didn't come to see me," Kate said. "All you came here for was that stupid coin. You don't care about me. You never have."

"That's not true, pumpkin. Honest. Of course I came here to see you."

It seemed even Kate could hear he wasn't sincere. "Liar!"

Taylor hugged Kate and Nick went over to them. "I'm sorry, Kate," he whispered.

"You get away from my little girl," Greg snapped.

Rocco stepped forward and Greg threw a punch. His brother leaned in and caught Greg's outstretched arm, twisting it up Greg's back.

Greg yelped. "Ow. You're hurting me. Let go!"

Rocco shoved him away. Greg stumbled and almost fell. "One last time. Leave. There is no coin. It's gone. We can't find it. It's missing and no one knows where it is. Do you understand?"

"I don't believe you. I'm going to fight you all the way, Taylor. I swear I am."

Taylor stood tall, clearly ready to do whatever it would take for her daughter. Nick felt the same for them both. "Leave, Greg. Now. You've caused enough hurt for one day."

Greg winced. He was losing. "C'mon, Katydid. You know I love you. That's why you told me the truth, isn't it?"

Kate looked up at Taylor but didn't speak. She just marched up the steps and into the cottage. Nick reached out and drew Taylor into his arms. He heard a car door slam and the engine revving as Greg drove away.

"Thank you," Taylor whispered against his cheek.

How he wanted to kiss her, comfort her.

Taylor let go of him and walked over to Rocco and gave him a quick hug. "Thank you."

Rocco shrugged. "Hey, family takes care of family."

Taylor offered a small smile and walked to the house. Nick turned to his brother.

"I'm impressed," Rocco told him. "You showed a lot of restraint."

"I didn't want to add any fuel. He's gone for now but not forever. He'll be back."

"We'll figure it out," Roc replied with certainty in his voice. "We'll talk later, okay?"

Nick nodded and entered the cottage. Taylor cuddled Kate as they sat on the couch, speaking softly. He kneeled down in front of them. "Are you all right, *bella giglia*?"

Kate wiped at her tears. "What's that mean?"

"Beautiful lily," Nick answered. "You are, you know. Beautiful. And in his own way, your father does love you. It's probably hard to understand but when people make bad choices and get themselves into a jam, sometimes they make even more bad choices and end up hurting the people closest to them. The thing is, Kate, I was hoping you'd have enough room in your heart for him and me. I think you're something special and you're mom's the best, and if you'll have me, I'd like us to maybe be a family one day? Do you think you have enough room in your heart for both of us?"

Kate nodded emphatically and Nick's heart soared. She leaned in and hugged him. One down. One to go.

He noticed Taylor swipe at her cheek. "It's getting late," she said. She stared at him, her lips parted just so, her gaze liquid blue. He wanted to kiss her and considered it for a split second. But what Taylor needed at that moment was a friend, not something more.

"It is. I have to get back. Diamante's waits for no one." Together, he and Taylor stepped onto the porch.

"My mother is coming. Perhaps later, we can gather the clan and put our heads together and figure out what to do."

Nick agreed. "Of course. As soon as we close. Let's ask Beth to watch Kate."

"That would be helpful. My heart breaks for Kate."

"I know. Mine does, too." Nick looked deep into Taylor's eyes. "When all this gets cleared up, can we have a talk about us...the future...?"

"Yes, definitely." Taylor slipped her arms around his waist. "I'd like that very much."

Nick held her to him, loving the feeling, loving her.

CHAPTER TWENTY-NINE

PRE-RUSH DINNER that afternoon became a subdued affair. But concern turned to focus later on as the restaurant got very busy very quickly. Customers came in hungry and left happy and sated.

Taylor was glad there was a crowd that night, but her concern kept seeping through her smile and rosy demeanor. Nick assisted more than once and Taylor felt bad, but knew she'd make it up to Diamante's one day. Once Kate's custody was settled, all would be right. Greg had no right to hurt Kate. And he had no right to make claims on herself or anyone else. Surely a court would see that.

Taylor's mother arrived just before closing and Mama Bella joined them when they congregated after the last customer had left. Tiny cups of espresso and plates of biscotti were on the table.

Since Mama wasn't aware, Taylor, with Nick's help, brought her up to speed about her ex and the custody issue. Then Nick added his promise of support.

Bella nodded. "Always. We are family. We take care of each other."

"I never thought things would get so out of hand," her own mother remarked.

Taylor had to agree. "I never expected to come back to Cantecaw or rediscover my wonderful second family. But I have. And I want to stay. Kate's come around, too. I'm so grateful. What we're found here—" she paused, looking directly at Nick "—is too important to let go of. So, here's the problem. Greg needs to give permission for Kate to live in another state. He probably won't do it unless he gets what he needs. Money. But I don't have it. However, it'll take money to fight him in court, to do what's best for Kate, so, what I'm proposing is a loan. I don't want anyone offering—"

Mama chimed in, respect shining in her gaze. "We no give. We make loan. You pay back with part of your salary every week."

"And your share of the profits from the tables in the back. No freebies." Nick sent her a quick smile.

Her heart filled with hope. "I can't thank you all enough. Everyone for your support." Taylor looked around the table, surrounded by love. Her mother said her goodbyes and went to pick up Kate. Rocco wished everyone well and exited with a jaunty wave. But Mama hovered.

When Nick went into the kitchen to put away

the cups and plates, Mama turned to Taylor. "You marry my Nico? You love him?"

Taylor pretended to frown. "Mama, at least allow me to tell him first."

"Tell me what first?" Nick asked, walking back toward the table.

Bella patted her cheek and disappeared into the kitchen. Taylor knew it was now or never. She stood up and faced him.

"Nick. I should have told you sooner. I shouldn't have let my fears get in the way. I should have trusted you, most of all myself." She held his face with her hands. "I love you. I loved you ten years ago. I love you more now." Taylor reached up on her toes and kissed him, only one of thousands to come, she hoped. She sank into an ocean of joy as he kissed her back.

"Ahem."

Mama Bella?

"Ahem."

Mama came up to them. "You are the best thing ever to happen to my Nico. Nico, she is the best thing for you. You get married, eh? Make grand-babies for me, yes?"

"Wow, Mom. Like Tay said, maybe give me a chance to at least ask first?"

She waved his complaint away. "You can still do your thing." Mama stared straight at her. "You say yes?"

Taylor nodded with all her might. Some bull-dozers couldn't be fought. "Yes, Mama."

"Good. Now I give you a wedding present." Mama Bella held out her hand. On her palm rested an 1821 nickel. "You remember one night, Nico, you come back to the restaurant. You go on and on about Taylor. Wanting to go to school then to the city, to a big job, but not wanting to go, too. Wanting to make a life for yourself, not wanting to leave her behind. I listen. Then you tell me Taylor gave you this nickel. Special. To remember her. You say it belong to both of you. And you ask me to keep it for you. Safe. So you never lose it."

Taylor stared. Of course, Mama knew where the coin was, she always knew everything. She knew the truth about her and Nick.

Nick's features softened and he blew out a huge breath of air. "I'd forgotten. Completely."

"I think, you hurting inside, *mi figlio*. Some-times we don't want to remember when we hurt."

Nick reached out and hugged his mother, lift-ing her off the ground. Then he opened one arm for her, and Taylor rushed in. "Thank you." He laughed. "Thank you, thank you and thank you."

"Mama," she said, "you've saved us all. You don't realize what you've done."

Mama looked tired. "I just thought it was a nice thing you two should have. What's all the excite-ment? It's a nice coin but—"

They filled Mama in on how much the coin was worth. She still seemed in disbelief when they saw her home. Afterward, Nick drove them up to the pier.

"This is where it all began," Taylor said, letting the sound of the ocean waves soothe her.

Nick held out the coin. "And where it can all end, if you want?" His tone was serious. "It might cause more problems than it's worth. We can throw it in the ocean, figure out the money, how to pay the lawyers for as long as it takes another way. Your choice."

She shook her head. "Too many lives it can help. Rocco and Beth need a new home, Mama needs to stop working and travel. So does my mom. Kate needs a fund for her college education. So does Roc Junior and their new baby."

"Do you want more children?"

The thought of possibly holding their baby in her arms one day was priceless. "Yes."

"Then let's make our dreams come true. And change the narrative on a few nightmares. I love you, Taylor Hughes. With all my heart and soul."

"I love you, too, Nick Diamante. With all my heart and soul."

"We're family. Today and always."

"Yes, we are."

EPILOGUE

"GOOD THINGS COME to those who wait. Isn't that right, Katydid?" Taylor smiled.

"They sure do, Mom."

Kate ran off to circle the wide-open field. Taylor called out to her to be careful. Machinery sat ready to remove more trees and enlarge the lot so they could begin building.

Nick came up behind her, circling her with his arms. He planted a soft kiss on the back of her neck and Taylor's knees gave way. She locked them a second later, but Nick felt the dip and she knew he was grinning.

"You nervous?" he asked, letting go.

"I thought I would be. But now that it's really here, I'm just happy. I never thought—"

"Neither did I." He dropped another kiss on her lips.

She laughed but tried to be stern. "Nick. Stop. People are already arriving."

"So? We are engaged, aren't we?"

"Marriage license. Check. Wedding. Soon. But

an engagement ring is not a permission slip to make out in public, in an empty lot, no less."

"Maybe later?" he joked and reached for her hand.

Happy, Taylor threw him a huge smile. Ever since Mama Bella gave them the coin, every day for the last month had been a new adventure, a new beginning.

Jax shut her car door and walked toward them. Instead of the usual chef's coat and sensible shoes, she wore heels and a classic little black dress.

"Hi, Jax." She waved and Nick did the same.

"Hey," Jax said. "I'm sorry Mama's not with me. She got going on a new kind of sauce again. I didn't have the heart to step in. Besides, some things should never change."

"And some things should," Nick said.

Rocco and Beth had moved into a four-bedroom house, big enough for their growing family, situated on the ocean side of a cozy avenue. She and Nick had bought one just like it across the street. South side of the Island. Mama Bella and Taylor's mother had just made arrangements to tour Italy for a month and there was this excitement about the trip that Taylor decided was unstoppable.

Greg? He'd agreed to not only Kate's living in a different state but acquiesced to Taylor having full custody when faced with what a family court judge had to say. After, she and Nick invested a portion of the money for him and he eventually cleaned up his debts and got his act together. Seemed once Kate had turned her back on him, she became important again. Taylor wished that it would stay that way this time.

And Taylor? She had a wedding to finish planning. Nick stood next to her, still clasping her hand with his. Together, she thought, today and always.

Friends and family gathered in the empty lot. They'd set up tables and chairs to celebrate the future. With food, of course. Lots and lots of food.

He squeezed her hand and smiled. She smiled, too.

"Welcome, everyone!" he said. "To our new restaurant—1821. I know it's hard to envision given the building isn't even started yet. But we hope you'll all enjoy many more Diamante meals here in the years to come. *Mangia*. Let's eat."

* * * * *